"We s̶_____ ̶o̶n̶e̶ ̶s̶i̶d̶e̶ ̶o̶f̶ Alex's mouth lifted in a tilted smile. "My brother was many things, Kit. But I am willing to wager that he was *not* a generous lover." His smile dropped away. "The fact that he had to depend on alcohol to convince a woman is testimony to that. *I*, on the other hand, would be willing to spend *hours* caressing." His fingers rubbed at the flesh of her neck. "Kissing." He leaned down and brushed his lips against her throat. "And fondling your delectable body until we *both* ached for the release we would find together."

Kit sighed and Alex shuddered. The mental images his words created affected him every bit as much as they did her.

"Inch by inch, Kit," he went on, unable to resist the temptation to describe what he would like to share with her, "my fingers will explore your flesh."

Kit's eyes closed, and she unwittingly leaned into him . . .

THE SCOUNDREL

And don't miss this passionate tale of
a legendary man and the woman who loved him . . .

The Buccaneer
by Donna Fletcher

Titles by Ann Carberry
from The Berkley Publishing Group

The
Scoundrel

Ann Carberry

JOVE BOOKS, NEW YORK

THE SCOUNDREL

A Jove Book / published by arrangement with the author

PRINTING HISTORY
Jove edition / September 1995

ISBN: 0-515-11705-6

A JOVE BOOK®
Jove Books are published by The Berkley Publishing Group,
200 Madison Avenue, New York, New York 10016.
JOVE and the "J" design are trademarks
belonging to Jove Publications, Inc.

PRINTED IN THE UNITED STATES OF AMERICA

10 9 8 7 6 5 4 3 2 1

To Cheryl Arguile/Emily Brightwell for her help and patience in guiding me through Victorian England. If Mrs. Jeffries ever makes a visit to the Old West, I'd be delighted to return the favor.

1

"It will take more than rubies to buy *my* bed!"

"My apologies, madam." Alexander Mac-Gregor's lips twisted in a sardonic smile. "But it wasn't my intention to *purchase* that noble, yet well-worn piece of furniture. I was under the impression that I was merely *renting* it."

"You bastard!"

A gold-link, ruby-studded bracelet sailed past Alexander's head and he ducked reflexively. He didn't even turn to look when the expensive trinket smashed into the wall behind him and fell to the polished wood floor. His eyes remained fixed on the woman opposite him.

Completely nude, she held an ivory-colored bedsheet clutched to her chest as if protecting a virtue long since tossed aside. Her honey-blond hair fell in luxurious waves about her smooth, almost translucent shoulders. An angry flush colored her high cheekbones and her dark brown eyes shone furiously in the lamplight.

Rumpled bedclothes lay bunched up around her in the huge four-poster. The doors to the stone terrace outside her room were standing open and a soft wind slipped through, carrying the scent of her perfume to him. She was the very image of sexual abandon. And Alexander knew that not so very long ago he wouldn't

have been standing across the room from her. He would
have been in that bed with her, reveling in Elizabeth's
very practiced "talents."

But after nearly six months of bedding Elizabeth
Beckwith, Alexander was thoroughly and completely
bored. These temper tantrums of hers were becoming
more frequent of late. And her greedy demands for
"love" tokens had recently gone over the top.

He'd already given her more jewelry than he had any
of his previous mistresses. The diamond tiara he'd given
her only last month alone was worth a king's ransom. In
fact, he had it on the best of authorities that Elizabeth's
husband, Sir Richard, had received quite a sum of cash
for the tiara when he pawned it the very next night.

"Oh, Alexander," she purred suddenly.

He shook his head and told himself to stop his wool-
gathering. If nothing else, in the last six months, he'd
learned that it was *always* wise to keep one's wits about
oneself when dealing with Elizabeth.

"I *am* sorry," she whispered huskily.

His right eyebrow lifted over suddenly wary blue eyes.
"Whatever for, Elizabeth?"

"Well," she sighed, leaning forward and allowing the
sheet to dip just low enough to give him a glimpse of her
breasts, "I shouldn't have snapped so, I know."

"Snap?" He chuckled and for the first time looked
behind him at the ruby bracelet. Bending down, he
snatched it up, admired it for a moment, then dropped
it into the pocket of his coat. "Hurling a gift at the
giver's head should hardly be referred to as 'snappish,'
don't you think?"

Her lips pressed together momentarily, then she

made a monumental effort at calmness. Alexander watched, fascinated as she forced all signs of anger from her face, then stretched back against the mound of feather pillows at the head of the bed.

Slowly she dragged the sheet from her body and just for a moment Alexander thought seriously about allowing himself one last romp with her delectable self. Then his gaze slipped up to her avaricious eyes and he thought better of it.

Lifting one lazy hand, she beckoned to him. "Come here, Alexander, and let me see the bracelet again." Her lips puckered in a promisory kiss and she whispered, "Please."

He cursed silently as his body, ever ready, leapt into life. Disgusted with himself, Alexander said shortly, "I think not, Elizabeth."

"What?"

"I said no." Lord knew he seemed to have no control over his body's physical response to the woman, but by thunder, he'd be damned if he'd act on his every impulse. He pushed his discomfort to the back of his mind. Besides, he told himself, the stunned expression on Elizabeth's face at his refusal was almost worth the pain. "Thank you, though," he added belatedly.

"No?"

"That's right, my dear." Stepping carefully to the small brocade chair near the door, Alexander scooped up his hat and coat, then turned back toward the bed. He almost smiled at the incredulity stamped on her features. "I've suddenly remembered a previous engagement. But I must say, I've enjoyed myself enormously these last few months."

"Surely you can't mean . . ." She sat up, gasping like a fish thrown on a dock.

His gaze ran lingeringly over her lush form one last time, then he sighed. "Good-bye? Yes, I believe that's just what I mean."

"But, Alexander . . ."

He opened the door and glanced back at her. Except for the numbing throb in his groin, he didn't actually mind ending this sordid little affair. The flaws in her character were beginning to overshadow the pleasures of her bed. Oh, her greed was no surprise, certainly. But she was getting far too blatant in her demands of late. It wasn't so much that he minded paying for her sexual favors with trinkets and such—but really, *some* illusions should be maintained.

Just like everyone else he'd ever known, Elizabeth was far more interested in the contents of his purse than himself. She'd just been more clever at hiding it than most. At least until recently.

Forcing a grin to his lips, Alexander said, "Oh, and don't worry about the rubies, Elizabeth. I'll just give them to Richard when I see him next, shall I?"

"What?" she screeched.

He winced. Really, her voice was capable of reaching abominable heights.

"I said," he went on, "I'll just give the bracelet to Richard directly. No sense keeping his pawnshop dealer waiting simply because you and I have reached a parting of the ways, is there?"

Her brown eyes wide open, Elizabeth rose up on her knees and in her fury dropped the sheet. Fists clenched helplessly at her sides, she screamed, "You upstart bastard!"

"Tsk, tsk, tsk." He shook his head slowly. "You disappoint me." Amazing, he thought, that in all the time they'd spent together, he'd never seen this side of her. Perhaps she was a better actress than he'd thought.

"I should have known better than to allow *you*, of all people, into my bed!" Her nose wrinkled slightly in distaste. "No matter your fine clothes or your elegant manners and speech. Under that facade of gentility, you're no better than that ridiculous father of yours."

Anger shot through him. Cold, furious. His fingers clenched in the folds of the coat draped over his arm.

"Keep your opinions about my father to yourself, madam," he managed to say through gritted teeth.

"I'll say what I like, Alexander. Though it's no more than everyone else in London says as soon as your back is turned." She snorted a laugh and tossed her luxurious hair back over her shoulders. "Your money is the key to your 'popularity,' you know. Without it, you would be just another bumbling Scotsman." Elizabeth snatched at the midnight-blue silk coverlet at the foot of the bed and threw it around her shoulders like a bulky cape. "And even the money wasn't enough to compensate for your father's ill-bred behavior."

He pulled in a long, deep breath but held his silence in the face of her tirade.

"And as for your *mother*!"

"Enough!" Alexander's deep-throated shout silenced her as thoroughly as if he'd clapped a hand over her mouth. Though doing his best to control the rising tide of anger coursing through him, Alexander knew that unless he left quickly, it was a battle he would lose. But as he watched the sanctimonious bitch across from him, he knew he couldn't leave before saying one last thing. "Before Richard pimps you out to some other poor fool, you'd do well to remember to hold your tongue. You sound no better than a common fishwife, my dear."

"My husband will call you out for this!"

"Oh, I hardly think so, madam." His lips twisted in a parody of a smile, he added, "Dueling, you know, is frowned on these days. And even if it weren't—if Richard were to call on *all* of your . . . *admirers*, he would have to pitch a tent on the dueling field."

She gasped.

"Besides, without your efforts in his cause, your dear husband might be forced to *work* for his money! And what would society have to say?" Wry amusement rippled through him at the very idea of Sir Richard Beckwith trying to *earn* a living. His anger now carefully banked, he waited for her reaction.

Elizabeth brushed aside the mention of her husband and gave Alexander a knowing look. As if she hadn't been screaming only a moment before, she said, "You won't be able to stay away from me, Alexander, and we both know it."

Color flooded her cheeks and her lips were parted in anticipation. It seemed that his sudden disgust for her only fueled her desire. Alexander shuddered as she dropped the coverlet, laid back down, and caressed her own flesh with her fingertips.

The uncomfortable throbbing in his groin increased tenfold. Even knowing her for what she was did nothing to eliminate the raw desire wracking him. His gaze followed the progress of her long, elegant fingers as her hands moved to cup her breasts. He saw the triumphant gleam in her eyes and knew she was mistaking the need shaking through him for something more.

And he could hardly blame her for her thoughts. The time spent in her bed had been pleasurable for both of them. Beyond the money spent on various gifts he'd bestowed on Elizabeth, Alexander had spent more time with her than with any of his former mistresses. Though the reason for that had nothing to do with sparkling conversation or a ready wit. On the contrary—Elizabeth cared less for the social trivialities than Alexander did. But as a mistress, she possessed one extraordinary talent. Elizabeth Beckwith was the most sexually driven woman he'd ever come across.

Her only mistake was in believing Alexander to be in love with her. If she knew him half as well as she professed to, she would know that "love" was an emotion Alexander MacGregor had no interest in experiencing.

When her tongue darted out to slide across her lips, Alexander silently reminded himself of everything she'd shouted at him. Was he truly no better than an animal that he could *still* feel desire for a woman who meant absolutely nothing to him?

Deliberately he drew himself up to his full height of six feet two inches. Alexander refused to be ruled by his own baser instincts. He looked into her brown eyes and forced a smile.

"I think not, Elizabeth."

Her hands stilled.

"Don't worry—though I won't be returning, I'm quite sure Richard will soon find *someone* willing to walk the well-traveled path to your bed." Then he jerked her a nod and left the room.

The fire in the library grate had been reduced to a few glowing embers. A chill began to creep toward him from the corners of the vast room and still Alexander didn't move.

He'd been shut away in the library for hours now. Ever since leaving Elizabeth's house. With the doors locked, the drapes undrawn, and the windows opened to the summer air, Alexander had watched the afternoon slip away to be replaced by the night. In the silence of his room, he listened to the sounds of carriage wheels on the street outside. Snatches of conversations drifted to him and the occasional burst of laughter grated on his soul.

There were any number of balls he could attend had he wished to spend yet another evening surrounded by insipid young women and their intrepid, son-in-law-hunting mothers. Despite everything Elizabeth had said, Alexander knew that those formidable women would be happy to overlook his ancestry in quest of his fortune. He had no doubt that even the fact that the Mac-Gregors were in "trade" wasn't enough to steal the sheen from his gold. He snorted and shook his head to rid himself of such dismal thoughts.

Certainly a ball wasn't his only choice of entertainment. He still might join John Tremayne, his business manager and closest friend, at the theater. Hell, there were any number of possibilities open to him. None of which, he admitted silently, interested him in the slightest. Instead, he sat alone in a room lit only by the glow of a fading fire.

And the time alone, coupled with the brandy he'd consumed, had done nothing to improve his mood. Glancing at the massive set of double oak doors to his right, Alexander frowned briefly. From the hall just outside the library came the unmistakable sounds of his butler, Harris, pacing.

The bloody fool would be out there all night, like some damned mother hen worrying over a lost chick. Alexander snorted. Chick indeed. He pushed a stray lock of midnight-black hair out of his eyes and deliberately straightened up in the chair. His life would be much simpler if he could only convince that butler of his that he no longer required a nanny!

Tugging his gold pocket watch from his vest, Alexander stared down at the clock face until the blurry numbers righted themselves. Ten o'clock. And Lord knew his body still ached for the release denied it earlier. He groaned and told himself that what he needed was a distraction. Cards? No, in his present condition, he couldn't be trusted to make intelligent wagers. Perhaps, he thought, a ride in the night air would be enough to cool his body's fires.

Decision made, he snapped the watch shut and attempted to tuck it back into its resting place. Once, twice, three times, his suddenly clumsy fingers skimmed across the gray vest. Mumbling a halfhearted curse, Alexander finally dropped the bloody watch and left it to dangle on its gold chain. He pushed out of the chair with a groan and caught himself as he staggered slightly, the brandy sloshing over the rim of his glass.

"Hmmm," he said aloud, staring down at the liquid soaking into his shirt cuff. "Now that's a bloody waste." A strangled laugh shot from his throat as he looked up at the portrait hanging over the mantel.

The burly, red-faced man with muttonchop gray whiskers seemed to glare down at the younger man.

"Aye, Father," Alexander said as if in answer to a question. "I'll be more careful in future. Can't have it said that the only remaining MacGregor son can't hold his liquor, now can we?"

In an instant he lifted the snifter in a silent salute, then brought it to his lips and tipped the remaining brandy down his throat. Can't be too careful, he told himself. The old man had only been dead a year or so. If displeased, it would be just like Douglas MacGregor to leap from the grave and mete out justice as he deemed fit. Alexander smiled slightly. Damned if he didn't still miss him.

Turning slightly, Alexander set the empty glass down on the table's edge. It tumbled off and hit the brown and gold carpet with a muffled thud. Frowning, he started to bend down for it when the room began to spin. Leaving the glass, Alexander straightened slowly, until he could reach out and curl his fingers over the mahogany mantel. He waited what seemed hours for his head to clear.

Then cautiously he stood away from the wall and tugged at the lapels of his coat. He took a few experimental steps and, except for his watch slapping against his thigh, felt that he was doing quite nicely under the circumstances.

It wasn't until he turned the key in the lock that everything went from bad to worse.

Katherine Simmons tightened her hold on the squirming toddler. But she couldn't blame Rose for acting up. The poor child had been traveling since morning. She hadn't had a nap or a decent meal in hours.

"Down, Kit?" the little girl whimpered, both chubby hands cupping her aunt's face.

"No, Rosie." Kit swallowed past the knot in her throat. "Not yet." She smiled at the girl, then glanced back at the street behind her. But for the occasional carriage, it was empty of life. No one strolled the sidewalks. No one sat in the yard, enjoying the night air. There were no friendly greetings called out. And no children laughing.

It was nothing like home. Kit swallowed heavily and fought back the tiny curl of distress beginning to unwind in her stomach. She didn't belong there. Neither did Rose.

For one split second she considered leaving. All she had to do was turn and walk down the path she'd followed to the door and hurry back to the train station. No one would ever know she'd been there. She wouldn't have to speak to a soul.

Then what? her brain taunted.

Where could she go? And if she had a destination, how would she get there? She'd spent almost her last coin on the train tickets to London. Reluctantly she looked back at the house. Its closed white door had a diamond-shaped leaded glass pane that successfully prevented anyone peering in. On either side of the wide door were tall, narrow windows with lamplight spilling out through the sheer film of white lace curtains.

Inside that house was warmth. Food. Safety. At least for Rose. All Kit had to do was ask for it. She shrugged the toddler into a more comfortable position on her hip and breathed in a gulp of flower-scented air. Biting down hard on her bottom lip, she told herself that she shouldn't be in this position. She shouldn't be forced into the humiliating prospect of begging for help.

"Biscuit?" Rose asked quietly and laid her head down on Kit's shoulder.

"Soon, baby. Soon." Stroking the child's back rhythmically, Kit felt her nervous embarrassment slowly turn to anger. It wasn't right. It simply wasn't right. By heaven, she wouldn't *ask* for his help. She'd *demand* it. Heaven knew it was the very least he could do. Rose wouldn't be made to suffer because of the accident of her birth—not as long as Kit had anything to say.

Before she could reconsider, she stepped up to the door, lifted the brass, lion-headed knocker, and let it fall.

Instantly it seemed, the door was thrown wide and a distinguished-looking man of about sixty was standing in front of her. His faded blue eyes swept over Rose, and Kit saw the flash of surprise there just before it disappeared.

When his gaze settled on Kit's own rumpled appearance, she forced herself to meet his eyes boldly.

Straightening her spine, she told herself that she had nothing to be ashamed of. Her peach muslin gown might not be fashionable, but it was clean and freshly pressed. Or it had been when she'd boarded the train that morning. Quickly Kit sidestepped the man she guessed to be a butler and hurriedly walked into the entry hall.

Her heels tapped against the checkerboard marble floor and seemed to echo on and on down the corridors of the house. She breathed deeply in a futile attempt to calm herself, but when the imperious butler asked, "May I help you, madam?" she jumped.

Spinning about, she said with as much dignity as possible, "I should like to see Mr. MacGregor, please."

The man's right eyebrow lifted slightly.

"I've come a long way and I won't leave until I've spoken with him." She felt it only fair to warn the butler that she would not be easily dismissed.

"I'm afraid," he began.

The double doors on the right swung open and a tall man in a wrinkled black suit stepped into the hall.

"Sir," the butler said quickly and stepped past Kit to reach his employer's side.

"What the hell's this about then?" the younger man demanded.

This is Alexander MacGregor? Kit thought. Quickly her gaze moved over the man she'd come so far to see. Tall and lean, with wide shoulders and a narrow waist, his black hair was a bit longer than it should have been and his sky-blue eyes were clouded over. His clothing in disarray, he swayed despite the butler's grip on his forearm. Heavy black brows drew together as he looked her over and Kit lifted her chin defiantly in response.

Drunk. Even with five feet of space separating them, she could smell the alcohol on him. Every breath he took fouled the air in the hall. Tired, hungry, and desperately worried about the child in her arms, Kit said the first thing that popped into her head.

"You're drunk."

He nodded and the effort that cost him sent him staggering. Only his butler's strong arms kept him from falling flat on his face. "Thank you, madam, for your insight. You may leave now." Staring down at the other man, Alexander MacGregor said thickly, "Call the carriage, Harris. I'm going out."

"Of course, sir. But first, might I suggest a change of clothes?"

"What?" The younger man's forehead wrinkled and he pulled his head back to look at the butler. After a moment MacGregor ran one hand over the front of his coat, sending his dangling watch on a pendulum swing. "Oh, well. Perhaps you're right."

"One moment if you please," Kit interrupted. She shifted Rose once more and took a half step toward the drunken man. "We have business to discuss, you and I."

He straightened up a bit, glanced at her from the corner of his eye, and slowly winked. "Good of you to offer, but I'm afraid I wouldn't be much use to you tonight."

"I beg your pardon?" Kit said and only glanced at the butler when he gasped.

MacGregor patted the butler's shoulder and ignored the man's horrified expression. "Perhaps if you came back tomorrow—"

"Tomorrow?" Kit's voice shook, despite her best efforts to control it. She couldn't leave. Not yet. Not until he'd agreed to take care of Rose. Besides, she hadn't the money to pay for a room in town. As foolish as it now seemed, she'd rather hoped to be allowed to stay in the house. With Rose. "I can't come back tomorrow," she said, unconsciously taking another step toward him.

"Whyever not?"

"Sir, if you would allow me," Harris said quickly.

"Now, now, Harris," MacGregor countered as he pushed away from the man's supporting arms, "if the woman is set on tonight, I shall just have to do my best to accommodate her." He added with a half grin, "Though I warn you, madam, I won't be at my best!"

"But, sir . . ." Harris's worried gaze shot from his employer to Kit and back again. "I don't believe you quite understand . . ."

"Nonsense," MacGregor shouted. "I understand perfectly. Harris, you're a wonder! Your thoughtfulness knows no bounds!" He slapped the older man's back and gave him a conspiratorial though crooked grin. "Always know just what to do and when to do it. Wish you hadn't let me drink all that brandy, though, I must say. By heaven, man, I've never known you to go quite so far to meet my needs before; I appreciate the effort more than I can say."

"Sir!" Harris sounded insulted. "I would never do such a . . ."

"Now, now," MacGregor assured him. "We'll say no more about it." He held up one unsteady finger to his lips. "No one need know."

"But . . ."

Kit wasn't quite sure what was happening. The disgusted expression on the butler's face was a mystery. Why on earth was the man so set on keeping her from speaking to MacGregor? What possible difference

could it matter to *him*? And as for MacGregor . . .
well, she thought determinedly, drunk or not, she'd
make him see it was his duty to do right by Rose.

MacGregor launched himself toward her with a staggering gait. Instinctively she reached out her free hand
to steady him. When she touched his arm though, she
felt a jolt of awareness bounce through her body. Up
close, the smell of alcohol was nearly overwhelming, but
there was something else too. Something alarming in its
strength.

He loomed over her. Even at her height of five feet
eight inches, he was much taller than she. And his very
nearness was most disconcerting. Kit looked up into his
eyes and found him squinting down at her.

"Have we met before, madam?" he whispered.

"No."

"Odd then, isn't it?"

"What?"

"This . . . feeling of familiarity." He rubbed one
long-fingered hand over his eyes, then looked down at
her again. "Almost as though . . . damnation!" Mac-
Gregor's eyes widened perceptibly as he stared at a
newly wakened Rose. "Who is that?"

Kit gave herself a mental shake. What in heaven was
she thinking? This was no time to be befuddled by the
very man she held responsible for her present problems.

"This is Rose," she said softly and couldn't resist smiling into the child's sleepy eyes.

"You've brought your *child* with you?"

"Sir . . ." Harris tried to speak but was shouted
down.

"What kind of woman drags along an infant while working?"

"Working?" Kit asked, thoroughly mystified.

"Well, what would *you* call it?" He sneered at her and took another step back. *"Courting?* For God's sake, woman! Have you no shame at all? The very idea of a streetwalker bringing along her child!"

Streetwalker? Rage rushed through her, almost blinding her with its fury. He thought she was a—and that she would bring Rose with her to—

"Harris," MacGregor shouted drunkenly, "I am appalled!"

Kit's hands were shaking. Rose began to cry in response to the noise and confusion. The tiny sobs issuing from the girl in her arms were the final blow. That the intoxicated half-wit before her should bring little Rose to tears was more than Kit could bear.

"Must the infant *bellow* so?" MacGregor shouted to no one in particular.

"Mr. Harris," she said quietly.

The butler heard her, despite his master's shouting, and turned toward her.

Kit held Rose out to the older man without a word and nodded her appreciation when he awkwardly held the toddler to his chest.

"Ah," MacGregor shouted anew, "so *that's* your plan, is it?" He waved his hands at the butler. "Leave your brat with my butler while we conduct 'business'?" Shaking his head, he walked toward her. "Damned odd, I think it, but very well. Long as Harris doesn't mind. C'mon then. No sense wasting time since you're already here."

As he stepped in close, Kit moved to meet him. Now that Rose was safe in Harris's arms, Kit gave her anger free rein. Everything she'd gone through to reach London raced through her tired brain. The worry, the nervousness. The humiliation of having to ask for what was, in justice, Rose's birthright.

Well, no more! her mind shouted. She might very well be forced to come to him for help, but she would not accept his insults into the bargain!

He reached out for her and the stink of him settled over her like an old blanket. Without wasting another thought on him, Kit raised her hand and slapped him with all her might.

Eyes wide, he spun about with the force of her blow. Already unsteady, Alexander staggered backward three steps, waving his arms wildly, then fell with a crash to the cold marble floor.

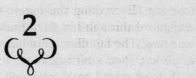

2

"Is he dead?" Kit took a half step closer to the fallen man and stared down at him fearfully. As soon as she'd heard his head hit the floor, her anger had drained away, leaving only a cold dread settled in her chest.

She turned and glanced at Harris, now holding Rose at arm's length in front of him. Keeping one wary eye on the crying child, the butler moved to his employer's side and looked down on him. Finally, the man muttered, "He's alive." His gaze shifted to Kit. "Been knocked senseless is all. Between the brandy and the hit on his head, I shouldn't wonder if he were unconscious all night."

Rose hiccuped, coughed, and let loose another wail, stronger than before.

Kit reached for the little girl and Harris gratefully released his charge. As soon as her small arms were safely around Kit's neck, she began to calm down. Whispering soothing, nonsensical words, Kit stroked the child's hair and tried not to think about how badly this meeting had gone.

Not only had she failed to win MacGregor's promise to care for Rose, she'd almost killed the man as well. What more could *possibly* go wrong?

From a distance, a chorus of hushed voices reached her. She looked up and saw a small crowd of servants hovering just beyond the main staircase. Three of the women were in their nightclothes, each of them clutching shawls about their shoulders. Two men, in their shirtsleeves and stockinged feet, looked no more at ease as they all stared at MacGregor, stretched out on the hall floor.

Kit's uneasy gaze passed over each of them and came to rest on the one member of their party whose face didn't register curiosity. Tall and angular, the gray-haired woman looked as though she'd been carved of stone. Her pristine white apron covered a severe gray gown and around her waist she wore a ring of keys.

The housekeeper.

Kit shivered slightly under that woman's hard glare and fought down the impulse to run. She could only hope that the MacGregor family would prove warmer and more compassionate than their housekeeper appeared to be.

Tearing her gaze from the woman's black, cold eyes, Kit looked back at Harris, bending over his unconscious employer to loosen the man's collar buttons. When he'd finished his task, the butler straightened slightly, looked down to the crowd of people at the end of the hall, and waved one hand. Hesitantly the two young men began walking toward them.

"Michael?"

Kit didn't stir an inch when a woman's voice called out. But she saw the relieved look on Harris's face as he pushed himself to his feet and looked toward the stairs.

Slowly Kit turned and watched an older, plump

woman at the head of the wide, circular staircase lean over the banister.

"Michael?" she called again. "What is it? I heard shouting."

"Ah . . ." Harris paused and Kit could almost hear him thinking, weighing his words. "It's Mr. Alexander, madam. He's had a fall."

This then was Mrs. MacGregor, Kit told herself and watched as the woman hurried down the stairs. As she ran, Alexander's mother tied the cords of an ancient-looking red wool bathrobe around her waist. Beneath the hem of the garment, her plain, white cotton night-gown was clearly visible. Her soft red slippers made barely a whisper of sound as her feet skimmed down the carpeted steps. One long, black braid, liberally streaked with gray, hung over her right shoulder, and as she drew nearer, Kit saw the unmistakable lines of laughter at the edges of her now worried green eyes.

"A fall?" she repeated as she ran past Kit and knelt beside her son's body. The older woman stretched out one hand and smoothed her fingers across Alexander's forehead. "Are you sure he's all right, Michael?" she asked.

"Quite sure, madam," Harris replied, "but if you wish I can have James fetch the doctor."

"Perhaps we should at that," she said softly as she leaned closer to her son's face. The fallen man took a deep, shuddering breath just then and exhaled on a rush. "Oooh!" Mrs. MacGregor sat back on her heels, fanning the air in front of her nose. Frowning, she glanced up at Harris. "I don't believe the doctor will be necessary after all, Michael."

"Yes, madam." He nodded and managed to hide a quick flash of sympathy that crossed his features.

"If you and some of the others would just carry him to his room . . ." The older woman's voice trailed off, but Kit heard the disappointment in her tone.

"Of course," Harris said smoothly and waved the other men forward again.

Kit braced herself. Now that the woman had assured herself that her son was all right, she would be turning her attention to the two strangers in her hall.

Guiltily, Kit told herself that whatever happened now was her own fault. That temper of hers had gotten her into trouble again. All her life, she'd fought to control it. And all her life, she'd been losing the battle. Oh, she'd succeed for a while; there might even be stretches of weeks at a time when she'd be able to deal with her anger reasonably. But inevitably something would happen to shatter her restraint.

And tonight, when she'd most needed that hard-won self-discipline, she'd allowed a drunken man's insults to deprive her of it.

Grimly Kit looked into the eyes of the other woman and felt her heart catch in her throat. Mrs. MacGregor's eyes were the exact same shade of green as little Rose's. Instinctively Kit's arms tightened around the toddler. For the first time, she realized that bringing the child to safety might entail being separated from her forever. And she didn't think she could bear that.

"Good evening," the older woman said as easily as if they were meeting in the park on a Sunday afternoon instead of the dead of night over her son's prostrate form. "I'm Tess MacGregor."

Slowly Kit took the woman's outstretched hand in her own and said quietly, "Katherine Simmons."

"Simmons?" Tess repeated, her gaze slipping to the wide-eyed girl on Kit's hip. "Did you say Simmons?"

"Yes."

"Then this must be . . ." Tess released Kit's hand and moved to stroke Rose's back.

"Rose," Kit provided. "Rose Simmons."

Startled, the older woman's hand paused, then after a moment, she sighed, "Ah . . . of course." A soft smile curved her lips and the faint lines around her eyes deepened in a familiar pattern. "A girl," she said wonderingly, "isn't that lovely?" She smoothed the child's deep brown hair back from her forehead and looked into the eyes so much like her own. Glancing at Kit, she asked, "May I hold her?"

Reluctant to part from the girl, even for a moment, Kit said, "I'm afraid she doesn't get on well with strangers."

"Oh," Tess countered quickly as she scooped the girl into her arms, "but we're not strangers. Are we, you little darling?"

She knew. Tess MacGregor knew all about Rose. Well, Kit's mind argued, why shouldn't she? Just because none of the MacGregor family had bothered to contact them over the last two years didn't mean that they were unaware of Rose's existence. In fact, Mrs. MacGregor's expression held all the wonder of one who'd searched years for a treasure, only to stumble across it unexpectedly. A small curl of fear began to worm its way through Kit's insides.

She watched the woman's hands move over the tiny

girl with a featherlight touch. Tess MacGregor's every motion told Kit that she'd already laid claim to the girl in her heart.

And as for Rose. Kit scowled as the little girl made a liar out of her.

Instead of being stiff and wary in a stranger's arms, Rose smiled up at her grandmother as if she'd been raised with her. The older woman fairly glowed with delight. Jealously Kit watched her niece pat the other woman's cheeks before asking, "Biscuit?"

"Oh, my dear," Tess cooed, "of *course* you shall have a biscuit! Two biscuits!"

Rose clapped her hands.

"And you, Katherine? You must be hungry as well." Tess said quickly, "I may call you Katherine?"

"I prefer Kit, Mrs. MacGregor."

"Oh, how nice! Kit it is then!" She reached out and squeezed Kit's hand. "And you must call me Tess."

Behind them, Alexander groaned and both women turned to look.

Cradling his employer's head in his hands, Harris glanced up at Tess. "We'll take care of him, madam," he said.

Nodding slowly, Mrs. MacGregor frowned momentarily at her unconscious son, then turned her gaze down the hall toward the servants clustered there. Kit saw the housekeeper move to the front of the crowd, her features still twisted in a mask of displeasure.

"Polly?" Mrs. MacGregor called and a young woman stepped out from behind the imposing housekeeper.

"Yes'm?" The girl dropped a half curtsy and her bright copper-colored hair danced around her head.

"Would you mind bringing up a tray with some sand-wiches and a glass of milk? Our guests will be spending the night."

Relief flooded through Kit. At least for tonight, she wouldn't have to worry. As to the inevitable meeting with Alexander MacGregor, she would worry about that later. Right now, it was enough that Rose would be fed and given a warm place to sleep.

"Oh, yes," Mrs. MacGregor added, "and a pot of tea for Miss Simmons, if you please."

Polly nodded, then hurried off down the hall and through a doorway toward, Kit supposed, the kitchen.

"The rest of you may go back to bed," Mrs. Mac-Gregor said quickly.

"I'll see the young *lady* to her room," the house-keeper offered.

The stone-faced woman's tone left no doubts about her opinion of Kit's character.

But before Kit could say something that would no doubt have only caused more trouble, Mrs. MacGregor spoke up.

"That won't be necessary, Mrs. Beedle."

The housekeeper frowned and Kit would have en-joyed the woman's discomfort but for the fact that Mrs. MacGregor seemed every bit as uncomfortable.

"I'll take them upstairs myself, thank you," Tess fin-ished and started walking, leaving Kit no choice but to follow.

As they climbed the circular staircase to the floors above, Kit dismissed thoughts of the housekeeper and the unconscious man she'd left behind her. She was far too caught up in gaping at her surroundings.

While Tess chattered happily at the little girl in her arms, Kit allowed herself the indulgence of staring openly.

The dark walnut banister she held was shined to perfection. Gaslight glittered on its polished surface, defining the intricate carvings that laced its edge and posts. A true craftsman had obviously taken great care with the delicate reproductions of vines and flowers entwining themselves along the banister's length.

Under her feet, a forest-green carpet stretched on forever, its surface free of the tiniest piece of lint or dust. On the pale rose walls, paintings of all shapes and sizes, in frames ranging from gilt to the homeliest wood, caught her eye. Landscapes hung beside still-life representations of fruits and flowers. And as she reached the upper floor, she was met by four identically sized portraits hanging directly opposite the staircase.

Kit's gaze moved over them quickly, as she was intent on keeping up with the swiftly moving Tess.

In the first portrait, an older man with gray side whiskers and a ruddy complexion looked out at the world with a well-pleased grin on his face. Beside him in an ornate frame of gold leaf hung a portrait of Tess MacGregor. Younger, thinner, yet with the same smile and shining eyes.

The next two portraits were obviously the MacGregor sons. She stopped dead. Kit barely spared a glance at Alexander's painting. After all, she'd left the real man only moments ago. Instead, her gaze was drawn to the painting hanging between Tess and Alexander.

It was a face she'd never forget.

Pompous. Smug. Cruel.

Ian MacGregor.

Her sister's seducer.

Rose's father.

Her jaw clenched, Kit stared up at the man who'd wrought so much destruction on her family. Not for the first time, she wondered what her life would be like now if Ian MacGregor had never spent that one summer in a house outside their village.

Would her parents still be alive? She would never know for sure. Certainly though, her sister Marian would be. Probably happily married too. Kit herself might even have married by now. But most important of all, there would be no Rose.

And despite everything, a world without Rose was hard to imagine.

Someone on the staircase behind her grunted and Kit turned to look.

"Don't drop him, dammit!" Harris's hushed comment came just before a telling thud and another, younger voice mumbling, "Sorry."

"Kit?" Tess called out, her voice distant. "This way, dear."

At the end of an impossibly long hall, Rose and her grandmother stood waiting. Deliberately Kit looked once more at the cold, imperious features of Ian Mac-Gregor before turning her back on the portrait and hurrying down the hall.

The bedroom was lovely. In fact, Kit had never seen a more beautiful room. Done in shades of peach and mint-green, in the soft gaslight it looked like a spring garden. Pale green curtains, edged with lace, hung at the windows. A peach silk coverlet lay across the high, wide

bed and matched exactly the fabric stretched across the
tops of the bedposts.

Two brocade chairs and a small table were clustered
before a now cold hearth and against the far wall were a
wardrobe, a mirrored dressing table, and a writing desk.
In her wrinkled muslin, Kit felt more than a little out of
place in such opulent surroundings. But Rose wasn't
having the least bit of trouble adjusting.

The child giggled and Kit turned to watch her jumping up and down on the mattress, steadied by the firm
grip of her grandmother's hands at her waist. After several minutes Tess MacGregor scooped the girl up in her
arms. Quickly then the older woman pulled back the
coverlet and laid Rose down on the cool, clean sheets.

As she pulled off Rose's worn shoes, Tess said quietly,
"There is so much we have to talk about, Kit. But I
think that can wait until morning, don't you?"

"Yes, Mrs. MacGregor. Of course."

"Tess, please." She glanced up briefly before looking
back down on her granddaughter. "I'm so happy that
you've come to us, my dear. You've no idea how I've
wondered about you and . . . Ian's child."

Kit inhaled sharply.

"Please," Tess said hurriedly as she straightened up
and looked at Kit, "don't misunderstand. I mean no
offense. Only that, well, we are all of us human, aren't
we, my dear? We all make . . . mistakes."

The kindness etched on the other woman's features
achieved what her son's rudeness had not. Tears filled
Kit's eyes and she blinked at them furiously. Now was
not the time for tears. Not when there was still so much
to be settled. Besides, Rose had had more than enough

upsets for one day. She didn't need to see the one constant person in her world crying.

But Tess saw the sheen of tears and reacted quickly. Taking a few short steps, she walked to Kit's side and drew her close for an all-too-brief hug. When she set her back again, Tess said softly, "Now, now. What's done is done. No more tears, do you understand? You have nothing to be ashamed of, my dear. As a woman, I understand all too well the, uh . . . shall we say 'desire,' to be as one with the man you love."

Comprehension dawned suddenly and Kit began to stammer in her haste to correct the woman.

"Oh, but I . . . no, I didn't . . ."

"Hush, hush, dear." Tess's fingers gave Kit's shoulders a comradely squeeze. "Didn't I say I understood? Why, when my Douglas was alive . . ." Her voice faded off and her eyes took on a dreamy cast.

"Mrs. MacGregor—Tess," Kit tried again.

"No, no." The older woman laid one finger across her lips. "We really mustn't be having this conversation in front of 'you-know-who,' anyway. We'll have plenty of time for long talks, my dear. You'll see." She glanced back at Rose and smiled.

The child was sitting up in the middle of the bed, tugging at the toes of her socks, trying, unsuccessfully, to pull them off.

"Tess, I really think you should know that—"

"Tut-tut-tut." Tess shook her head slightly. "I know all I need to know. My son's child has come home at last. And I have her mother to thank for it." Impulsively she bent forward, kissed Kit's cheek, and bustled out of the room.

Good heavens. Stumbling toward the bed, Kit plopped down on the mattress as soon as she could. Her knees were weak and her stomach was in knots. Even Rose crawling into her lap wasn't enough to distract her mind from this latest development.

Tess MacGregor thought that she, Kit, was Rose's mother. Why, the very thought of lying with Ian Mac-Gregor was enough to bring cold chills to her spine. Even before he'd deserted her sister without so much as a backward glance, Kit hadn't been able to understand Marian's infatuation for the man.

The perpetual sneer on his face had done nothing to endear the man to anyone. And his haughty behavior had offended every person he'd come in contact with. When word from London had drifted to the tiny village of Oxgate that Ian MacGregor was dead—not a soul could be heard to whisper "God rest him."

No. Everyone in Oxgate had recognized Ian for what he was. Everyone save Marian, of course. Instead, Marian's trusting nature and gentle spirit had led her to see in Ian exactly what she wanted to see. At the time though, no one in the family was much concerned with her infatuation. At the time Kit hadn't thought Ian Mac-Gregor human enough to have the same desires as a normal man. But she'd certainly been proven wrong about that.

It appeared that he was human enough to want a woman. Just not man enough to do the right thing by her.

Kit sucked in a gulp of air and wrapped her arms around the child in her lap. Deliberately she pushed all thoughts of her sister and the worthless man she'd loved out of her mind. There were far too many other things to worry about now.

The first being, should she tell the MacGregors the truth?

As Rose's "mother," Kit was obviously welcome at the house. Of course, Alexander was hardly in a position to argue right now. She would have to deal with him in the morning. But if his mother's reaction was anything to judge by, Kit might do better to simply let Tess's assumption stand. After all, the MacGregors might feel no obligation whatever toward Rose's *aunt*. In fact, they might very well insist that she leave Rose with them and go away.

Instinctively her arms tightened until little Rose squealed a protest. Go away? Leave the child who had become so much more than a niece to her? She might never see the girl again.

No matter how friendly Tess MacGregor seemed, it would be wise, Kit told herself, to remember that Ian was her son. And a man that cold and ruthless had to have learned his behavior *somewhere*.

Her mind whirled from one thought to the next, each new possibility worse than the one before. What if they *did* send her away? What could she do? She could hardly go to the law. Kit glanced around at the elegant furnishings of her room. Now, it looked different to her. Now, its very opulence was a threat. The MacGregors were a wealthy family.

They knew influential people. They moved in the highest circles of society. What chance would a village rector's daughter have against such money and power?

None, her brain taunted. None at all. She would lose Rose forever.

On the other hand, even the MacGregors might hesitate to separate a mother from her child. If she went along with Tess MacGregor's notion, all Kit had to lose was her reputation. And what was *that* compared to the loss of Rose?

A knock on the door startled her out of her thoughts. "Yes?"

"It's Polly, miss. I've brought your meal."

"Oh, yes. One moment." Kit stood up, then set Rose down in the middle of the bed.

As she turned toward the door, the little girl asked, "Biscuit, Kit?"

"Yes, Rose. A biscuit." She took a deep breath and added, "Mama will get it for you."

"Alex! Are you listening to me?"

Warily lifting his head from the cradle of his hands, Alexander looked up into his mother's determined green eyes. "Yes, Mother. I *am* listening. There is really no need to shout."

He hadn't slept well at all, and since rising at the abominable hour of seven A.M., he had been wreathed in pain. It seemed as though every saint in heaven were bent on making him pay for his drinking the night before. Now, added to the mess, was his mother.

"I wasn't shouting, dear." She clasped her hands together at her abundant waist and said again, "When you speak to Kit, I want you to be . . . *nice*."

"Nice?"

"Friendly. Polite."

"I understand the term, Mother." He sighed and let his head fall back into his hands. The world was so much easier to bear when surrounded by the darkness of his cupped palms. "I simply do *not* understand why you are so concerned with the way I speak to this 'Kit' woman."

"Alex, are you blind?"

Would that it were so, he groaned silently. His eyeballs grated in their sockets and he had no doubt that blindness at least would obliterate the pain.

"Didn't you see the child?" his mother went on, her voice creeping higher and higher with her every word. "The little girl? Were you so woofled that you don't remember that precious child?"

A child? Yes, his brain sluggishly reminded him. There *had* been a child at the house last night. He remembered thinking at the time how odd it was that a whore would bring along her offspring. Ah well, he told himself, perhaps the governess was unavailable. He snorted a silent laugh, then stifled the groan that followed.

All at once, his mother's choice of words struck him.

"Woofled?" He spread his fingers far enough apart to allow him to glare at the woman opposite his desk through one bloodshot eye. "*Woofled*, Mother? Really!"

"Do you prefer another term? Drunk? Intoxicated?"

Her foot tapped in a quick, no-nonsense beat and Alexander recognized the stern expression on her usually placid features.

"Hammerish?" she went on. "Lit to the guards? Loaded to the gunwales?"

"Enough, Mother!" His own shout nearly split his

skull in two. Gritting his teeth, Alexander cautiously lifted his head again, then leaned back in the maroon leather desk chair. His long, manicured fingers curled over the arms of the chair and he forced himself to look up. "You've made your point. Quite colorfully too, I might add."

Tess MacGregor's lips quirked and she moved her hands to her hips. "Even if you don't like to remember it, Alex, I'm not ashamed that I started out my life in the kitchens of fine houses like this one. And I'll have you know that most often, *your* behavior is worse than any I encountered while in service."

"So you've said." Silently he added, time and time again. Still, he looked up into the face that had seen him through nightmares, bouts of measles, and the lonely times when he was sure no one in the world cared for him. He'd always thought there was nothing he wouldn't do for Tess MacGregor, the one woman in the world who'd never betrayed him.

"I've never been ashamed of you or who you were, Mother. You must know that."

"It's not who I was, Alex." Her voice had gentled and it smoothed over his aching head like cool water. "It's who I *am*." She waved one hand across her blue day gown with the lace-edged collar and cuffs. "Silk purse or no, there's a sow's ear underneath, still."

"Mother . . ."

"All right, all right." She shook her head, then immediately smoothed the sides of her upswept hair unnecessarily. "I didn't come to talk about me. *Or* you and your bad habits."

He winced.

"I want to talk about Kit."

"Tell me again. Who *is* she?"

"Don't you remember anything about last night?"

Oh, yes, he remembered *some* things quite clearly. Like the fact that Harris had procured him a whore. A surprising event in itself. *And*, he remembered the fact that the whore had hit him with something. Alexander ran one hand over the back of his head gingerly. From the feel of the lump on his skull, it had to have been something heavy. A poker, perhaps? He shook his head and immediately regretted it.

As soon as his mother left him alone long enough to recover, Alexander had every intention of demanding the woman's name and her whereabouts from Harris. Then he would go call on the bitch and settle up with her.

"Alex!"

"Yes," he sighed finally. "I *do* remember last night. At least parts of it."

"Good." She jerked him a nod. "Then you're prepared to discuss Kit."

"Kit." He blinked his eyes cautiously, then narrowed his gaze to stare up at his mother. "The woman who hit me?"

"More of a slap, really," the woman countered quickly. "And she told me all about it, Alex."

He frowned, wondered exactly how much his mother had been told, then asked, "What about her?"

"I want you to insist that she and the child move in immediately."

"What?" His head must be more clouded than he'd thought.

Tess MacGregor crossed her arms beneath her ample bosom before adding thoughtfully, "I only hope she's forgiven you your outrageous behavior."

"*My* behavior?"

"Yes. *Yours!*" Her lips thinned as she frowned at him. "Imagine! Calling her a . . . and expecting her to . . ."

Had his *mother* been there? Good Lord. What on earth was Harris thinking?

"No matter now. It's over and done." She seemed to be speaking more to herself than her son. "I'm sure Kit will see that you made a terrible mistake."

"A mistake?"

"Stop repeating my every word, Alex."

He stifled the groan threatening to erupt from his throat and forced himself to be civil. The quicker he finished this business with his mother, the sooner he could find Harris and straighten out this mess.

"Sorry."

"Good. I've already talked to her and she seems a lovely girl," Tess supplied.

His mother had spoken with the woman? About what?

"I've assured her that the past isn't important in the least."

Past? *Whose* past?

"The only thing that matters now is that she's here. And she's brought the baby."

Ah yes. The baby again. He had a vague memory of the child's earsplitting cries the night before. But why were the brat and her mother still here?

"D'you mean to say," Alex asked, "that they spent the night here?"

"Naturally."

Alex shook his head carefully. The only explanation was that he was still drunk—*or* his mother had taken to drinking on the sly.

"Now," she continued, "when I send her in, you *will* be nice, won't you?"

"Fine." He was ready to promise *anything* if it would end this interview. "I'll be . . . *nice*." At least, he told himself, until he figured out just what was going on.

"Good." She nodded sharply. "And you'll insist that she and the child move in immediately."

"Move in?" he asked, sure that he was lost again. Squinting against the brilliant sunlight flooding through the floor-to-ceiling windows of his study, he asked, "Where?"

"Well, here of course!"

"Here? In our home?"

"Where else?"

"I should think *anywhere* else," Alexander shot back. Another muffled groan worked its way up his throat and he began to rub furiously at his temples.

"Alex, how can you say that?" Her thick, deft fingers tugged a lace-edged hankie from the sleeve of her gown and she dabbed it at the corners of her eyes. "Your own brother's child! Oh, the shame of it!"

Ian's child? Good Lord.

3

"Ian's child?" he said aloud, the pain in his head momentarily forgotten. That streetwalker was the mother of his brother's child? Why in heaven had she brought the creature here? Alexander thought wildly. Hadn't his own father sent money to Ian's lightskirt more than two years ago to prevent this very situation?

And how, he wondered an instant later, did Tess MacGregor know of the child's existence? No one was supposed to have told her. Alexander knew *he* hadn't. His father had been adamant about keeping it from her. And it was a safe wager that a truth of *any* kind had never left Ian's lips!

Good Lord. "Ian's bastard." He didn't realize he'd said that aloud until his mother gasped in outrage.

"Don't you ever let me hear you refer to that precious little girl in those terms again, young man!"

Young man? She hadn't called him that since he was fourteen years old and had thrown a cat in the lake to see if it could swim. Alexander shifted uncomfortably in his chair. What was even more amazing than her using that phrase . . . he still reacted to it.

"Your pardon, Mother." He nodded, then asked, "But how did you find out about the child? Father expressly swore us to secrecy."

"Hmmph! Douglas MacGregor never kept a secret from me in his life!" A brief frown crossed her face. "Except one." Sadly she admitted, "He always refused to tell me where the child was. He did slip one time and mention the mother's last name. Said it was better that way. Don't quite see how, though."

She sniffed again and Alexander scowled. Bloody hell. *Now* what? Desperately he tried to think. Of all days to have a damned hangover! As the fog in his brain began to slowly clear, one thought did occur to him.

"All right, Mother. Ian *did* leave a child."

She smiled.

"But," he countered quickly, "who is to say that *this* child is his?"

"What do you mean?" Indignant color raced up her neck to her cheeks.

"Hear me out, Mother." Alexander lifted one hand in appeasement. "All either of us knows is the last name of Ian's . . ."

Her eyes narrowed perceptibly.

"Woman friend," he hedged and she relaxed a bit.

"Your father didn't tell you about her, either?"

"No." And that implied lack of confidence still rankled. But he was letting his mind stray from the point.

"How are we to know that this Kit person is the actual woman?" he asked. From what he recalled, she didn't look like *anyone's* mother. Determined, he went on, "For all we know, she could simply be an acquaintance hoping to pocket some easy money."

"Oh, no, Alex." Tess shook her head emphatically and three or four strands of gray-streaked hair slipped from her coronet. "She's not like that at all."

"You don't know that." He sighed and pushed himself to his feet. Immediately little men with hammers began beating on the backs of his eyes.

"I tell you I *do* know it." She hurried around the desk and followed him as he walked to the nearest window. "Besides, even if I doubted her story, one has only to look at the *child* to believe. The little darling is the *image* of Ian."

There's a sobering thought, Alexander told himself. One could only hope for the child's sake . . . *if* this incredible story was true . . . that she hadn't inherited her father's character, or lack of it, as well as his looks.

"And as for the child's mother."

"Yes?" Despite himself he was curious. If he was to believe his mother's tale, then the woman who'd struck him the night before wasn't a common whore. Merely a woman with incredibly poor judgment and even worse taste in men.

Still, from what his muddled brain could remember, she'd been a rather nice-looking creature. Of course, in the state he'd been in last night, he acknowledged, *Mrs. Beedle* would, no doubt, have possessed enough charm for him.

"Well," his mother said, obviously searching for just the right words, "she seems a quiet soul. Pretty, of course."

"Of course." To give him his due, Ian had never suffered for likely looking female companionship.

"But there is more to her than a pretty face, I'll wager."

"Mother, you only just met the woman!" He turned toward the slice of sunlight pouring in through the sparkling glass panes, winced, and turned away again. "How could you possibly know anything of the kind?"

"It's a feeling, Alex." She tilted her head back to look up at him. "All I'm asking is that you give her a chance. Speak to her. Then come upstairs and meet your niece."

He frowned and she said quickly, "Alex, I want that little girl here. She's my own granddaughter and I . . ." She dabbed at her eyes with the hankie again and Alex was lost.

He knew only too well how desperately his mother had wanted a daughter. The three babies born to her in the years following his own birth had all been girls. And not one of them had lived a full year. With the deaths of each of his sisters, Alexander had seen his mother's pain deepen until he, only a child at the time, had been afraid she would die of grief.

Thankfully though, she'd recovered and there'd been no more children born to the MacGregors. And though she'd never spoken of it, he'd always been aware that she still mourned the daughters she'd wanted so badly.

Looking into her anxious eyes now, there was nothing else he could say but, "All right, Mother. I'll listen to her."

A delighted smile creased her face and faded only a bit when he warned, "But if I think she's lying, she's not staying. Neither is her child."

Kit stood at the head of the stairs and pulled in one long, deep breath after the other, hoping to calm the bees buzzing around in her stomach.

She lifted one hand and checked for the tenth time that every hair was in place. Glancing down at the front of her simple, flower-sprigged peach muslin gown she smiled halfheartedly. Since her bags had been left with the stationmaster at the depot, she'd been forced to wear the same dress she'd arrived in last night. It was still unfashionable and certainly out of place at the Mac-Gregor house, but thanks to Polly, it was clean and freshly pressed. As Kit began the long walk downstairs, she heard the soft, unfamiliar rustle of heavily starched fabric accompany her.

With Rose in the maid's capable hands, Kit could concentrate fully on the coming interview. She smoothed her damp palms against the sides of her skirt and told herself firmly that she *must* hold on to her temper. No matter the provocation, she could not afford to make a blunder of this "chat." As it stood already, Kit knew that Alexander MacGregor wouldn't be feeling very kindly toward the woman who'd slapped him into unconsciousness.

Still, the brief chat she'd had with his mother had gone well. Tess MacGregor had thankfully accepted Kit's refusal to speak about Ian. Sighing, she admitted that she wasn't at all sure she could discuss that man without offending the one woman she couldn't afford to displease.

At the bottom of the stairs, Kit stood stock-still in the empty hall. Though no one was in sight, she couldn't help feeling that there were eyes watching her. Judging her. And finding her lacking. Her jaw clenched tightly, Kit reminded herself that *she'd* done nothing wrong. It wasn't through any fault of her own that she'd been forced to come to this house.

If the unseen eyes wanted to place blame, they need look no further than Ian MacGregor.

That thought firmly in mind, she willed herself courage and turned toward Alexander MacGregor's study. Even if Polly hadn't pointed it out to her earlier, Kit felt sure that she would have found it on her own. Though it might sound fanciful, she was almost positive that she could actually *feel* the man's indignation.

Still, she and Rose hadn't been thrown out onto the street yet. Surely that was a good sign. Wasn't it?

Almost defiantly, she crossed the marble floor, stopped in front of the double doors, and knocked. The rapping of her knuckles sounded thunderous in the silence.

After a long moment, a deep voice called, "Come in."

She steeled herself, turned the gold knob, and stepped inside.

Closing the door behind her with a soft click of the latch, Kit stood in the shadows, waiting. A big room, it was definitely furnished with a man in mind. Heavy burgundy drapes had been pulled against the morning sun. But even in the dim light, she could make out the walls of books, the paintings, each of which depicted some sort of hunting scene, and even, in the far corner, a lion's head, stuffed and mounted on the wall. She dragged her gaze away from the poor beast and looked at MacGregor.

Elbows propped on the enormous desktop, he held his head in his hands. Unwillingly, she suffered a pang of conscience. But with her next breath, Kit reassured herself that his injury wasn't completely her fault. Had he been sober, he never would have fallen.

When he finally raised his gaze to hers, Kit swallowed heavily. Even in his deplorable condition the night before, there'd been no denying that Alexander Mac-Gregor was a handsome man. But now, with his hair combed into submission, his jawline freshly scraped, and his well-tailored clothes neatly done up, he was something else entirely.

Blue eyes, deeper in color than her own, stared at her warily, appraisingly. She straightened her spine, lifted her chin, and waited. No matter how long it took, she was going to make him be the first to speak.

He couldn't speak. Alexander swallowed heavily and willed his features to remain blank. But the effort was monumental. Surprisingly, the fog in his brain lifted as if pierced by a brilliant shaft of sunlight. Even the pounding ache behind his eyes was all but forgotten. Every inch of his body felt suddenly, vibrantly alive. He must truly have been drunk as a lord the night before to have considered the woman a common whore.

Through sober eyes, he could easily see there was *nothing* common about her.

His gaze swept over her quickly, thoroughly. Her dress, though obviously worn, fit her like a calfskin glove. And the figure it clung to was magnificent. Her full breasts rose and fell rapidly with her nervous breathing and her hands were clasped loosely at her narrow waist, almost defining the curve of her hips.

Taller than most women, she held herself like a queen under his direct stare and he couldn't quite stifle a small burst of admiration for her.

The woman's shining, light brown hair was pulled

back from her heart-shaped face into a loose knot atop her head. A few stray wisps of curls though had pulled free and lay against her smooth, milk-white flesh. Her wide blue eyes were set under finely arched brows and her full lips were pressed together—no doubt, he told himself with an inward chuckle, in an effort to hold her silence. She had a small, straight nose, lightly dusted with freckles, and she wore tiny pearls on her ears.

Altogether, she was a delightful surprise. As a matter of fact, he couldn't remember the last time he'd felt such an instant attraction for any woman. Not even Elizabeth had so affected him. Still, Alexander reminded himself sternly, he already knew that she wasn't the innocent she appeared to be.

But for the life of him, he couldn't understand why in heaven a woman like *this* would have taken up with Ian!

Deliberately Alexander leaned back in his chair and adopted a more casual pose. Calming the inexplicable fires coursing in his blood was no easy task, but he was up to the challenge.

As he watched her silently, Alexander realized exactly what she was doing. Hiding a smile, he congratulated himself. He too could play this waiting game. And he was willing to wager that he'd had much more practice at it than she had. Since taking over the family's shipping interests, Alexander had been to more meetings than he cared to think about. And at every one of those meetings, he'd forced the other fellow to be the first to speak.

The silence lengthened. The ticking of the mantel clock became the heartbeat of the room. A cool breeze lifted the draperies at the window and scattered across the loose papers lying on his desk. They fluttered wildly in the air for a moment, then settled to the Oriental carpet below.

Minutes crawled by, each longer than the one before.

Watching her face, Alexander was sure the woman was ready to crack, when a discreet knock sounded at the door.

Damn.

"What is it?" he shouted and scowled when the woman across from him smiled.

"The tea you ordered, sir."

Blast it.

"Very well, Harris. Bring it in." Alexander waved his fingers at the woman. "Come and sit down, Miss . . . Simmons."

Once she was seated opposite the desk and Harris had poured tea for both of them, Alexander dismissed the butler. But not before seeing the smile the older man directed at the woman. Hmmm. Was *everyone* in his house beguiled so easily?

When the door closed behind the other man, Alexander lifted the delicate, rose-patterned china cup and took a small sip of tea. Stalling. He was still stalling, hoping she would speak now that he'd broken the silence. He was very curious to hear her reasons for appearing on his doorstep out of nowhere, in the middle of the night.

He heard her cup rattle in its saucer then, and for some odd reason it bothered him to know that she was so nervous.

"I understand," he said, tossing his bargaining tactics aside, "that you've brought my brother's child to us."

Again, the rattle of china on china. This time louder.

Carefully she placed the cup and saucer on the edge of his desk and folded her hands in her lap before speaking.

"I've brought *my* child, yes."

One heavy black eyebrow lifted. He hadn't missed the emphasis she'd placed on the word "my." By the same token, he also hadn't missed the tone of her voice. Soft, easy on the ear, Alexander was inordinately pleased that her voice matched her appearance. How hideous it might have been to be forced to listen to an atrocious accent.

Instead, she had the self-possession of a well-educated woman. Interesting indeed. No, he told himself firmly, this was no common whore. At least not in the usual sense. If she was indeed the mother of Ian's child though, it didn't say much for her virtue *or* her morals.

"Fine." He nodded at her. *"Your* child. However, I've been informed that you also claim my late brother as the father."

"I haven't claimed anything, yet," she countered. As she continued to speak, her voice lost the quavering note. "Until now, I haven't been given the opportunity to explain my presence."

"My mother," he began.

"Your mother is a lovely woman," she cut him off expertly, "but she decided quite without my help that Rose was her granddaughter."

"Are you denying it?"

He waited, breath held. Unreasonably, he realized that he desperately wanted her to do just that. Deny it.

For a count of five, she gave no answer. Then finally, quietly, she said, "No."

"It is Ian's child, then?"

"*She* is, yes."

"And why should I believe you?" Even to his own ears, his voice sounded cold.

"I brought proof," she said and stood up.

Tearing his gaze away from the swell of her bosom, Alexander waited.

She slipped her hand into the pocket of her skirt and pulled out a small piece of paper, folded in two. Without a word, she handed it to him.

His fingers touched hers and Alexander felt the warmth of her to his toes. He glanced up quickly, to see if she'd felt anything, but her features were masked. Telling himself he was imagining things, Alexander focused his attention on the note in his hand.

Carefully unfolding it, his gaze fell on his father's elegant script. Without thinking, he read the note aloud. " 'Reverend Simmons.' "

"My father," she interrupted.

A *parson* the father of a fallen woman? How very biblical. He started again. " 'Please accept this donation for the needy members of your flock.' " Flock indeed, Alexander thought grimly. It was so like his father to couch his real intent behind layers of confusion. He continued, " 'I hope this *one hundred pounds* will be of some use, especially in the care and feeding of unfortunate girls and their offspring.' "

Alexander glanced up at the woman. High color flushed her cheeks a bright crimson.

" 'Care and feeding,' " she muttered thickly, "sounds as if he's donating to a zoo."

That was precisely what it sounded like. Not for the first time, Alexander realized from whom Ian had inherited his cruel streak. Admittedly, though, the son had far outstripped the father in terms of pettiness and cruelty.

Douglas MacGregor's sometimes cruel actions were simply thoughtless mistakes.

And thanks to his father, Alexander was now in the unfortunate position of having to apologize to his brother's mistress.

"My father, well," he groped for the proper words, "I'm certain he didn't mean that, Miss Simmons."

"I think that is precisely what he meant, Mr. Mac-Gregor."

Alexander's eyes narrowed thoughtfully. He'd thought her high color due to embarrassment. He was just beginning to realize that rage was the cause. Not humiliation. The woman was veritably *seething*. Not that he could blame her, really.

But there was something else wrong too. Silently he reread the note. One hundred pounds. One hundred? Surely that wasn't right? It seemed to him that he clearly recalled his father mentioning the sum of one *thousand* pounds. Yes. It was a thousand, he was sure of it.

Because Douglas MacGregor wanted to make sure that he would never be troubled by Ian's by-blow in future.

Carefully Alexander studied the numbers on the note. Tilting it into the light more fully, he could only just make out the faintest of lines. But it was enough to convince him.

The third zero had been erased. Rubbed out almost entirely.

Ian.

Alexander muttered a vicious curse under his breath and directed it at his brother, in whatever afterlife was granted to malicious, greedy bastards like himself.

Instantly the scene played out in that very room more than two years ago rushed into his mind. In memory, Alexander saw again his father, his brother, and himself sequestered in the study. He watched Douglas Mac-Gregor hand over a thousand pounds cash along with the note to Ian.

"Take this to the girl's father, Ian."

"Thank you, Father." The oldest son smirked a bit as he added, "I *do* appreciate this. She might have built this entire unfortunate situation into a bloody scandal, y'know." Ian sniffed and tucked the bills into his inside pocket.

"And she'd have the right, by God!" When Douglas MacGregor's voice thundered, even his grown sons jumped to attention. "If ye must take yer pleasure where you find it, ye fool—make damn sure it's a married woman! For the love of heaven, stay the hell away from virginal village girls!"

"She told me . . ." Ian's lie faded off into nothingness.

"Don't lie to me, man! I'm yer father and I know ye for what ye are." Douglas shook his fist in helpless rage. "But God help me, I'll not see yer mother hurt by the likes of ye!"

Alexander studied his older brother's face and couldn't even find pleasure in watching his discomfort. He knew Ian too well for that. Any remorse or regret the man displayed now was merely an act. A performance designed expressly to help him achieve his own ends. Alexander knew that once out of sight of their father, Ian would go on just as he was, without another thought about the family, or the woman he'd ruined.

"And see that ye get her father to sign a receipt," Douglas added slyly, proving that he knew Ian every bit as well as he claimed.

Ian blanched.

"I want to know that my money went where it was intended."

Father and son stared at each other in the dimly lit room. It was not the first time that Alexander had watched his father wait, to make the other man speak.

Finally, Ian nodded his agreement. "I'll be back in a week or so. *With* the receipt."

"Ye'll be back in three days. *With* the receipt," Douglas countered.

Ian jerked his father a nod and stormed from the room, never even glancing at his younger brother.

Douglas sat down in the big leather chair and stared at his work-worn hands for a long moment before looking to Alexander.

"If I see signs that you've become like *him*," he warned, "I swear to the Holy Mother, I'll kill ye myself."

And, later, when Ian had brought the receipt, it had contained no mention of the amount of money tendered.

"Mr. MacGregor?" The woman's voice demanded his

attention and dragged Alexander away from his memories.

"Yes?"

"Do you accept my proof?"

"Yes," he sighed heavily. There was little else he could do. Even from the grave, Ian had managed to make a mess of the MacGregor family. Alexander now knew that Ian had given the mother of his child a measly one hundred pounds and kept nine hundred for his own use.

"Then you'll help me take care of Rose?"

"Rose?"

"My . . . daughter."

"Ah, of course." Damned strange, he told himself. Hard as he tried, he couldn't seem to imagine this woman handing over her virtue and her future to Ian. He shook his head. That was hardly of utmost importance now, however. "We shall have to talk about this, Miss Simmons, you and I. And then I will do whatever I think best for the girl."

"But . . ."

"Sit down, if you please. This may take quite a while."

"Well, Michael?" Tess whispered as she came up behind the crouching butler.

Harris jumped, startled. Straightening away from the study keyhole with as much dignity as possible, he said, "There's been no shouting as yet, madam."

She sighed. "That's a good sign. Wouldn't you say?"

"I wouldn't know, madam." His tone stiffened slightly.

"Ah, Michael," she urged, laying one hand on his forearm, "don't be angry with me."

He glanced down at her hand before raising his gaze to a spot just an inch or so above her eyes. Looking past her dispassionately, he said, "Listening at doorways is most undignified, madam."

"I know." Her hand dropped away and she looked down before she saw the glimmer of disappointment cross his face. "I'm sorry I asked you to eavesdrop, Michael. But this means so very much to me, you know. That child . . ."

Harris cleared his throat uncomfortably, and despite his best efforts, his gaze slipped down to hers. "I understand completely, madam."

"Then you forgive me?" She smiled hesitantly.

Anything, he thought. Aloud, though, he said only, "Think nothing of it, ma'am."

"The best thing for the child, as I'm sure you'll agree," Alexander said with a nod at the girl's mother, "is that she stay here for the time being . . ."

"The time being?"

"Well, certainly. After all, this is not something to be decided on a whim, is it?"

Kit watched him carefully. He hadn't said anything about *her*. Did he expect her to leave Rose with strangers?

"Rose and I have never been separated," she hinted, hoping he would say something to put her out of this misery.

"I'm sure."

"She's uncomfortable with strangers."

"Undoubtedly."

"She's never been away from home before."

"I'm sure she will adjust to her new surroundings."

Kit's jaw clenched to keep from screaming at him. He seemed to be deliberately avoiding the one issue she most needed him to address. A quick glance at his shuttered features, though, didn't tell her anything.

"Perhaps," she said in desperation, "it would be best if you were to settle a small sum on Rose. Then we could simply go back home. Where we belong."

"I'm afraid not," he answered and stood up. "It seems my mother is quite intent on getting to know her granddaughter."

"But—" Kit stood up too and faced him. No matter what, she would not be separated from Rose. Not now. Not ever.

"Miss Simmons!" he snapped, then clapped one hand to his forehead. "I'm quite certain," Alexander continued in a much quieter tone, "both you and your daughter will be made relatively happy here. Why don't we simply leave things at that for now. Shall we?"

Her heart started beating again. They were safe. For the moment. "Of course."

"Thank you." He swept her a mocking bow, then muttered, "Now, if you'll excuse me, I need to find something for this damned headache."

4

Almost guiltily, Kit picked up a cookie from the tray at her side and nibbled at the edge. The delicate, nut-flavored shortbread melted in her mouth and she told herself she would have to be careful that she didn't become too used to such luxuries.

Leaning back in the comfortable old rocking chair, Kit stared blankly at the morning sunshine pouring through the nursery window and gave her mind free rein to wander.

In the few days since arriving at the MacGregor house, she and Rose had been treated lavishly by nearly every member of the household. The servants, save for one, seemed to have taken their lead from Mrs. Mac-Gregor, *Tess*, Kit mentally corrected. It seemed as though the older woman couldn't do enough to make sure both Kit and Rose were happy and well cared for.

The nursery, Kit thought, was proof enough of that. She looked around the large, well-appointed room and couldn't quite contain a smile.

Rose's bed, from its polished cherry-wood headboard to its pale yellow eiderdown coverlet, was literally buried under a mountain of toy animals. Lining the walls were stacks of books, a rocking horse, toy trains, and even a tiny carriage so that Rose could take her new "babies" for walks.

Kit glanced at the little girl, seated on the floor across the room from her. Rose's soft brown hair fell in shining waves to the shoulders of her white, lace-dotted gown. Her stockings lay crumpled around the chubby ankles of her widespread legs while she determinedly pushed a bright red ball to Polly. Laughing delightedly, the young maid seemed willing to play the game interminably.

Rose looked happy. In fact, she was the very image of a well-fed, well-cared-for child of a wealthy family.

Quite different, Kit admitted with a sudden frown, from the child's situation only a few weeks ago. And though she tried to stop herself, Kit wasn't able to stifle the tiny pangs of jealousy. It wasn't right, but she found herself almost resenting the very care she'd come to this house to demand.

Oh, she was grateful that so far everything had worked out so nicely. And, as far as she was concerned, this special treatment was only what Rose deserved. Still, everything the MacGregors did for Rose without a second thought made the child's former life look like a prison sentence.

All the small indulgences Kit had tried to provide before seemed trivial compared to daily life at the Mac-Gregors. And despite her best efforts to curb her resentment, Kit continued to experience brief flashes of anger at the circumstances.

Her own parents, though good, honest people, had never had more than two coins to rub together. Then, when Marian had found herself in the family way, things became even harder. Even the collections at Sunday service dropped to hardly more than a handful of coins. It seemed that even though the villagers remained friendly enough, they hardly thought it necessary to give more than a few pence to a minister who'd been unable to keep his own daughter on the straight and narrow path.

Old frustrations simmered deep within her as Kit remembered the look on her father's face after Ian Mac-Gregor had made his last call on the Simmons family.

"One hundred pounds," he'd mumbled, his gnarled fingers rubbing the back of his neck. "My daughter's virtue and reputation sold for one hundred pounds."

Of course, he'd *had* to accept the money, as much as he'd hated to. Her father had not been a man to allow his family to suffer for his pride's sake.

And bitter as it was to admit it, Kit thought, the money *had* come in handy more than once. In fact, after her parents' deaths, what little had remained of that one hundred pounds had seen them fed and clothed and finally financed Kit's and Rose's trip to London.

"More!"

Rose's shriek snapped Kit from her thoughts and she shook her head, ridding herself of the last of the memories. It would do no good to relive them yet again. Still, she told herself as she stared about her at the lovely room, one hundred pounds was nothing to people like the MacGregors.

Despite their seeming generosity now, only two years ago they'd expected a child to be raised and fed on a sum less than would be spent on a new suit of clothes for the master of the great house.

Alex MacGregor.

Kit grumbled under her breath at the thought of the

irritating man. He and his housekeeper were the only two people in that house who'd made it perfectly clear they were unhappy with the present situation.

Oh, Alex was a bit less obvious in his distaste than his housekeeper. *He* simply stared at Kit as though she were some unusual creature released from the British Museum for a brief stay with polite society.

And she seemed to run into him quite a bit considering the size of the MacGregor house. Time and again, they seemed to be thrown together, though she'd only seen him once in the nursery. For some reason, he preferred to visit with his niece when she, Kit, wasn't present. According to Polly, though, Alexander was becoming quite a favorite of Rose's.

But then, she was only a baby. She hadn't learned yet to guard herself against a smooth tongue and languorous eyes.

Kit forced herself to breathe slowly as she recalled the insolent way Alex's eyes followed her every movement. The habit he had of licking his lips slightly when watching her, as if he was preparing to feast himself on her person. And as long as she was being honest with herself, she had to admit to the strange, quivering sensations that coursed through her every time his deep voice rumbled through a room.

And only last night . . . she thought, but immediately quelled the memory. She refused to think about that right now.

Yes, Alex was unsettling, but she could deal with that type of bother. Heaven knew he wasn't the *first* to think he could steal past her defenses. Though thinking as he did that she was Ian's former mistress, he was the first to have reason to believe he'd succeed.

Alexander MacGregor might be difficult, but Kit didn't doubt her abilities to watch out for herself.

If truth be known, it was Mrs. Beedle, the house-keeper, who was beginning to worry Kit. The stiff-lipped older woman had made no secret of her distaste both for Kit and Rose. Barely polite when Mrs. MacGregor was within earshot, Mrs. Beedle dropped all pretense when she and Kit were alone.

Only an hour ago the housekeeper had stopped Kit in the hall outside the nursery.

"I know what you're after, my girl," she'd whispered.

Kit turned her head from the strange gleam in the woman's black eyes, but forced herself to stand her ground. After all, the mistress of the house had made her and Rose welcome. What did she have to fear from a housekeeper?

"What do you want, Mrs. Beedle?"

"Nothing the likes of you could give me, girl," the woman answered, leaning closer.

Kit glanced around the empty hall, looking for some-one, anyone, to distract the woman long enough for Kit to make an escape. But there was no one. The corridor in front and behind her stretched on forever, with no sign of life. The only witnesses to Mrs. Beedle's rude-ness were the stiff, formalized paintings of animals, country lanes, and the occasional angel or saint.

Kit kept her voice calm, refusing to give the woman the satisfaction of knowing she'd upset her.

"Rose is waiting for me in the nursery, Mrs. Beedle. If you'll excuse me . . ." She tried to step aside.

The housekeeper moved to block her. "Rose. Too pretty a name for a bastard if you ask me. And you needn't bother with your polite manners. *I'm* not fooled. You're no more a lady than she who pretends to run this house!"

Rage boiled up inside Kit and it was only with a monumental effort that she kept from slapping the woman's bony cheeks. She'd almost come to expect the nastiness directed at her. But that the housekeeper should belittle the very woman who not only paid her salary but had been Rose's salvation was too much. Kit opened her mouth to give the shriveled old woman a taste of her own medicine, but before she could speak, Tess Mac-Gregor appeared at the stair landing.

In an instant Mrs. Beedle's hate-filled features relaxed into a vacant, disapproving frown that was plainly directed at both Kit *and* her mistress. Then she walked past Kit, nodded at Tess, and descended the stairs.

"Is everything all right, dear?" Tess asked, ignoring the other woman as she closed the distance between her and Kit.

"Yes," Kit answered, deciding to keep the ugly confrontation to herself for the time being, "everything is fine, thank you."

"Splendid!" Tess hooked her arm through Kit's and steered the younger woman toward the nursery. "Why don't you and I go and visit sweet Rose and I'll tell you about my little surprise."

"Miss?"

Kit sighed and looked up as Polly's voice recalled her to the present. "Yes?"

"It's near eleven o'clock, miss." The young woman grinned. "You'll be expected now in your room."

"Oh, dear." Kit's lips pressed together sulkily. It was indeed time to deal with Tess's "surprise."

"It won't be so bad, miss." Polly reached for Rose and pulled the toddler onto her lap. "You'll see."

Kit pushed herself from the chair and took a couple of steps toward the door. "That's easy enough for *you* to say, Polly."

"Yes, miss." The girl bit back a smile and dipped her head to Rose's.

With no escape in sight, Kit left the nursery—and her quiet harbor—behind.

"Ian's child?"

"Quiet, man," Alexander ordered with a quick look over his shoulder. Just as he'd expected, John had spoken without thinking. It was for that very reason Alex had insisted on meeting in an out-of-the-way public house rather than his own club. "For God's sake, d'you think I want all of London to hear about this?"

"Sorry," John Tremayne lowered his voice and leaned across the tavern table, "but when did all this happen?"

"A few days ago." Alexander sighed, slid to the corner of the booth, and leaned back against the brick wall. Drawing his right foot up, he propped the sole of his polished boot on the nicked and scarred arm of the settle, then glanced again at his friend.

John's open, friendly face was a mask of stunned surprise. He ran his fingers wildly through his shock of blond hair, leaving it standing out at odd angles. His wide blue eyes looked about to pop from his head and his oversize Adam's apple bobbed up and down his long, thin throat like a cork on a fishing line.

Alexander sympathized. He had no doubt at all that he himself had looked much the same when he'd first heard the story.

"But how? Why?"

"How?" Alex snorted, lifted his near-empty glass of beer, and drained the last of its contents. Slamming the mug back onto the table, he said, "I assume the creature's mother took a train to London. As for why, that should be clear to you, John. And if it's not, perhaps I've got the wrong man looking after my finances."

"Huh?" The other man started, hesitated, then nodded slowly, saying, "Oh, of course. She wants money."

"Precisely my opinion."

"Is she blackmailing you then?"

"No."

"No?"

"No." Alexander frowned, signaled the barmaid for another beer, and scowled at the man across from him. "She didn't have to."

"What?"

"My mother has all but adopted the woman!"

"Ahhhhh . . ."

An expression of complete understanding settled on the other man's face. John Tremayne knew Tess Mac-Gregor every bit as well as Alex. The son of the Mac-Gregor groundskeeper in Scotland, John had been raised with Alex and Ian. At Tess's insistence, he'd even been taught by their tutor. And when he was ready, she'd packed him off for college, brushing aside his reluctance to accept a loan from her.

In time, he'd become Alex MacGregor's business manager as well as his closest friend.

"Well then," John said quietly and smiled his thanks as the serving girl brought them two fresh beers, "there's nothing to be done about it, is there?"

"Doesn't seem to be, no."

"Is she so appalling, Alex?" John grinned. "By the look on your face when you speak about her, my guess is that she's a three-headed troll with a harpy's tongue and a wart on her nose."

Alex frowned, lifted the beer, and took a long, deep swallow. A troll? Hardly. His body tightened just at the thought of her.

Bloody hell, she was driving him over the edge! Instantly his mind recalled the image of her as she'd been only the night before.

As was his habit, Alex had strolled into the house in the wee hours of the morning after a particularly disappointing night at the card table. He hadn't been able to get his mind off his brother's mistress long enough to stay even against two of the worst cardplayers he knew.

In the stillness, his own boot steps on the marble floor sounded like a marching band and somehow made him feel a bit—*lonely*. But he shrugged away the nonsensical notion and told himself that all he needed was a good night's rest.

Gaslight shone on the empty hall and he made a mental note to speak to Harris in the morning. Though he'd already insisted that the butler not wait up for his return every evening, he'd now have to convince the older man that he also didn't require a night-light left burning in welcome.

Alex tossed his greatcoat over the end of the oak banister, climbed five stairs, then stopped and reached up for the gas jet on the wall sconce. The flame lowered and the hall was thrown into darkness.

Someone gasped.

Immediately Alex turned the flame back up, then spun around. Kit Simmons stood below him in the hall, her fingers curled around the handle of a cup. As the gaslight scattered the shadows, she pulled in an unsteady breath.

The breath rushed from Alex's body in the same instant. His gaze swept over her, noting the bare feet peeking out from under the hem of her virginal-looking, plain white nightdress. Her deep brown hair lay across her right shoulder, tamed into the confines of one thick braid, knotted at the end with a piece of yellow ribbon. Then his sharp eyes settled on the gown's buttoned-up, lace-edged collar encircling her slender neck. Hardly the type of night apparel he'd expected from a woman of her character. And yet, perhaps it was the perfect choice. The yards of material covering her body practically screamed to be tossed aside. In his mind, the buttons slipped free, the simple cotton fabric fell to the floor, pooling around her ankles, and her delectable figure was bared to his gaze.

His throat tight, Alex noted the quick rise and fall of her breasts and knew that his open perusal was making her very nervous.

"You startled me," she finally whispered and her voice was like a gunshot in the quiet, shattering his fancies.

To compensate for feeling the fool, Alex's own voice came harsher than he'd planned.

"What are you doing prowling about the house at this hour?"

She lifted her chin defiantly. "I wasn't 'prowling.' I simply went to fetch a cup of warm milk."

"It couldn't wait until morning?"

"It's not for me," she countered quickly and walked to the base of the stairs. "It's for Rose."

"Oh." He watched her climb the stairs until she stood on the step just below him. At a loss for words suddenly, he blurted out, "We have servants, y'know. You might have called one of them to get you the blasted milk."

Disgust flashed across her features before she said, "You would have preferred that I wake Polly out of a well-earned rest?"

"Well."

"She works hard enough as it is," Kit continued, fixing her gaze firmly on his face. "I wouldn't think of asking her to run about in the middle of the night."

"That isn't the point."

"That's exactly the point. And you must think so as well, despite what you say."

"What in heaven are you prattling about?"

"You." She tossed a quick glance at the empty hall behind her. "Where is Harris? Shouldn't he be here to open the door for you and see you settled?"

"Hmmm."

"Exactly. You've told him not to wait for you, haven't you?"

"Well," Alex said, giving in to the ridiculous urge to defend himself. "I'm a grown man. There was no need."

"And I'm a grown woman."

"On that score, madam, you have my agreement." She was close enough to touch. The gaslight illuminated her features, giving her fair skin the sheen of fine porcelain. A faint scent of lavender came to him and he inhaled sharply, drawing it deep inside him.

"Uh . . ." Her tongue darted out to smooth over her lips and Alex barely managed to squelch the groan building in his throat.

"If you'll excuse me, Rose is waiting for her milk."

"Of course," he muttered and stepped back to allow her to pass.

She lifted the hem of her gown slightly, lowered her gaze to the steps before her, and began her climb to the upper floor.

Alex curled his fingers into the palms of his hands to keep from touching her as she slipped by him. But he allowed himself the pleasure of watching her every movement. The sway of her hips. The delightful flash of ankle and the pull of her nightdress against her body with every step.

By the time she'd reached the upper landing and then passed from his sight, Alexander was in torment. His body tight, his mind a jumble of thoughts, he was no longer in any condition for sleep. Instead, he went back downstairs, crossed the hall to his study, and poured himself a generous splash of brandy.

"Alex!"

John's voice splintered the rest of his memories and Alex blinked as he looked at the other man.

"Good God, man, have you gone deaf?"

"What?"

Frowning, John said, "I've been practically shouting at you and you haven't heard a word."

"Sorry. A lot on my mind."

"Apparently." John's eyebrows lifted as he asked yet again, "So, you didn't tell me. Is she really as bad as you've made out?"

"Actually . . . no, she's not. In fact, she's rather an attractive woman." Certainly an understatement, he added silently.

"In that case"—John grinned—"I shall stop by the house today. It's past time I visited with Tess, anyway."

Alexander scowled as he lifted the glass to his lips. The idiotic smile on his friend's face assured him that the man was eager for a meeting with Ian's former mistress. Indeed, why wouldn't he be? John Tremayne was well noted for his success with women. Indeed, seemingly without effort on his part, John never suffered for female company. From the lowliest scullery maid to the occasional duchess, women fell before John's guileless features and boyish charm.

And, for reasons he didn't quite understand himself, Alex would just as soon not have John Tremayne anywhere near Kit Simmons. But for the life of him, he couldn't think of a way to prevent it.

"It's a disgrace, that's what it is." Mrs. Beedle shifted her bony bottom on the hard-backed kitchen chair and reached for the nearby teapot. As she poured herself a second cup of tea, she went on, "Isn't bad enough—having a mistress that used to clean kitchens herself! No, now we're to treat a *harlot* as if she were a lady!"

"She seems a nice enough thing," cook said, barely

looking up from the vegetables she was slicing for supper. "Real helpful she is. Don't ask special favors of no one."

"I should think not!" Mrs. Beedle took a long drink of the cooling brew and set the china mug down on the table again. For the love of heaven. Hadn't she overlooked the appalling inadequacies of Mrs. MacGregor? Hadn't she lowered herself far enough, agreeing to work for a family who made their money in *trade*? The fact that the MacGregors paid her almost double what she'd made when she'd worked for the late earl was neither here nor there. One had to be able to hold one's head up, after all.

And after a lifetime of protecting her own virtue, *she*, Theodora Beedle, was now expected to wait on and cater to a woman of accommodating morals? It was more than could be expected of anyone! "A girl like that . . . no better than she should be, that's what *I* say! And that —that—*child*."

"Here now, Mrs. Beedle, that's a sweet baby." Cook looked up, thought better of it immediately, and lowered her gaze to the pile of carrots before her.

"Makes no matter," the housekeeper said. Pointing her index finger at the woman opposite her, she added, "You mark my words, Elmira. No good ever comes from sin. None at all. That child is the spawn of the devil!"

"Devil my arse," another voice chimed in.

Mrs. Beedle gasped, turned toward the staircase, and frowned at Polly as the young maid ran down the last few steps. "Mind your language when you speak to me, girl."

"Wasn't speakin' to you, ma'am." Polly walked past

the housekeeper, stepped up to the nearest cupboard, and reached for a teacup. "I only come downstairs for a quick cuppa." She shrugged, pushed the teakettle onto the hob, and winked at cook before adding, "I didn't have any idea it was *you* talkin', ma'am. I just heard somethin' foolish and talked right up."

"Foolish, is it?"

"Well, ma'am, now that you ask me, yes." Dropping down onto a chair beside Elmira, Polly snatched one of the freshly peeled carrots, bit off the end, and went on. "The very idea, that lovely little girl bein' the spawn of the devil—"

"And what would you call it then, missy?"

"I call her Rose." Polly grinned up at Elmira when the cook smothered a chuckle.

"All well and good for *you* to say so."

" 'Ere now"—Polly's eyes narrowed just a bit—"what's that supposed to mean?"

"Only that it's not surprising to find that you sympathize with the harlot and her ill-gotten offspring." Mrs. Beedle tugged at the cuffs of her gray gown, lifted her pointed chin, and said, "Birds of a feather, y'know."

"Are you accusin' me of somethin'?"

Elmira laid one beefy hand on Polly's shoulder in a none-too-subtle attempt to calm the girl.

"Not at all. I'm only telling you that when *your* belly is full, you'll not find the same grand treatment from the 'lady' of this house that the other slut has."

"Why you dried up old . . ."

"Keep in mind, my girl, that *I* am in charge of the servants in this household." Pushing herself to her feet, Mrs. Beedle glared down at the young maid. "Before you say too much, remember that without a character, you would be hard put to find employment elsewhere."

Polly bit down hard on her bottom lip. There was nothing she'd like better than to lay the sharp side of her tongue against the old harpy. And she'd do it in a heartbeat but for one thing. The old bitch was right.

Oh, Polly knew that Mrs. MacGregor wouldn't let her be discharged. But Beedle could have Polly out on the street before the mistress knew anything about it. And for the first time in her eighteen years, Polly was happy. She enjoyed working for the MacGregors. Oh, Mr. Alex was no prize, certainly. Handsome is as handsome does, as Polly's mother used to say. But old Mrs. MacGregor was a darling. Kind and always smiling.

And they weren't stingy with their food, neither. Since coming into service with the MacGregors two years before, she'd never known a hungry night.

No. She was in no position to defy Mrs. Beedle. Besides, she told herself, in a few weeks they'd all be off to the country house, leaving the old bitch behind in London. Surely, Polly thought desperately, she could hold her tongue a few more weeks.

Steam erupted from the teakettle's spout and Polly leapt to her feet, glad of the excuse to turn her back on the woman. Quickly she moved the pot off the fire and kept her back to the housekeeper for good measure.

"Nothing to say?" Mrs. Beedle snorted. "I thought not. Elmira! See that supper is served precisely at seven o'clock tonight."

"Yes'm."

A muffled, far-off crash followed the cook's reply.

And from a distance came the unmistakable sounds of glass splintering.

"What in heaven is going on out there?" Mrs. Beedle lifted the hem of her gown and hurried across the room. The ring of keys at her belt jingling with every step, she pushed through the door to the main hall.

"Dinner *precisely* at seven, then, cook?" Polly mimicked.

"That's right." Elmira sighed. "As it is every night."

"That old harridan is goin' to push me too far one day and I'm goin' to have a go at her!"

Elmira glanced at the younger woman and shook her head. "Her kind get their comeuppance soon enough, Polly girl. They always do."

"I'd surely like a front row seat for that!"

"Save one for me as well, then." Elmira winked.

Polly laughed, poured hot water into the now cool pot on the table, and replaced the heavy crockery lid. As she covered the little flowered pot with a tea cozy, a child's scream echoed through the house.

5

"**D**o please stand still, miss, else you'll be stuck with one of these pins."

Kit looked down at the woman kneeling at her feet. "I *am* sorry. I'm simply not accustomed to this sort of thing."

"Ah well." The young woman clucked her tongue and checked her measuring tape again. She wrote something down on a small pad of paper, then said, "There's nothing to it, miss. You'll see. Why, we're near finished as it is."

Thank heaven, Kit sighed silently. When the dressmaker's assistant gave her a gentle nudge, Kit obediently made a half turn and stopped. It seemed as though she'd been standing still while being poked at and measured for days.

It simply wasn't right, she told herself for the twentieth time. She didn't need any new dresses. Now that her own bags had been delivered from the station, she had more than sufficient clothes for her needs. True, they weren't exactly fashionable—but then, she thought with a smile, she hadn't received many invitations to balls lately anyway. What did it matter if more than one of her gowns had had the hems and sleeves turned? They were certainly good enough for her.

Kit could understand Mrs. MacGregor's wanting to order new clothes for Rose. In fact, she'd enjoyed helping to select fabric and designs. It was a pleasure seeing the little girl dressed in velvets and laces.

But for heaven's sake, Kit thought. *She* wasn't a member of the MacGregor family. There was no need for the older woman to completely outfit *her* as well as Rose. And she'd tried to tell Tess MacGregor that only a few hours ago. The moment Tess had explained her "surprise."

"Nonsense," the woman had replied, "you're a part of this family now. Besides, Alex insisted."

Knowing that Alex MacGregor had had a hand in all this had somehow made it even harder to bear. But when Kit tried to object, Tess rushed on. "My dear, you're the mother of my only grandchild. If you'll allow it, I'd like to think of you as my daughter."

The woman's kindness stabbed at Kit's heart. What would Tess have to say if she knew that Kit was lying? Would Rose's destitute *aunt* be as welcome as her *mother*? Or would the *aunt* find herself out on the street?

Though the lie came hard, Kit swallowed back the urge to confess. Better she be a liar than be separated from Rose.

Rose. Thoughts of the girl brought a smile to Kit's face despite the sudden prick of a needle in her calf.

"Sorry, miss," the younger woman whispered.

"It's all right," Kit assured her quickly.

"If you don't mind my sayin' so, miss," the assistant continued softly, "Mr. MacGregor's not goin' to like the fabrics you've picked very much."

"What?"

The woman pushed herself to her feet and looked up at Kit, still standing on a low stool. "It's just that when Mrs. Talbot, the lady I work for, sent me here, she said you was to have whatever you wanted."

"Yes . . ." Confused, Kit waited.

"Well, miss," she sucked in a gulp of air and forced herself to say, "I don't think Mr. MacGregor wanted you dressed all in gray and brown."

"No?" She'd chosen plain, serviceable material purposely. If she was going to have new clothes, at least they would be practical! What possible use would she have for silks and satins? Besides, a voice in the back of her brain whispered, if she was forced to leave the Mac-Gregor house, she would have the proper attire necessary to find a position as a governess.

Thankfully, her late father had seen to her education. A scholarly man, the Reverend Simmons had enjoyed helping his daughters discover the world around them. And because of him, Kit was capable of supporting herself if the need arose.

Her eyes squeezed shut as if closing off the thought entirely. Leaving the MacGregors would mean leaving Rose.

"Oh, no, miss," the girl continued. "Why, I remember him tellin' Mrs. Talbot that he thought bright, clear colors would look best on you, what with your hair and all."

Surprise flooded her. Why on earth was the man taking such an interest in her clothing? Was he afraid she'd shame him somehow? And if so, why was he allowing her to stay?

Bright, clear colors, he said, had he? Just what bright color did he have in mind, Kit wondered. More to herself than the other woman, she said quietly, "Red, I suppose?"

"Oh, my, miss! That *would* be lovely!"

Kit smiled at her. The dressmaker's assistant was, after all, only trying to do her job. But behind her smile, Kit's thoughts were on Alex. As they had been too often of late.

Why was he so concerned with her wardrobe? The last few times she'd caught him looking at her, Kit had had the distinct impression the man was looking *through* her clothes, not *at* them. In fact, every time his blue eyes rested on her for even the shortest bit, her breathing came short and fast and the most unusual *heat* seemed to engulf her.

Kit felt the familiar flush racing across her flesh and she turned a nervous glance toward her closed bedroom door. She wouldn't put it past Alexander MacGregor to suddenly arrive home and come blundering into her room demanding to speak to her! Immediately she crossed her arms over her near-naked bosom. Then, shaking her head, Kit told herself she was being ridiculous. He would have no reason to come searching her out.

Still, standing in the middle of her room wearing nothing but her underclothes did little to quell her uneasiness.

A taunting voice in the back of her mind sounded out then, asking why she should be uneasy? Hadn't Alex already seen her in her nightdress? Inwardly she groaned as she finally allowed herself to recall the night before.

The two of them, only inches apart, surrounded by the pale nimbus of gaslight. He'd smelled of tobacco and brandy and there was a faint shadow of whiskers along his jawline.

She'd certainly noticed his good looks before that instant. Kit still remembered quite clearly their initial meeting and the jarring shock that rippled through her at the touch of his hand.

And yet, not until they were together in the dark had she felt the almost overwhelming urge to feel his arms slip around her. To taste his mouth with her own.

From the moment she'd joined him on the stairs, Kit had felt the danger emanating from him. Not that she feared he would harm her physically. No, the danger she sensed from him was directed more at her virtue.

Perhaps it was the silence of the night. Perhaps it was because they'd seemed to be alone in the world. And then again, perhaps it was because she was no wiser than her sister Marian had been.

Suddenly, deliberately, Kit pushed the disturbing memory away. What was it about the MacGregor men? she asked herself. Or did it have nothing to do with them at all? Was there instead some fatal flaw in the Simmons women? Would she really allow herself to lose all sense—as her sister had—because of a handsome face?

Kit dragged in several deep breaths and squared her

shoulders. No. She'd seen firsthand what happened when a woman took a misstep.

First, her own body betrayed her with the faint stirrings of a new life. Then, more often than not, her seducer moved on to his next conquest, leaving the foolish woman's life and reputation in tatters. His own guilt and responsibility was easily assuaged with a few pound notes.

"Are you all right, miss?"

"Hmmm?" Kit shook her head. "Yes, yes, I'm fine." And will be, she added silently, as long as she kept her wits about her.

"Can I tell Mrs. Talbot you've changed your mind about the color of the new gowns then?"

"No, I don't think so."

"Mr. MacGregor won't like it, miss."

"Then Mr. MacGregor won't have to wear them."

"If you say so, miss." The assistant gathered up her pins and measuring tapes. "I'll be off now and you should have the first of your things in two days."

"Thank you," Kit started, "but there's no hurry—"

A child's scream sliced through the air and stopped Kit midsentence.

Rose.

Ignoring the other woman's baffled expression, Kit jumped off the stool, snatched up a dressing gown from the foot of her bed, and raced for the door and the staircase beyond.

"Look at what you've done, you miserable child!"

Rose jammed the middle two fingers of her right

hand in her mouth and stared up at the angry woman through teary eyes.

Mrs. Beedle's breath came in short, furious pants. Blood thundered through her veins and she pressed her palms to the sides of her head as if to quiet the painful throbbing. Briefly she looked away from the product of sin quaking before her, to the destruction littering the once pristine marble floor.

A small oak pedestal table lay on its side and scattered all across the hall were delicately flowered shards of what had been an antique china vase. Mrs. Beedle swallowed convulsively, stifling the moan of distress lodged in her throat.

She remembered when that piece had first been delivered to the house. More than five years it had stood proudly in the entry hall, its fragile beauty a reminder that not only those who deserved great works of art possessed them.

But more than that, from the moment it arrived the vase had become, in Mrs. Beedle's mind, her own. She hadn't even allowed the maids to touch it, insisting instead on dusting the beautiful ornament herself. Over the years it had become a comfort to her. The delicate vase represented everything in life that she'd wanted and never had. Everything she'd deserved and never received.

And since she was the only person in the house to take the slightest notice of it, the vase's presence reinforced her own belief that the MacGregors, even with all their wealth, were incapable of appreciating beauty for its own sake.

Now a child of sin had destroyed it without so much

as a second thought. Just as the child's very existence signified moral destruction. Mrs. Beedle's sharp black eyes glanced about the hall. Where was the creature's mother? Didn't the harlot know enough to keep the child locked away in the nursery? Had she no shame at all? Did she not even have the sense to keep a watchful eye on the brat? Was it left to Mrs. Beedle to do *everything*?

Rose took a half step back and sucked even harder at her fingers. Soft brown hair flew untidily about the girl's round face and there was a tear in the hem of her new white dress. Her pale green eyes filled to overflowing with tears, the child's voice was garbled as she asked, "An' Kit?"

Pure, hot anger raced through the older woman's body. She shook with the strength of it. All her life, she'd guarded her virtue, protected and defended her name. Even her marriage had been short-lived. As soon as she'd discovered the indignities of the marriage bed, Mrs. Beedle had left her husband's home—her virtue bruised but intact.

And this is what she'd come to. Looking after the bastard spawn of a loose woman.

"Rose sorry," the little girl said, her chin wobbling.

"It's little use dressing trash in lace," Mrs. Beedle muttered, ignoring the child's apology. "Underneath, it remains trash." One long-fingered hand shot out and curled around Rose's pudgy forearm. Yanking the child's fingers from her mouth, Mrs. Beedle went on talking in a rushed, harsh whisper. "If there's no one else to teach you to respect your betters, the job falls to me." A long, dry tendril of gray hair pulled free of its knot and fell to lie along her cheek.

She stared into the toddler's watery green eyes and took courage from the fear she saw. "The devil's in you, child, and it's up to me to tame it. If you're to live in *this* house, you'll do well to remember who's in charge."

Backing up, Mrs. Beedle dragged the whimpering girl toward a high-backed, mahogany bench set against the wall. Seating herself, the housekeeper pulled the tiny body across her lap, flipped up the tattered, lacy hem of the girl's skirt, then raised her hand high overhead. "I'll whip the devil out of you, child! If it takes me all day!"

Her open palm smacked against the girl's behind and Rose screeched in pain.

Grimly Mrs. Beedle held the squirming child in place and lifted her hand again. "Crying will not deter me from my duty!" she shouted just before she smacked Rose a second time.

She didn't hear the front door swing open. She didn't notice the shaft of late afternoon sun that splashed across the marble floor and sparkled on the broken pieces of china. She didn't hear the hurried boot steps or the shouted commands to "Stop!"

In fact, Mrs. Beedle noticed nothing until her up-raised hand was suddenly caught in an iron grip and the wailing child snatched from her lap.

It was all Alex could do to keep from snapping the bony wrist he held so tightly. Instead, he sucked in air through gritted teeth and with his free hand cradled the weeping toddler close against his chest. Rose's small arms encircled his neck and held on with every ounce of her puny strength. "Hurts," she choked out and Alex swallowed another rush of anger. Her short legs locked around his middle and the heels of her new shoes dug into his ribs. He felt her hot tears and shook with the force of her sobs.

Alex fought desperately for control. He'd never experienced such a powerful surge of rage. For the first time in his life, he completely understood what people meant when they said they'd "seen red." From the moment he opened the door and spied Mrs. Beedle beating his brother's child, he'd been near suffocated by a choking haze of anger. Alex wanted nothing more at that instant than to put his fist through a wall. *Anything* to release the tightly coiled anger threatening to strangle him. But he was forced instead to be still. The little girl he held was in no condition to be treated to yet another example of an adult's untempered fury.

Glaring down at the woman who'd run his household for the last six years, it was as if he were seeing her for the first time. Of course, Alex admitted silently, he'd hardly paid her the slightest bit of notice over the years at all. He hadn't thought it necessary. The house was always in good order, meals on time, and the servants went about their business and left him to his. As it should be.

And yet . . . staring down into the woman's small, shining black eyes, Alex realized that *nothing* was as it should be.

Suddenly disgusted, he threw her wrist from him as if tossing away a bit of garbage. As she cupped her injured hand with the other, she began to talk in a futile attempt at an explanation. As if there *were* an excuse for her behavior.

Immediately Alex cut her off and heard himself shout, "What the bloody hell do you think you were doing?"

Rose cried a bit harder and Alex cursed himself under his breath as he began to pat her back awkwardly. The little girl hiccuped, nestled her wet cheeks against his throat, and thrust her fingers back into her mouth.

"The child broke the vase, Mr. MacGregor," Mrs. Beedle said firmly. "I was . . . *chastising* her."

"Is *that* what you call it?"

"Alex . . ."

He didn't even turn when John stepped up behind him. *"Chastising?"* Alex repeated. "The child's little more than an infant!"

"Rose!" Kit's voice called out from the top of the stairs, but Alex didn't look. Instead he kept his gaze riveted on Mrs. Beedle.

"Infant or no," the woman said as she pushed herself up from the bench, "the devil's own must be made to learn."

"Devil?" The woman is unbalanced, his brain shouted. "Good God!"

"Rose?" Kit's voice was closer now and Alex heard her run across the hall and come to a stop beside him. Good, he thought. With the child safely deposited with her mother, Alex could deal more adequately with the tall, defiant-looking housekeeper.

He didn't glance at Kit, but tenderly pulled at the child's limp form in an attempt to hand her over.

Rose, though, wouldn't be budged. She tightened her

grip on his neck and shook her little head wildly. She felt safe with the big man. He'd come to her room to see her whenever Aunt Kit wasn't there. He even played ball with her once and laughed really loud when the ball hit his nose. Now, with his arms around her, Rose knew the mean lady couldn't hurt her anymore. She squeezed his neck again, harder this time.

A short spasm of unexpected pleasure shot through him. Alex had naturally assumed that Rose would be more comforted by her mother. That she would feel . . . *safer*. Apparently, she preferred him. Odd how good that knowledge felt. Surrendering to the situation, he once more began to pat the girl's back as she cuddled in closer.

"What is it?" Tess called out from upstairs. "I heard a scream. Is the baby all right?"

"Yes, Mother." Alex managed to make himself heard over the flood of servants streaming into the hall.

"Alex, what the devil is going on here?" John demanded, poking at his friend's shoulder.

"Yes, what happened?" Kit's question joined his.

"She's the devil's own, I tell you, sir!" The housekeeper raised her voice too, and Alex winced at the shrill tones she reached. "Spare the rod and spoil the child! It's what has to be done, sir!" Mrs. Beedle finished flatly and glared at him as if waiting for Alex to back down before her superior knowledge.

"Here," Polly's voice cut into the stunned silence, "is she on about the devil again?"

"Hush, girl," Elmira hissed.

"What has to be done, madam," Alex ignored everyone but the woman standing before him and roared out his own opinion, "is your packing! I want you out of this house before nightfall, do I make myself clear?"

"You can't discharge me!"

"I believe I just have," he countered. Then softly he whispered, "Hush now, Rose. All is well." Frowning at Mrs. Beedle, Alex added, "When you've finished packing, come to my study. I shall have your wages and a bit more in lieu of notice."

"You'll never get another like me to work in this place!"

"One can only hope," Alex said gravely.

"Amen," Polly muttered before being shushed again by the cook.

"Not with the likes of her"—Mrs. Beedle jerked a nod at Kit—"and her bastard living here!"

"Don't push me, madam." Alex drew himself up to his full height, towering over the frustrated housekeeper.

"You'll regret this." Mrs. Beedle leaned in closer and Alex almost backed up. Her eyes shone desperately and spittle dotted her chin as the words rushed from her throat. "You just see if you don't! No one treats Theodora Beedle like this! I've worked for the best families in London!"

"May I be of assistance, sir?"

Harris's cool, calm voice snaked through the chorus of shouts and it was with relief that Alex turned to his unflappable butler.

"Thank you, Harris." Suddenly disgusted with the entire scene, he sighed and said, "Please escort Mrs. Beedle to her rooms and assist her with her packing. Then bring her to me in my study."

"As you say, sir."

Harris walked past him and Alex was almost positive he saw a hint of a smile on the other man's face. Then, shaking his head, Alex turned to face the crowd around him.

"Are you going to tell me what's happening?"

"John, you're sounding peevish. It's most annoying."

"Give her to me," Kit demanded.

"I tried to," he said. "She didn't want to go." Alex turned to look at her and his jaw dropped. In the heat of battle, he hadn't realized that in her haste to reach Rose, Kit had come downstairs in her underwear.

His lips curved slightly as he told himself that he'd be willing to wager that *she* still didn't realize it. Not being one to miss a golden opportunity though, Alex allowed himself the pleasure of a quick, yet thorough study of her remarkable figure.

The swell of her bosom above the lace edging of her chemise drew his gaze unerringly. But after a moment, he also found himself admiring her narrow waist and rounded hips beneath the full, baggy pantaloons she wore.

Then John's whispered comment of male appreciation shook Alex from his reverie.

Frowning, he stepped in front of his old friend, blocking the other man's view of Kit. Hitching Rose a little higher, Alex asked quietly, "Were you planning on wearing that dressing gown you're holding? Or is it merely an accessory?"

"Hmmm? What?"

Alex leaned down a bit, allowed his half smile full rein, and said, "I do, of course, find your choice of afternoon wear most appealing personally. However, I believe the servants might misinterpret it."

"What are you . . ." Kit's question faded off into shocked silence. Her blue eyes narrowed, then widened again in a split second of realization. Hurriedly she turned her back on him and shoved her arms through the sleeves of her dressing gown.

Alex all but groaned aloud as the garment fell in soft folds around her. The sheer fabric did little more than satisfy convention. In fact, the pale blue diaphanous gown only defined the very form it purported to hide.

An all-too-familiar discomfort settled low in Alex's body and he grumbled something unintelligible in response.

"Papa?"

"Eh?" He pulled his head back and stared down into the now smiling face of the little girl in his arms. "What did you say?"

"Papa?" she said again.

At least, Alex was fairly certain that she said "papa." Since she was trying to speak around her fingers, it was a bit difficult to be sure.

Her tear-streaked face was flushed, her hair stood out around her head in a soft brown halo, and her lips were curved in the sweetest smile Alex had ever seen.

He knew in an instant that he was in serious trouble.

"Now, darling girl," Tess crooned gently, "close your eyes and sleep."

Rose curled up on her right side, put her folded hands together under her cheek, and burrowed deeper under her blankets.

Tess sat quietly beside the little girl, her fingers tenderly smoothing through the soft brown curls on her granddaughter's head. Softly she began to hum an old lullaby and smiled as the child's breathing became even, regular.

"That's right, precious baby, sleep and dream of hot cocoa oceans and sugarplum mountains." She bent low, planted a tender kiss on Rose's forehead, and promised quietly, "No one will ever hurt you again, darling. Grandmother promises."

Just the memory of that evil woman laying a hand on her dear little Rose made Tess shudder. At the moment she wanted nothing better than to run through London until she found the wretched Mrs. Beedle and then settle with her as she should have done years ago.

It was all her fault. Oh, no one had said so, but Tess knew it was true. As mistress of the house, she should have discharged the woman in her first month as housekeeper. But if she were to be honest, Mrs. Beedle had always intimidated her.

Tess knew very well what the stiff-necked housekeeper thought of her. And in a strange sense, she could even understand it. Mrs. Beedle *had* worked for the best houses in England. For her to have to take orders from a woman who was herself once a kitchen maid must have been galling. Not that Tess had ever given many orders.

Despite the years of easy living, she'd never quite become accustomed to the life of "lady of the manor." In her mind and heart, she knew she would always be Tess Taylor MacGregor, scullery maid, originally from Newcastle. And all the fine clothes and diction lessons in the world wouldn't change that. Not that she would change it if she could.

As far as she could see, the easy life her husband had provided for them had done her sons more harm than good.

One son had used women for his own pleasures, then cast them aside without another thought. And the other son had made the mistake of trusting the wrong woman at a much too tender age—with the result being that now he trusted *no* woman.

Tess sighed heavily. She still wasn't sure what had caused Ian to be such a wastrel of a man. Certainly it was nothing he'd learned from his father. Douglas Mac-Gregor was a fine, hardworking, honest man his whole life. Perhaps *too* hardworking. Perhaps if he'd spent more time with them, the boys wouldn't have—

This would do no good at all, she told herself firmly. What's done is done. And now Douglas and Ian both were gone from her. Still and all though, she had Alex. And Rose now too, thank God.

Tess blessed whatever saints had led Kit Simmons to bring the child to London. And every night since their arrival, Tess prayed that they wouldn't leave. Not just for Rose's sake, she told herself, but for Kit's as well.

She'd become very fond of the young woman, though for the life of her, she couldn't understand what Kit had seen in Ian. Tess was no doting mother, blind to her children's faults. She'd known Ian for what he was and was privately surprised when other women didn't recognize him as a bounder immediately.

Especially a woman who appeared to be as intelligent as Kit.

Carefully Tess stood up, walked to the nearest window, and lifted the curtain aside to peer out at the walled garden below. She wasn't surprised to see Kit, seated on the bench at the base of the oak tree, reading quietly.

The young woman had laid claim to the garden soon after her arrival. Perhaps she too, just like Tess, found peace there in the quiet.

Thoughtfully Tess stared down at her and remembered the look on Alex's face when he turned and saw the young woman in her undergarments. A soft smile curved Tess's lips as she suddenly realized just why that certain expression on Alex's features had seemed so familiar at the time.

He looked much like his father had when Douglas first began courting Tess so many years before.

Could it be possible?

She dropped the curtain back into place and turned back around to face her sleeping granddaughter. Her brain raced with one wild thought after another.

After all, they had no assurances that Kit and Rose would stay with them. There was nothing to stop Kit from taking her daughter and leaving just as suddenly as they'd appeared. And that, Tess thought, would be impossible to bear.

The only way to be absolutely sure that Kit never left would be to make her a *real* member of the family.

Her motives were not entirely selfish, she told herself. It was past time that Alex should be married. And who better than Kit?

Her index finger tapping gently against her chin, Tess

told herself that perhaps it wouldn't be as difficult as it sounded. She'd seen for herself that Alex was interested. Perhaps all he needs, she thought, is a push in the right direction.

6

Kit finally gave up and closed the covers of the book. For the last half hour, she'd been staring blankly at the same page and hadn't read a word. She was alone in the garden. There was no one watching. There really was no point at all in continuing the pretense of reading. Especially since the afternoon light was quickly fading into dusk.

Leaning her head back against the cragged surface of the oak tree's thick trunk, Kit closed her eyes and willed herself to calm down. The hideous scene with Mrs. Beedle was over. The woman had, in fact, already left the house. Amid a flurry of veiled threats and dire warnings of future trouble, the housekeeper had been "escorted" through the back door by an unshakable Harris.

Rose was upstairs, being tucked in for a nap by her doting grandmother. And Alex had, thankfully, taken himself off somewhere.

There was no earthly reason for her temper to still be on the boil.

But it was.

Kit's eyes snapped open and she stared up through the leafy branches overhead at the small patches of late afternoon sky. Deliberately she drew in long, steady breaths. The sweet, heady scent of summer roses filled her, bringing a reluctant half smile to her lips. She told herself to concentrate on the whispered hush of leaves brushing against each other in the breeze. The now familiar, steady beat of horse's hooves on the street beyond played out a soothing rhythm. In the boughs above her, birds chattered to each other and occasionally one would swoop to the ground in search of food.

She sighed as the peace of the garden crept over her. For a moment Kit thought she might succeed in forcing the memories of Rose's screams and Mrs. Beedle's vicious rantings into a dark corner of her mind.

But the moment she began to relax, her brain drew up the image of that scene in the hall. Again and again, Kit relived it all. The servants crowded around. Alex, holding Rose closely, protectively. The blond stranger staring at her as if she'd lost her mind.

That last thought she pushed away firmly. At the moment she wasn't the least bit interested in recalling her state of dress—or rather *un*-dress—during the confrontation. What she wanted, no, what she *needed* was the opportunity to face Mrs. Beedle herself. To have the satisfaction of slapping the smug expression from the harridan's features.

Instead, Kit thought disgustedly, she was sitting in the rose garden, pretending to read a book in the growing dark.

Of course, she was more than pleased that the dreadful woman was gone. And Kit knew that she wasn't the only one. The entire household seemed to breathe easier. It was as if a bank of hovering dark clouds had lifted with the woman's departure.

Strange, how one person could so affect an entire house full of people.

"Am I interrupting?"

A too familiar, deep voice splintered her thoughts and Kit looked resignedly toward the glass doors leading from the garden to the parlor.

Alex MacGregor, looking very pleased with himself, stood leaning negligently against the doorjamb, his gaze locked on her. Kit bristled slightly at her body's response to him, but managed to say quietly, "Not at all."

"Good." He stepped clear of the doorway, crossed the few feet of ground separating them, and seated himself beside her on the narrow bench.

Kit, holding her book in one hand, gathered her skirt with the other and made to rise. "I was just leaving."

He stopped her with one hand on her forearm.

Her flesh tingled warmly and Kit drew away, a bit hastier than she should have.

Alex's left eyebrow rose questioningly.

She chose to ignore the whole business. "If you'll excuse me, I really should go and check on Rose."

"I won't excuse you." His lips quirked slightly, taking the brusqueness from his tone, but there was no mistaking him. "My mother is with Rose, there's no need for you to go as well."

"She *is* my—"

"Daughter," he finished. "Yes, I know. And my mother is her grandmother. I assure you the child is quite safe."

"Of course she's safe," Kit countered. Really, the man appeared to misunderstand her deliberately. "I didn't mean to intimate otherwise."

"Good." He took the book from her hand and set it down on his other side. "Then you will do me the favor of staying put for a moment or two longer."

"Very well." Kit released her iron grip on her skirts, then futilely tried to smooth out the resulting wrinkles. Cupping her hands in her lap, she waited. Long, silent moments passed and Kit began to feel as though she should say something. Anything.

She was in no mood to play that waiting game once more.

Her conscience began to needle her too. She hadn't as yet thanked him for his handling of the situation with Mrs. Beedle. And though it irked her to know that she owed him her gratitude, Kit wasn't one to back away from a debt.

"I appreciate what you did this afternoon." She kept her eyes fixed on her clenched hands. "With Mrs. Beedle, I mean."

"Hmmm?" he said. "Oh. Your thanks are unnecessary, I assure you. The woman was so unbalanced it was a wonder she could stand upright."

"Even so," Kit answered, surprised at his modest tone, "you dealt with an ugly problem before it could become even more unpleasant." She looked up at him briefly and saw him nod.

Odd, she told herself. That wasn't as difficult as she'd imagined it would be. Still and all, Kit wanted nothing more at that moment than to conclude their interview as quickly as possible. There was something unnerving about being that close to Alex MacGregor.

Since he appeared to be in no hurry to say whatever

he'd come to say, she prodded him by asking, "What was it you wanted to see me about?"

He didn't answer.

The continued silence stretched out in front of her like a living, breathing being. It grew more powerful, more intimidating with each moment that passed. Finally, Kit risked a glance at him from the corner of her eye. Her breath caught in her throat. Alex MacGregor was studying her with the avid interest of a lion watching his next meal.

Her heartbeat quickened and swarms of butterflies again took up furious residence in her stomach. She lowered her gaze to her hands and wasn't surprised to see her fingers clenched tightly.

His left leg was much too close to her. The dove-gray fabric of his trousers was pulled tight around his muscular thigh and when he shifted his position until his leg was actually *leaning* against her own, Kit jumped as if she'd been burned.

She half turned away, but it did no good. He simply moved to follow her. Her brain whirled with fragmented thoughts, each chasing the other, each demanding precedence, and none of them making the slightest bit of sense.

What was he doing? And why?

A touch as soft as the summer wind suddenly moved across the back of her neck. Kit held perfectly still. If she were to admit the truth, even if only to herself, she couldn't have moved if she'd wanted to. Her legs had turned to jelly.

Back and forth, over the same sensitive patch of flesh, Alex's fingers skimmed gently. The short tendrils of hair that lay against her nape twisted with his every caress until they tugged at her, adding their own gently felt distraction.

Kit leaned forward a bit, hoping to shake him free without looking as though that was her intent. Instead, though, his fingers only slid farther down her back. Her eyes slid shut, her lips parted, and a shuddering sigh escaped her. Even through the fabric of her gown, his fingers left a trail of warmth that seeped into her bones.

Unsteady as she felt, Kit knew she had to get up. Get away. Keep some distance between them.

Pushing herself to her feet, she took two stumbling steps and stopped, surprised to find herself standing on solid ground. Only a moment before, she would have sworn she was stranded in the middle of shifting sands.

"Kit," he said and she felt the earth tilt a bit.

"Yes." She hoped her voice sounded stronger to him than it did to her.

"Why don't we stop all this nonsense?"

Nonsense? What nonsense?

Soundlessly he stepped up beside her. His hands cupped her shoulders and turned her around to face him. He moved one hand to cradle her chin and tilt her head back until her eyes met his.

And what she saw in his gaze did nothing to dispel the nervousness wracking her body. Kit had had her share of admirers in the past. She wasn't completely innocent of a man's wants and needs.

But never before had she seen desire stamped so frankly on a man's features. And she hadn't the slightest idea what to do about it.

Perhaps, she thought, her best course would be to ignore it.

"Nonsense?" she finally asked. "What do you mean, Mr. MacGregor?"

His full lips twisted into a sardonic grin and she knew her little ploy had been quite transparent.

"*Mister*, is it? I'd thought we'd done with that, Kit."

"Of course," she agreed, forcing a bantering tone, "*Alex* then. I'm afraid I still don't know what you're talking about."

"I think you do." His left hand followed the curve of her throat, his thumb stroking her pulse point.

Her heart pounded erratically and Kit was positive he knew it. There really was no point at all in pretending any longer.

"All right then, Alex. I believe I *do* know to what you're referring. I simply prefer not to acknowledge it."

"Why not?" he whispered and bent low to press his lips to her hairline.

Kit took a half step back, but he followed.

"Naturally, as a guest of your mother's, I wouldn't want to offend her by behaving in an unseemly manner," she said hopefully.

"Ah, but this is *my* house. You are *my* guest." His gaze moved over her features slowly, admiringly. "Therefore, I think *I* should be the one to decide what is and is not unseemly, don't you agree?"

She swallowed. This was going very badly indeed. She was hardly in a position to risk insulting him. As he'd just pointed out, she was a guest in his house. In the blink of an eye, Kit could find herself, new wardrobe and all, sitting on the front steps.

With Rose lost to her forever.

"I . . ."

"Of course," he went on, "I wouldn't want you to feel —*obliged* to me in any way."

"Thank you." Easier said than done, she told herself.

"But a man would have to be blind not to notice certain 'signs,' shall we say?"

"Signs?"

His right hand moved to cup her cheek. "Mmmm. Signs of interest."

"You're mistaken, Alex."

"Am I?" He smiled again. "I don't think so. Why, even now, Kit, your blood is racing through your veins." His thumb pressed gently against her traitorous pulse. "Your breathing is fast and shallow."

Her tongue darted out to slide across her suddenly dry lips.

He bent quickly and slanted his mouth over hers for just an instant. When he straightened, his smile had broadened. "And your mouth is dry."

"You are mistaken," she repeated, more firmly this time, and deliberately stepped free of his grasp.

"We shall see." He seemed to accept her retreat. "But I would like you to think about something if you would."

"What is that?"

Alex stepped up close to her again and raised his hand to cup her breast. His fingers pressed gently into her flesh, demanding a response.

Kit gasped, shuddered, and twisted away. No one, *ever*, had attempted such a liberty! And even more appalling was her own reaction.

She'd had to fight to keep from leaning into his palm. Heat flooded her cheeks and a damp warmth coursed through her lower limbs. Over the roaring in her ears, she heard him speak.

"You're no frightened virgin, Kit. And I would much appreciate it if you would stop pretending to be." His already deep voice roughened. "We both know that you were my brother's mistress."

Kit cringed. How soon she'd come to regret *that* lie.

"And, if you would give me the . . . *honor* of proving it to you, I would like to show you that I can be much more *generous* than my brother."

Oh, Lord. She stared up at him. Was he *actually* suggesting what she thought he was?

"Besides," he added with a last, lingering touch at her neck, "I believe we would get on well together, Kit."

Yes, she thought. He was. What was she going to do?

"Now, if you'll excuse me," Alex sighed, "I have a few business matters to attend to before supper."

She nodded.

"I'll see you in an hour, then. We'll continue our little talk after we've eaten."

Kit didn't move until his footsteps had faded away into a silence that held no peace. Then she quietly slipped through the parlor and up the stairs to the sanctuary of her room.

She had only an hour to think of some way to discourage him.

When the garden was empty, the curtains drawn across an upstairs window dropped back into place.

* * *

Alex bent closer to the mirror and tilted his head this way and that, studying his reflection. No, he hadn't grown a wart on the tip of his nose. He looked just as he always did—well groomed and impeccably dressed. Though he'd never actually taken the time to consider whether or not he was a handsome man, he was willing to admit that his features were not unpleasant enough to frighten small children and animals.

"What then does she find so thoroughly *resistible* about me?" he wondered aloud. When his reflection couldn't answer him, Alex turned away from the gilt-framed looking glass in disgust.

Thoughts of Kit Simmons were perilously close to driving him over the edge. The woman did everything she could to avoid him. She all but wore blinders to keep her eyes from straying toward his. In fact, she'd made it patently clear that she didn't care for him one bit.

Except for those few moments when he'd held her. Alex perched gingerly on the edge of his desk and stretched his legs out in front of him. In his arms, Kit Simmons was a warm, responsive woman. But generally speaking, it seemed as though she could hardly bear to be in the same room with him.

And that particular blow was one he'd never experienced before.

From a woman.

There'd been others, though. He'd grown up with the best of everything, but he'd also learned early in life that the MacGregor *money* was all anyone was interested in. And because of their wealth, the members of London society were willing to overlook the fact that Douglas

MacGregor had been an upstart Scotsman who'd had the temerity to marry a kitchen maid.

Oh, they despised his ancestry. The fact that he'd been born into a line only recently "crawled out from under a rock in Scotland." They loathed the fact that Alex wasn't bothered in the least by their gossiping tongues or their snide comments, usually whispered just loud enough for him to overhear. Mostly, though, he thought with a grin, they hated the way their precious daughters looked at him.

But money was an all-forgiving entity. And to get hold of his fortune, more than *one* set of parents had been more than happy to disregard the rest. But *never* had a woman looked at him as though she couldn't be bothered. Particularly any woman who wanted something from him.

As this one most certainly did.

Alex pushed away from his desk and straightened his black wool coat. Yes, Kit Simmons wanted something. Hadn't she said so that first day? Hadn't she openly asked for money so that she and Rose could go back to their village of—what was the name of the place again? Oxtail? Oxenfoot?

He shook his head. It didn't matter. She hadn't received the settlement. And she wasn't about to, either. His mother would be crushed if Rose were to leave now. Wryly, he admitted that even *he* would miss the child. Strange, how quickly he'd become used to his daily visits to the nursery. *More* than used to them, really. He actually found himself looking forward to seeing the little girl. She seemed to change almost by the moment.

But it wasn't only Rose he didn't want to see leave.

Kit Simmons had somehow managed to worm her way into his thoughts. By night, his dreams were filled with shadowy images of her magnificent figure, naked beneath his hands. And, he told himself, now that he'd seen her in her drawers, he'd be getting even less sleep.

By day, he found himself trying to find ways to make her speak to him. To look at him with interest rather than disdain. All in all, she was taking up far too much of his valuable time. Which is precisely why he'd suggested their "association" become a closer one. Alex had learned one very valuable lesson in his thirty-two years.

Once he'd lain with a woman, it was easier to eventually distance himself from her. It was the wanting, the desire, that made a woman attractive. Once that desire was satisfied—once the "chase" was ended, his interest began to wane.

"And so it will be with Kit Simmons," he declared to the empty room. Then, feeling just a bit foolish for talking to himself, Alex left his study for the dining room.

Kit felt the beginnings of another blush and did all she could to stop it. Every time she allowed herself to remember what Alex had said to her, how he'd touched her, shame flooded her. And there was no way to keep from remembering. His voice seemed to echo on and on in her brain, teasing her—toying with her.

As if that weren't enough, she was forced to sit at the supper table with a perfect stranger who'd seen her in her underclothes! John Tremayne's pale blue eyes had scarcely left her during the entire meal. Not that she was concerned in the least with Mr. Tremayne's opinion of her. But at the same time, if she was going to be living at the MacGregor house, she would no doubt be seeing the man from time to time. Now, Kit would always wonder if he was imagining her undressed!

Thankfully, no one had mentioned the embarrassing incident to her and though she knew it was impossible, Kit was willing to pretend that everyone had forgotten her momentary lapse. Especially in light of the fact that she now had much more pressing matters on her mind.

Giving a quick, furtive glance around the supper table, she noted pleasantly that no one appeared to be paying her the least bit of attention. With the supper dishes cleared away, and the footman pouring brandy for the men, Kit found herself wishing that the Mac-Gregors followed the tradition of the ladies excusing themselves from the table. But no such reprieve was in sight.

Hesitantly she glanced at Alex. Their gazes locked. It was as if he'd been staring at her for some time, just waiting for her to look at him. His eyes held all manner of suggestions. In those blue depths, Kit saw desire, suppressed laughter, and a challenge.

Clearly, he had no intention of forgetting either her memorable appearance in the hall earlier *or* their conversation in the garden.

Kit straightened her shoulders and lifted her chin. She wouldn't be intimidated by him. And she wouldn't be forced into his bed as if she were the common street-walker he'd taken her for on the night she'd first come to this house. And it wasn't only her own reputation she was thinking of, either.

Every time Alex MacGregor hinted that she, as Ian's

mistress, was less than honorable, he insulted not only Kit but Marian as well. Her sister was no more a whore than Kit herself was. The only real mistake Marian had made was thinking herself in love with a gentleman who was revealed to be unworthy of the name. And since Marian could no longer defend herself, it was left to Kit.

Alex MacGregor would find that she was no easy tumble into bed, despite the fact, she thought, that her own body was working against her.

If she'd thought he was a threat to her virtue before, he was doubly so now.

And it wasn't merely her physical reaction to his touch.

Since the moment she'd looked down from the top of the stairs and seen him cradling Rose protectively against his broad chest, Kit had felt—*differently* about him. And it wasn't just the fact that he'd saved the child from that raving lunatic—Kit would have expected nothing less from *anyone* in the same situation.

But there'd been something in the way he held Rose. Something tender . . . *gentle*. Something that she hadn't seen in him before.

And that tenderness was more of a threat to Kit than any of his blustering, his long, heated looks, or his ultimatums.

"Kit?"

"Hmmm?" She shook herself slightly, tore her gaze away from Alex's, and turned to his mother. "I beg your pardon?"

Tess glanced thoughtfully from her son to Kit and back again.

Kit fought to keep her features blank, unreadable.

Despite her kindnesses, Tess had to have a somewhat low opinion of her morals as it was, believing as she did that Kit was the mother of an illegitimate child. She certainly didn't want the older woman to think that Kit had lost one MacGregor brother only to go after the other.

Particularly since Alex MacGregor was the *last* thing she wanted.

Willing steadiness into her unsure fingers, Kit reached for the crystal water glass in front of her.

"I was saying to John," Tess began slowly, "that I think it would be best if we left London early this year."

"Whatever for?" Alex cut in.

"Calm yourself, dear." Tess waved one hand at her son negligently. "I didn't mean you, of course. I know you and John still have business to take care of."

Alex nodded, picked up his wineglass, and took a small sip.

"But," his mother went on, "after that awful scene today, I do believe it would be best for Rose if we left for the country right away." Before anyone could speak, she added quickly, "The poor child was so upset by that terrible woman, I do believe she needs a complete change."

Relief rushed through Kit with the force of a spring flood. What a wonderful suggestion, she thought gleefully. With Alex in London and her safely in the country, perhaps he would rethink his preposterous suggestion. Surely he would come to realize that any . . . association between them would be disastrous.

"Best for Rose?" Alex asked with a half smile.

"All right now. We both know that I don't enjoy being

in London," Tess admitted as she laid her folded napkin on the lace-covered tabletop. "I much prefer the country and I think Rose will too. There's so much for her to do there. So much room for a child to run and play."

Neither of the men had a thing to say to that and after a long moment of silence, Kit hesitantly spoke up.

"I think it's a lovely idea. If you like, Tess, Rose and I could be packed to leave by morning." She felt rather than saw Alex's gaze shift to her. Deliberately she ignored him.

"Thank you, dear," the older woman said, "but I think it would be best if you remained in London for a few days yet."

"What?" In seconds, terrible visions rose up in Kit's brain. Had it all been a trick? Had Tess MacGregor merely *pretended* to make Rose's "mother" welcome? Had she planned all along to separate them? "You want Rose to go without me?" Even her voice sounded haunted, shaken.

"Oh! Forgive me, my dear girl!" Tess reached across the wide table for Kit's hand and gave it a gentle pat. "Of course I see now that I worried you." Shaking her head, she continued, "I said it badly, I know. Certainly, you shall come to the country house." She smiled gently. "I've seen the love between you and Rose and you may rest assured that I will allow nothing to damage that. But your new wardrobe won't be delivered for several days, and it seems a shame for you to travel without it, don't you think?"

Wardrobe? Kit almost laughed aloud in relief. She hadn't misjudged the woman after all. But really, there

was no need to worry about a wardrobe! Until a week or
so ago, she'd only owned four dresses.

Still, she didn't want to hurt Tess's feelings. Carefully
she said, "There's no need to worry about my clothes,
Tess. What I have will be more than sufficient until the
dressmaker can send my new things on." Besides, she
added to herself, it was much more important that she
put some distance between her and Alex.

"I wouldn't hear of it!"

Kit's hopes plummeted as soon as that simple statement left Tess's mouth. In the little time she'd known
the older woman, Kit had come to learn that once her
mind was set, there was no shaking it. Now, Kit recognized the set of Tess's chin and knew without a doubt
that she wouldn't be swerved from her plan. Still, it was
worth a try.

"Don't you think . . ."

"As soon as your new clothes are ready," Tess interrupted, "Alex can escort you to the country." As she
pushed herself up and away from the table, she added,
"You'll see I'm right, dear." Hands at her thickened
waist, Tess nodded to the men, each in turn. "If you'll
excuse me, I'll just go set Polly to gathering Rose's
things for the journey." She took a few steps toward the
door, then turned around suddenly. "Kit, would you
mind terribly if I took Polly along with me, to help with
Rose?"

"Of course not," she managed to say, still avoiding
Alex's interested gaze. Inwardly she groaned. With Polly
gone as well as Rose, she wouldn't have *anyone* to act as
a buffer between her and Alex.

"Splendid." Tess smiled, then asked, "John? I wonder

if I could impose on you to fetch a small traveling case from the attic? I'm afraid Harris is off somewhere tending to other duties and I'd really like to get started."

"Certainly." The blond man tossed his napkin to the table, bowed toward Kit, then grinned at Alex. "I'll just pop on home after. We can talk at the office tomorrow?"

Alex nodded.

Kit watched the two people leave the room and wondered frantically how she too could make her escape.

"Sherry?"

She started and looked up at him. He'd moved to the sideboard and was resting one large hand on the neck of a crystal liquor decanter. "I'm sorry?"

"Sherry. I asked if you'd care for some sherry."

His lips were curved in a knowing smile and his eyes held the same gleam she'd noted there before.

Though she knew she should keep a clear head about her, Kit told herself that perhaps a small sherry would help to calm her rapidly worsening case of nerves. "Yes," she answered softly. "Thank you."

Alex had already poured a drink for each of them. He set her glass in front of her, then took the empty chair beside her. Staring into his snifter of brandy, he said casually, "You don't approve of my mother's plan?"

His voice rumbled along her spine and it was all she could do to stay in her chair. Lifting her glass, Kit took a sip of the sherry and paused long enough to enjoy the trail of warmth it created. Finally, though, she said quietly, "I'm really in no position to approve or not, am I?"

"I suppose not," he conceded. "Although it wouldn't matter if you were."

"I beg your pardon?"

One black eyebrow lifted over his amused blue eyes. "I said it wouldn't matter if you approved or not. Once Mother sets her mind to something, she generally finds a way to make it happen."

Kit nodded and kept her eyes on the amber liquid in her glass.

When he touched her, she jumped. Her gaze flew to her forearm and she watched nervously as he ran the tip of his index finger over her flesh.

"Do I make you nervous, Kit?" he breathed.

7

Kit swallowed, looked him directly in the eye, and lied. "Of course not."

"Did Ian make you nervous as well?"

She just managed to suppress a shudder at the mention of his brother's name. Her fingers tightened on the stem of her glass and as he leaned in closer still, his familiar scent washed over her.

"Tell me," he whispered, his mouth just a breath away from her cheek, "which brother do you prefer?"

Everything stopped. Her breath. Her heart. Even the blood in her veins seemed to freeze over. Slowly then she raised her gaze to his and recognized the challenge written in his eyes.

Deliberately she took another sip of sherry and as the liquid fire raced down her throat, she told herself that she *must* make her stand here. If she was to survive in this household, she had to convince Alex MacGregor that she wasn't interested in warming his or anyone else's bed.

"Quite frankly," Kit said quietly, "I don't think especially highly of either of you."

His eyebrows shot straight up. "I beg your pardon?"

Kit set her glass of sherry down on the table before

continuing. "You asked which brother I preferred—I answered you."

"Hardly the answer I was seeking," he said.

"Nevertheless . . ."

She was nervous. He could see it in every inch of her. And yet, she stood up to him anyway. Silently Alex admitted to a grudging bit of admiration for her, but he pushed it aside quickly. He wasn't interested in the least in her somewhat belated attempts at acquiring character.

However, his curiosity was piqued enough to ask, "Just what exactly is it that you find—*lacking* in the MacGregors?"

A muffled snort of laughter shot from her throat but she disguised it behind a pitiful attempt at a coughing fit.

Frowning, Alex said, "You find the question—*amusing*?"

"Not at all," she replied, letting her hand fall from her mouth back to her lap. The soft curve of her lips slowly straightened and thinned as she finished, "I find your question—*limiting*."

"Indeed?" Somehow, Alex knew he was going to regret asking but he heard himself say, "In what way?"

"You asked what *it* was I found lacking in you Mac-Gregor brothers."

"Yeesss . . ."

"The question implies that there could only be *one* glaring fault."

"I see." And he did. Alex shifted uncomfortably in his chair but, dammit, he would see this through. If he ever hoped to get a night's rest again—he *had* to. "And you are of the opinion that those faults are too numerous to mention?"

"No . . ."

He knew there was more coming.

"I could list them all for you," she said with a sweet smile that never reached her suddenly cold eyes, "but it would, no doubt, take considerably more time than we have at present."

"I am at your disposal, madam," he replied through gritted teeth. Bloody hell.

"Kind of you, I'm sure," Kit said with a brief nod, "but I'm afraid I'm simply not up to a complete tally tonight."

"Very well," Alex offered, determined to make her declare herself, "we will forgo a thorough inventory for now. But perhaps you wouldn't mind touching on this mountain of imperfections." He locked his gaze with hers and challenged, "If you were forced into choosing *one* of the myriad defects my brother and I suffer from —which would it be?"

"Honor."

"Honor!" he barked, a harsh laugh scratching his throat. "You, madam, are a fine one to speak of honor!" Lifting his glass, Alex swallowed the last of his brandy. Surprised by her answer and despite himself a bit stung, he silently had to agree with her assessment—at least as far as Ian was concerned.

Alex was the first to admit that his late brother had been a pitiful excuse for a man.

However, he told himself, no one had ever questioned *his* sense of honor—especially to his face! *Alex* had never made a habit of deflowering virgins! On the contrary, excepting that one regrettable instance when he was fool enough to believe a "virtuous" woman's lies —he had devoted his time to married women. Or, at the very least, widows.

He preferred women who would make no claim on him. Those who, like him, were interested in pleasure without becoming entangled in society's webs of courtship and marriage. No, he told himself, he'd always been scrupulously honest with the women who'd come to his bed. He'd promised them nothing and remained on friendly terms with most of them long after the affair had concluded.

Elizabeth Beckwith's furious features leapt to mind but he ignored the reminder of his last paramour. She'd become greedy, that was all. Not for him, of course, but for the tokens he'd given her. His *honor* was very much intact, he told himself.

He leveled his gaze on the woman opposite him. Considering Kit Simmons's past, she was in no position to be throwing stones of any size. Perhaps it was time to remind her of that. Setting the empty snifter onto the table, he cocked his head and gave her a mocking half smile.

"Honor, madam?" he repeated politely. "Are you or are you not the same woman who bedded my brother, gave birth to his bastard, accepted a cash settlement, and then came trotting to London when the money ran out?"

He watched her reaction and wasn't surprised at all to see a rush of color fill her cheeks. He'd struck a nerve. It should've made him happy, knowing that he'd repaid her insult—but it didn't. Alex watched as her hands clenched and unclenched at her sides. She took several deep breaths before answering him.

"Yes"—she nodded slowly—"I *am* that woman. And who better to know the men in your family for what they are? Let me tell you about the *honor* I've seen from the MacGregor men." Pushing herself to her feet, Kit looked down at him and went on in a quiet, fury-filled voice. "I didn't simply 'bed' your brother. I made the mistake of falling in love with him." Her lips curled distastefully but she rushed on before he could interrupt. "A serious mistake, I grant you. But at least it is one I have accepted responsibility for. I'm a rector's daughter, Alex MacGregor . . . not the village whore!"

Magnificent, he told himself.

"I believed all the pretty lies your brother told me. I trusted him when he spoke of *love* and *forever*."

Alex bit down hard on the inside of his cheek. He knew all too well what his brother had been like. In fact, every time Ian had been drunk, he'd bragged to his younger brother about the many conquests he'd made. For all Alex knew, he might very well have nieces and nephews scattered all over England.

"One night," Kit said, her voice low, "after filling my head with more of his lies, he persuaded me to go on a moonlight stroll." She glanced behind her at the closed door that led to the servants' hall and the kitchen beyond. Apparently satisfied, Kit turned back to him, lifted her eyes, and stared at the wall behind him as if seeing another time, another place. Lowering her voice even further, she went on. "He too offered me sherry" —her lips curved in a humorless smile—"to ward off the cold, he said." She shivered. "And all the time, he talked of what our life together in London would be. The parties, the balls. The people he would introduce me to. He told me how beautiful I was." Her voice dropped until Alex could hardly hear her. He leaned forward, caught in the spell of her words. "It was cold out that night, but he put his arms around me and told me his love would keep me warm. He kept insisting I drink the sherry, that it would do me good." One tear fell from the corner of her eye and rolled down the line of her cheek. Alex was sure she was unaware of it. "But he gave me too much. He seduced me. Ian MacGregor took advantage of her love. He used her, then cast her aside without so much as a second thought."

Alex's brow furrowed. She? Her? In her haste to tell it all, Kit didn't even seem to notice that she'd begun to speak of herself as she would someone else.

"And you mentioned a 'settlement,' didn't you?" Her eyes shifted back to him. "You're quite right. I did accept his *generous* offer. What choice did I have? A village parson earns barely enough money to keep body and soul together. With another mouth to feed . . ." Kit shook her head. "One hundred pounds. One hundred pounds to care for his child. Less than the amount he would have spent on a new horse."

"There is something you should know about that," Alex said quickly, determined that she know his father had meant for her and the baby to be well taken care of. Somehow, after hearing her story, it was important she know that his father had *tried* to do what he thought best. But she stopped him with an upraised hand.

"And as for you, what honor have you shown?"

Alex stood up, refusing to be looked down on any longer. In the state she was in, he had no doubt that she was about to tell him exactly what she thought of him too. And by thunder, he preferred to face it standing on his own two feet. Before she could start, he pointed out one thing. "I welcomed you and your child into this house."

"Oh, yes," she shot back, "after your mother fell in love with her granddaughter. And my 'welcome' isn't quite so secure as Rose's, is it?"

"I haven't said anything of the kind."

"Haven't you?" She crossed her arms over her chest and hugged herself tightly. "Didn't you inform me only an hour ago that you wanted me to play the part of your mistress?"

"Yes . . ."

"Is that the welcome you bestow on all the guests in your home? Or is that special treatment reserved only for those you've already decided are no better than whores?"

"I . . ." Dammit, Alex thought disgustedly. For God's sake! Did she really think that he bedded every female who entered his house? She really was carrying this a bit far! Because he was willing to admit that there was a certain . . . *attraction* between the two of them— he was a dishonorable fiend?

Hell, even *he* couldn't believe that he wanted a woman who'd given herself willingly to his brother! But by heaven, he did. Alex wanted Kit Simmons more than he'd ever wanted anyone or anything in his life. She was constantly on his mind. She'd disturbed his well-ordered life. She and her child had turned his house upside down.

Why, Alex couldn't go anywhere in the house without stumbling on some evidence of their presence. If he wasn't stepping on some toy or sitting on a forgotten doll, he was inhaling the soft lavender scent that Kit left behind to mark her passage.

Dammit, he'd hardly gotten any work done all week. Several times, John had said something about one of their ships only to have to repeat it because Alex's mind had been firmly fixed on Kit Simmons!

He rubbed one hand across his jaw roughly. Oh, he wanted her. But he hadn't meant to imply he thought of her as a whore. That certainly wasn't how he saw her. Not since the moment she'd walked into his study the day he was suffering from a hideous hangover.

He *was* willing to concede that she'd shown appalling judgment, believing in Ian. But she was definitely no common strumpet.

By the same token though, for God's sake, why was she so intent on acting the part of outraged virgin? It wasn't as though he was asking her to sacrifice her virtue. And if they were to enjoy a . . . *close* association, who would be hurt by it?

Dammit, at least *he* was willing to admit to desire!

"So," she said quietly and his thoughts scattered, "you can see why I am less than impressed by the Mac-Gregor family . . . save your mother, of course."

"Of course," he ground out. And if he were in a mood to be reasonable, he might have agreed with her. But Alex was in *no* mood to be reasonable. "Thank you so much for sparing my mother your condemnation."

She had the grace to flush slightly. "Are you saying I have no right to my feelings concerning you and your brother?"

"No!" Alex raked one hand through his hair, glanced at the still closed door, and found himself imagining the cook, the footmen, and even *Harris* bent over double listening at the keyhole. Lowering his voice, he told her, "You have every right to the malice you bear my late brother." Throwing his hands wide, he added, "Frankly it amazes me that Ian died at sea! It would have been more appropriate for him to have been shot down by any number of the women he'd misused over the years. Hell, if I'd been born female, I might have shot him myself!"

She blinked.

"But," Alex said and grabbed her upper arms in a firm yet gentle grip, "as to your feelings about me . . . I think you've been a bit precipitate."

"I have?" she asked and tilted her head back to look at him.

Alex wasn't fooled by her calm. He could see the still burning flames of confrontation dancing in her eyes. But at least she was listening.

"You have." His thumbs moved in lazy circles over her arms. "I will admit to desire . . . but not to black-mail."

"Blackmail?"

"Blackmail. I did not threaten you with eviction, madam." His shoulders lifted and fell in a graceful shrug. "I merely . . . *suggested* that we might find plea-sure in each other's company."

She shifted nervously in his grasp, but he didn't release her. He had every intention of taking advantage of her momentary befuddlement.

"I *do* desire you, y'know," he whispered and leaned closer to the lavender scent clinging to her. There was no harm in admitting to that much, surely. It wasn't necessary for her to know that *desire* was almost too small a word for the need gripping him. "Unlike my brother, though, I don't make a habit of promising what I have no intention of delivering."

"Such as?"

"Such as love. Marriage. *Forever*."

She bit her bottom lip at the reminder of her own speech.

"I *would* be willing to promise you one thing, madam." Alex's right hand slipped along the top of her shoulder to the back of her neck.

"What?"

"I can promise you that when *I* seduce you, you won't be drunk. I want you to be as eager for me as I am for you."

She shook her head. "I won't be seduced."

"We shall see, madam." One side of his mouth lifted in a tilted smile. "My brother was many things, Kit. But I am willing to wager that Ian was *not* a generous lover." His smile dropped away. "The fact that he had to depend on alcohol to convince a woman is testimony to that. *I* on the other hand would be willing to spend *hours* caressing." His fingers rubbed at the flesh of her neck. "Kissing." He leaned down and brushed his lips against her throat. "And fondling your delectable body until we *both* ached for the release we would find together."

She sighed and Alex shuddered. The mental images his words created affected him every bit as much as they did her.

"Inch by inch, Kit," he went on, unable to resist the temptation to describe what he would like to share with her, "my fingers will explore your flesh." His speech fanned her cheek and he smiled when she inhaled a jerky breath. "In the soft glow of candlelight, I will watch as your eyes darken with passion. I'll clasp your naked body along mine, delighting in the feel of your soft, smooth skin, and I'll hold you tight until the tremors wracking you are stilled."

She swayed slightly and Alex steadied her with a hand at her waist.

"And when neither of us can survive another moment of glorious torment," he said softly and paused to brush his lips against hers, "I will slide into your warmth, joining our bodies as they were meant to be joined." Kit's eyes closed and she unwittingly leaned into him. His body tightened in response but Alex fought down the urge to press her against his arousal. Instead, he continued in a strained tone, "Your legs will lock around my hips, capturing me deep inside you, and together we'll reach the shattering end of our journey."

"No," she whispered halfheartedly.

"Yes," he countered and raised his hands to cup her face. Alex waited until her eyes opened and she was looking deep into his own before he added, "And when that journey is completed, we will begin again."

His mouth came down on hers and Kit knew nothing except the incredible feel of his warmth. The tiny, rational voice in the back of her mind was silenced by the flood of raw sensation that raced through her in a matter of seconds. When his arms snaked around her middle, drawing her close, Kit groaned softly and gave herself up to his kiss.

Alex's words still echoed in her brain when his tongue slid across her lips, coaxing them into parting for his entry. He stole her breath with his gentle invasion and Kit moved against him, instinctively seeking more. The rigid proof of the desire he spoke of pressed against the juncture of her thighs, and Kit's knees buckled.

Alex's arms tightened around her waist in response. Her fingers crept up the length of his arms to the back of his head and entwined themselves in his thick black hair. She held on to him tightly as he moved his mouth to her throat, lavishing soft, damp kisses along the line of her neck, only stopping when halted by the high, buttoned collar of her muslin gown.

One of his hands slipped around between their bodies and deftly loosened the top three buttons, allowing his talented mouth access to even more of her flesh. She heard him groan with pleasure just before she let her head fall back on her neck in a silent plea for more.

His strong left arm held her pressed firmly to him while his right hand moved to cup her breast. Lightning-like jolts shot through her at this most intimate touch and like before, she was shaken from her abandon.

What on earth was happening to her? Eyes wide, Kit stared blankly at the subtly shaded mural stretching across the high ceiling above. The angels and cherubs sat on their painted clouds, looking down on her with what seemed to be disappointment. Her fingers clutched spasmodically at his shoulders and even the persistent nibbling at her throat wasn't enough to recapture the wantonness she'd experienced only moments ago.

Twisting her head to one side, Kit pushed back from him, and when he released her, she stumbled a few steps before regaining her balance.

"What?" he ground out in a voice raw with need. "What is it?"

"I . . ." She shook her head and somehow managed to move her trembling fingers enough to button up her collar once more.

"You what?" He swallowed heavily, then forced a deep gulp of air into his lungs.

"I won't let this happen," she said haltingly. Then, remembering the part she was playing, she added, "Not again."

Alex nodded stiffly. Pulling at the lapels of his elegantly cut black jacket, he straightened his shoulders and with both hands smoothed his hair back before speaking.

"You said we MacGregors lacked honor."

"Yes."

"May I assume that honesty is another virtue you value highly?"

"Naturally."

"Then, madam," he said, his voice gravelly, "I suggest you do a bit of soul-searching yourself."

"What?"

"If honesty is indeed something you cherish, perhaps you should ask yourself why you continue to lie to me and to yourself."

She shook her head slightly, confused.

"Honesty should compel you to admit that you want me every bit as much as I want you."

"That's not—"

"Careful," he said quickly, "I feel yet another lie approaching." His lips curved in a taunting smile. "Despite what you say, Kit, *no* woman responds to a man like that unless she *feels* something."

"You're wrong," she said and knew it for the lie it was.

"As I said earlier, madam, we shall see."

"Alex . . ."

"If you'll excuse me"—he turned for the door—"I believe I'll go and arrange for the carriage to be brought around in the morning."

He left without another word, and when he was gone, Kit was left to deal with her troubling thoughts.

Alex went straight to his study, locked the door, then crossed the room to the crystal decanter of good Scots whiskey. Pouring himself a healthy measure, he walked to the terrace doors and flung them wide. Knowing he was far too wound up to sit still, he instead opted for a brisk walk in the garden.

His body felt as tight as a noose around a felon's neck. If he didn't get some relief soon, he'd go mad. Perhaps he should countermand his mother's decision and pack Kit off to the country. It was ridiculous for him to continue to torture himself with her presence. What was that old saying? Out of sight, out of mind?

Or was it absence makes the heart grow fonder?

Fond? It wasn't *fondness* driving him to drink! And

what he was feeling had nothing at all to do with his heart!

A rustle of movement in the nearby bushes told him he'd disturbed a rabbit with his pacing. Well, hell, why should *any* creature have any peace if *he* wasn't?

He stopped suddenly and stared blankly at his mother's roses. Kit hadn't really been *serious* when she said she'd *loved* Ian, had she? Could it be possible that his despicable brother had actually succeeded at something he, Alex, had not? Oh, to be sure, even if it were true, Alex had no doubt at all that the "love" was strictly one-sided. He didn't believe his brother had been capable of any genuine feeling, yet alone love.

But still. It was bloody annoying to know that Ian of all people had inspired true love in a woman's heart when all Alex had ever known was greed and sexual desire.

He lifted his glass to his lips and took a long drink of the whiskey. Surprisingly, the liquor didn't taste as good as he'd expected it to. Alex shook his head, stared down at the amber liquid, then slowly upended the glass, spilling the liquor into the grass at his feet.

She'd even taken away his enjoyment for good drink. He took several deep, long breaths of the cold night air, welcoming the chill that crept through his bones. Perhaps it would be enough to quench the fire still raging in his blood.

Not likely, he told himself. There was only one cure for what he suffered from. And that cure would be denied him because she didn't love him.

On the other hand, Alex thought as he tossed the

empty glass into the air and caught it deftly on his palm, if she *did* love him, his problem would be solved.

He smiled slowly in the darkness. Instead of seducing her, he would try wooing her.

It couldn't be *too* difficult. *Ian* had managed it. And by God, if Ian could do it, Alex told himself, so could he!

8

O n the wide street, hansom cabs moved swiftly, their horses' hooves tapping out a steady rhythm that began to sound like the heartbeat of the city. Gentlemen in black silk hats and knee-length frock coats, umbrellas furled and tucked under their arms, moved quickly along the walk as if marching to a drummer's beat. Sporadic sunshine filtered through the scuttling gray clouds, bringing just enough warmth to counteract the brisk spring breeze.

And yet, Kit shivered. Too much was happening. Too quickly. In the short span of a week, her life had changed in such a drastic way that she hardly knew which way to turn anymore.

Rose jumped up and down excitedly on the burgundy leather carriage seat, her laughter spilling out into the noisy London morning. Her short fingers curled over the edge of the seat back, she looked up at the footman and crowed, "Ride?"

James, a too thin sixteen-year-old, grinned at the baby. "That's right, little miss. We're goin' for a ride, we are."

Smiling from her post on the sidewalk, Kit gratefully realized anew just how quickly children were able to put unpleasantness behind them. Though yesterday's incident with Mrs. Beedle was still very fresh in Kit's mind, obviously Rose had completely recovered.

"That'll do now, Rosie," she said, "you'll be all mussed before you even get started." Reaching for the little girl, Kit added, "Let me straighten your bonnet, sweetheart."

Dutifully Rose wobbled closer and tilted her chin up. As Kit tugged and twisted the pale yellow ribbons back into their original shape, the little girl asked, "Go for ride, An' Kit?"

She inhaled sharply and looked up at James's suddenly stonelike features. If he'd heard Rose, it was apparent that he wasn't going to let on. She only hoped that he would continue to do so. Kit glanced warily back over her shoulder at the house's open front door.

No one there. Thank heaven.

Kit turned back to the child watching her through wide green eyes. Gently she said, "Mama, Rose. Remember?" She lowered her voice even further, hoping James wouldn't hear, and bent close to the girl. "You call me mama now."

Rose chewed at her lip for a long moment. Her right foot moved to cover her left and she tilted her head as if in deep thought. Finally, she nodded. "Mama."

"That's my girl," Kit crooned and lovingly tucked one long brown curl beneath the white lace bonnet. She worried about confusing the child and constantly fretted over the rightness of teaching her to lie. But there was no help for it. So much depended on the MacGregors continuing to believe that she was Rose's mother.

Especially after the events of yesterday afternoon. Kit bit back an embarrassed groan. She *still* couldn't believe how easily she'd allowed herself to be carried away by Alex's smooth words and ardent kisses. Right after she'd vowed that he wouldn't succeed in seducing her, no less.

For heaven's sake, why was he so insistent on conquering *her*? Surely there were dozens of women in London who would welcome his notice. All of them, no doubt, wealthier, prettier, and far more eager than *she*.

Alex, she was certain, had never before had to work so diligently at wearing down a woman's defenses. Her lips curved in a wry smile. He had the appearance of a man well used to getting whatever he wanted in life. Every time she refused him there was an unmistakable expression of surprise etched on his features.

If his presence wasn't so blasted unnerving, Kit might almost enjoy watching his consternation.

Rose pulled at the front of Kit's blue and green gingham dress and talked to herself unintelligibly.

Kit smiled at the girl, but her thoughts were, as so often lately, elsewhere. She'd been prepared, even before reaching London, to hate the MacGregors on principle alone. But Tess, she'd found out soon enough, was impossible to dislike.

And even Alex was a puzzle. Oh, he was certainly arrogant. Demanding. Self-assured. But, she admitted grudgingly, he was also kind to Rose. Understanding and generous toward his mother. An indulgent master to the servants.

And altogether discomfiting toward her.

She'd expected to dislike him solely on the grounds that he was a wealthy, selfish man. Kit had mentally endowed Alex with all of Ian's nasty traits. She'd failed to consider the possibility that like her and her sister Marian—he and his brother weren't necessarily two of a kind.

Kit sighed heavily. Of course, the *most* important thing she'd failed to consider was her own response to him. Not for a moment would she have entertained the notion that she could feel herself drawn to the brother of the man who'd ruined her sister. Not once would she have thought that she would be in danger of losing her own virtue to the same family that had claimed Marian's. And though the turmoil her body experienced whenever he was near was driving her mad—the *real* question was why Alex wanted *her*?

A poor, provincial woman. The daughter of a village rector. The supposed mother of an illegitimate child. Hardly the image of a woman destined to be sought after by wealthy, influential men. What *was* it that kept driving him so relentlessly in his pursuit of her?

Was it simply because she was ready to hand—living right in his own house?

She frowned, somewhat insulted at the thought.

Then she recalled his questions about her feelings for Ian and wondered if he was in some way trying to prove himself against his brother's memory.

A half laugh caught in her throat. If he only knew what she *really* thought of his precious brother, he wouldn't be trying so hard to win the same regard.

Rose placed her hands on either side of Kit's face and her little fingers tapped gently. "An' Kit go for ride too?"

She tossed another hasty glance at the still empty doorway to the house. Fortunately, no one had come down yet. Kit didn't bother to peek up at James. It was far too late now. He either would or wouldn't keep silent about what he'd overheard. There was nothing she could do about him; all she could hope for was that Rose wouldn't make the same mistake in front of Tess.

Or Alex.

God forbid.

Looking back at the girl, she shook her head. "No, darling. *Mama* has to stay here a bit longer."

Rose's chin quivered and Kit knew exactly how she felt. Since the day of her birth, the little girl and her aunt had never been separated.

"Rose stay too?" the tiny voice asked.

Kit wrapped her arms about the girl and held on tightly. She closed her eyes at the heartbreaking feel of chubby fingers tugging at her neck. As long as she lived, she would remember the feel of those fingers moving trustingly on her flesh. Tears welled up in her eyes, but she blinked them back. She didn't want the baby upset by all this. Heaven knew, the child had already had to adapt to enough changes in the last week.

Deliberately lightening her voice, Kit leaned back, looked into Rose's watery eyes, and said, "No, Rose. You don't want to stay here."

The girl sniffed and rubbed her nose with the back of her hand. She nodded her head so hard, her bonnet tilted down over her forehead.

Kit pushed it back gently and said, forcing excitement into her tone, "Rosie gets to ride on a train with her grandmother. And Polly."

Another sniffle and a half smile accompanied the demanding statement, "An' Kit ride the train too."

"Oh, Rosie," Kit whispered.

A babble of voices interrupted her and Kit turned to watch Tess, followed by Polly, Harris, and Alex, come down the wide front steps. Briefly her anxious gaze rested on each of them in turn. Had any of them heard Rose call her "Aunt Kit"? But she couldn't tell a thing from their expressions.

"You'll like the train, little miss." James leaned down to smile at Rose. "You'll likely see lots of cows and horses and such out the windows."

"Horsey?"

Kit glanced at the boy gratefully when she heard Rose's pleased question.

"Michael," Tess said as she came closer to the waiting carriage, "the moment Kit's new things arrive, I want you and Alex to bring her to the country."

"Of course, madam." Harris's lips twitched slightly as he handed a small leather bag up to James. Most of the luggage had already been stacked in the coach.

"Mother." Alex rolled his eyes and stepped up to her. Leaning down to plant a kiss on her forehead, he finished, "You've already told him that at least two dozen times this morning."

"Have I?" she asked, frowning at Harris.

"Closer to ten times, I'd say, madam," the butler assured her.

"I am sorry, Michael, but this is most important." She turned a smile on Kit before looking back at the man. "Remember now . . . the very moment . . ."

"Two dozen and one," Alex said quietly.

"Eleven," Harris answered.

"Oh, I don't know why I bother with the both of you

at all." Tess turned away from them, stepped up close to Kit, and took the younger woman's hands in her own. "Try not to worry, my dear. I shall take very good care of our Rose."

Kit forced a smile she didn't feel and nodded briefly. "I'm not worried, Tess. Really." Surely one more lie couldn't make her soul much blacker. "Hopefully I'll see you all in just a few days."

"Of course, dear." Tess patted her hands. "Of course. The time will *fly*! You'll see."

Kit very much doubted that, but she didn't see what good it would do to say so.

"Polly, you and Rose get settled in the coach now, else we'll miss our train."

"Yes, ma'am," the young maid answered and climbed into the carriage.

"Pardon me." A new voice was added to the bustle and Kit looked up to see a middle-aged matron, elegantly dressed in violet silk, tapping Alex on the shoulder with the handle of her closed parasol.

Immediately he stiffened and stepped back out of the woman's way.

She gave him the briefest of nods, then her gaze slid to Tess.

"Good, morning, Lady Shivington," Tess offered.

The woman's long, curved nose twitched just before she sniffed pointedly. Then, with an even briefer nod, she sailed past the MacGregor party, her oversize bustle bobbing and swaying. Only a step or two behind Lady Shivington, her maid, clutching at stiffly starched black skirts, raced to keep up with the imperious woman.

Kit watched Tess's face and saw her kind features

change swiftly from anger to disappointment to acceptance.

"Our neighbor," the older woman said by way of an explanation, "and she certainly seems to be in a hurry this morning, doesn't she?" Her tone deliberately brighter, Tess added, "But then, so are we!"

Kit's admiration for her hostess soared. It can't have been easy, she thought, being snubbed so blatantly by your neighbor. Kit herself had been totally ignored by the intruder, but she hadn't expected any acknowledgment. The MacGregors on the other hand had every right to expect if not friendliness, at least a showing of well-bred courtesy!

No, Kit thought, outraged on behalf of the woman who'd been so kind to her, despite the other woman's title, Tess MacGregor was the *real* "lady." And for tuppence, Kit would be willing to chase the hawk-faced female down and tell her so.

Just then, she looked up and studied Alex's carefully controlled features. For a moment he and Harris stared at each other and Kit wasn't surprised in the least to see the same helpless anger she was experiencing on the butler's face. She'd already noticed more than once the telling glances Harris sent his mistress when he thought no one was looking.

Her gaze shifted back to Alex and she saw that his eyes were locked on the now distant form of the retreating woman. If looks could burn, Kit told herself, Lady Shivington would surely burst into flame at any moment.

"Alex," his mother said quietly, apparently reading

his expression as easily as had Kit, "please. It doesn't matter."

Trying to make herself as inconspicuous as possible, Kit turned away, but she really couldn't help overhearing.

"It *does* matter, Mother."

"Not to me," she replied, laying one hand on his forearm, "it never has."

Kit looked back in time to see Alex wave one hand in the direction of Lady Shivington. "But if the old b—"

"Alex!" Tess cut him off and tossed a worried glance over her shoulder at the carriage. "The *baby!*"

His brows drew together and he shoved his hands into his pants pockets. Lips clamped firmly together, a muscle in his jaw began to twitch noticeably. But after drawing several long, deep breaths, Alex finally nodded his compliance.

"Thank you, dear," his mother whispered.

Alex's expression softened into a genuine smile and Kit's breath caught at the beauty of it. He really was the most unexpected man!

"It's time, madam." Harris's quiet voice broke the strained silence and everyone, it seemed, breathed a little easier.

Quickly Kit reached into the coach, pulled Rose close, and gave her an all-too-brief hug and kiss before turning the child over to the waiting maid.

Polly settled the baby on her lap and began to whisper a story that started Rose giggling almost immediately.

Apparently, Kit thought with a sigh, Polly was every bit as excited as her charge was to be riding a train. "Be a good girl, Rosie," Kit admonished. But Rose was already babbling about her coming ride.

Reluctantly Kit turned away and came face-to-face with Alex. Her heart began to pound frantically and she instinctively crossed her arms over her bosom. Vaguely she heard the whispered, hushed conversation between Tess and Harris on her right. From the corner of her eye, Kit watched Tess nod sharply in her direction, then lean in close to the dignified butler to whisper something else.

Alex, handsome in a black suit coat and trousers, seemed to tower over her. Only a half step from her, he also appeared to be enjoying her discomfort. His lips barely curved in a hint of a smile, his gaze burned through her with the same desire she'd seen and run from the day before.

Kit licked her lips nervously and started when he mimicked her action. Knees wobbly, she leaned back against the carriage behind her for support.

"Now, Kit dear," Tess announced and stepped up beside her, "while you're in town, I want you to use the carriage and see something of London. James will be more than happy to accompany you anywhere you choose to go."

"Oh, I don't know."

"Tut-tut-tut." Tess brushed aside her hesitation. "Surely there are any number of things in town to interest you. The museum perhaps? Bond Street? Oh!" she said suddenly. "That reminds me. There is a certain milliner on Bond Street, a Miss Michele, who does the most divine hats! I insist you go there tomorrow at the latest and choose one for yourself!"

"Thank you, Tess, but I really couldn't do that."

"Nonsense! I told you, I insist." Tess leaned in and kissed Kit's cheek. "I have an account there myself. Just tell Michele that I want you to have anything you'd like."

"Well . . ." Kit couldn't imagine herself shopping on Bond Street at all . . . much less having a hat designed for her especially.

"I shall expect to see it when you arrive at the country house, mind."

Nodding absently, Kit told herself that by the time she reached the MacGregors' country home, Tess would have forgotten all about the hat.

"Alex," his mother ordered, "I expect you to make sure Kit goes to see Michele."

"I would be delighted to, Mother."

He grinned wickedly at her and Kit had to remind herself to breathe.

"Good! That's settled, then." The older woman gave Kit a quick, hard squeeze, then turned to face her son. "Alex! Come give me a kiss so we can be off!"

Alex grinned, moved in close, bent down, and kissed his mother's cheek. "Enjoy yourself, Mother," he said. "I've wired ahead. Jeffords and one of the footmen will meet you at the station and see you home."

"Thank you, dear." She patted his arm, then cautioned, "Look after yourself, now."

"I will."

"And Kit as well," Tess went on, blithely unaware of the heated gaze her son was directing at that woman.

"It will be my pleasure."

His voice rumbled through her and Kit almost groaned.

"Michael," the older woman went on, "lend me your hand, please."

The butler handed his mistress up into the carriage, saw her settled, then quietly closed the hinged door.

"We'll see you all very soon," Tess sang out, clearly delighted to be heading for the country. Then, half turning to the driver, standing at the rear of the coach beside James, she said, "All right, Henry. We mustn't be late."

Henry nodded, flicked his whip with a snap over the horse's head, and the carriage pulled away from the curb.

Kit waved until the carriage was lost in an anonymous sea of black carriages and hansoms. She didn't even notice when Harris went back into the house, leaving her and Alex alone.

"She hasn't left the country, y'know," Alex said, hoping to make her turn and face him. It didn't work.

"We've never been apart before."

"Perhaps it'll be good for both of you." At the very least, he assured himself, it would give the two of them time to talk. Alex started at the thought. He'd never wanted to "talk" with a woman before.

He stared at her as yet another startling conclusion struck him. Kit was . . . *different*. Immediately he shook his head, hoping to dislodge the uncomfortable thoughts.

"Perhaps."

Her voice sounded as if it were echoing off the walls of a tomb. For God's sake. The world hadn't ended. Just the opposite, in fact. Her world had just opened up. She'd been offered the chance to look around London, the greatest, busiest, liveliest city in the world. In *his* company!

He was willing to concede that their association so far hadn't been exactly—*friendly*, but he could think of any number of women off the top of his head who'd adore the opportunity of spending time with him. The fact that he had no interest in those women was neither here nor there.

But dammit, if she was going to adopt this funereal air for the next several days, he would accomplish nothing!

And with his next breath, he said as much.

"Are you going to spend the next few days mourning your daughter as though she were lost to you forever?"

"I beg your pardon?" She spun about suddenly to face him.

"You heard me correctly."

"I am not . . . mourning her." Kit tossed another glance at the crowded street as though she could still see the MacGregor carriage. "But I will miss her."

"Completely understandable," he said, "but at the same time, I think you should keep in mind that Rose will probably not be pining away for you."

"What?"

"Don't misunderstand, madam. I'm not implying that the child is completely insensitive to your parting." He gave her a half smile but didn't bother to wait for her to answer it. "I'm only trying to point out that Rose will no doubt be having much too fine a time to be heartsick for long."

"Perhaps . . ."

"My mother was quite right, y'know. There is a large garden and a nursery twice the size of this one, with an unlimited number of toys and books scattered around."

A reluctant smile tilted her mouth slightly and Alex took heart.

In an effort to see that smile widen and grow, he added slyly, "And I haven't even mentioned the puppies."

"Puppies?"

"Yes. One of our dogs, Cleopatra, gave birth to nine puppies a month or more back." Alex grinned when he saw Kit's blossoming smile. "They should be just old enough now to want to do a little romping with Rose."

"She'll love that."

"Then you agree that your daughter will survive your parting until you're reunited?"

"I suppose so."

Excellent. He slid his palms into his pants pockets again to keep from rubbing his hands together in gleeful anticipation.

"Fine. Then I insist on obeying my mother's command and showing you about London."

The smile dropped from her face like a stone into a pond. "Thank you, but that won't be necessary."

"I disagree."

"That's unfortunate."

"True." Dammit, she had the lamentable ability to turn a perfectly enjoyable conversation into a contest of wills seemingly without effort. But he refused to be set down like a schoolboy. "I had hoped that we could commence our tour on friendly ground."

"I hardly think that likely."

"Apparently not," he conceded, putting the reins to his simmering temper. Why must she make everything so difficult? "Nevertheless, the tour *will* be made."

She shook her head, lifted the hem of her shabby dress, and half turned toward the door Harris had left standing open. "I think not."

He stopped her with one hand on her arm. Dammit, he'd tried to be civil. Congenial. *Charming.* She wouldn't have it, though. So niceties be damned.

"I have some business to take care of," he said, his voice tight. "Expect me back within the hour. Be ready to leave."

She glared down at his hand on her arm until he released her. Then, her chin high, Kit left him on the walk, marched up the steps, inside the house, and quietly shut the door behind her.

Alex fumed silently for a long moment, staring at the door with a force that should have blown it in. Did she really believe that he would allow her to hide in her room until it was time to escort her to the country? Was she really foolish enough to think that he would be put off by her disagreeable manner?

"Hah!" he laughed aloud. Surely, he'd already proven *that* assumption false. A more frustrating female he'd never met, and still, he wanted her more than he'd ever wanted anything.

He snorted and muttered a curse under his breath.

A gasp of outrage startled him from his furious thoughts.

Alex looked up to see yet another overdressed, middle-aged matron glaring at him as if he'd just splashed mud on her.

"In *my* day," she informed him haughtily, "a *gentleman* did not curse in front of ladies!"

He swallowed the next curse that leapt to his tongue and inclined his head at her. "Your pardon, ma'am." As her rigid countenance shriveled even further, he told himself that in *her* day, she had probably considered herself fortunate if a man spoke to her at all!

Still grumbling to himself, he stalked off down the sidewalk, determined now more than ever to go through with the plan that had occurred to him only that morning.

9

E ven a blind man could see that all was not well at that house.

When Alexander MacGregor stomped down the sidewalk, Mrs. Beedle scurried back farther into the shadows of the alley. She watched him pass by and smiled at the look of fury carved into his features.

No matter that he fired her, she told herself. It was plain to anyone that *he* was no fonder of the upstart slut than she was.

After a few minutes, she stepped calmly out of the alley, glanced down at the MacGregor house, then deliberately turned her back and walked in the opposite direction.

He probably only dismissed her to placate that mother of his, Mrs. Beedle thought. If left to his own devices, he no doubt would have sided with his housekeeper. After all, that slut and her child had disrupted his entire household with their presumptive demands.

Yes, she told herself, it was possible that she'd misjudged Alex MacGregor. Why, she must have been blind not to have seen it before. It was *obvious* that he'd been forced to discharge her. He knew how important she was to the smooth running of his household. He was probably searching right now for a way to be rid of the woman and her child so that he could welcome Theodora Beedle back to her rightful place.

Her thin lips curved in a fond smile. She'd been unfair. Forcing his hand by thrashing the spawn of Satan like that. She should have been more circumspect. More discreet. She realized that now.

Straightening her narrow shoulders, Mrs. Beedle stepped out of the alley and stared after her former employer. Now that she knew how he felt, she would, of course, do all she could to help him. And she knew just where to begin.

In the cold silence of her hotel room the night before, Theodora Beedle had remembered something.

"Aunt Kit," the child had said.

At the time, she hadn't paid attention. She'd been much too involved with seeing just punishment doled out. But later, alone, that one phrase had haunted her. "Aunt Kit."

Odd way for a child to address its mother. If the slut *was* the mother. And the more Mrs. Beedle thought on it, the more it made sense. If that harlot was the real mother, why did she wait until *now* to come looking for money? Of course Kit Simmons wasn't the brat's mother. She was merely a slattern, probably a "friend" of the mother's, looking for an easy life at someone else's expense.

But how to prove it?

Her mind whirling, she mentally sorted through her memories of everything she'd heard about the slut. What had she said the name of her village was? Ox something . . .

Oxgate! That was it! Oxgate.

With that information and some of the money she'd been able to put by over the years, Mrs. Beedle knew she would be able to find out the truth. Or at least enough of the truth to enable Alex MacGregor to rid himself of the woman and the brat—and to return his housekeeper to her rightful position.

Slowly she started the long walk back to her rooms. As her plan took shape, Mrs. Beedle smiled.

Other pedestrians gave the odd woman with the evil smirk a wide berth as they passed.

Alex was barely out of sight when Kit raced out of the house in the direction of Hyde Park. She'd paused only long enough to snatch up her cape and now she clutched tightly at the black wool garment and kept her head down, eyes on the path. She needed time. Alone.

"Here, cabby!"

The driver pulled his horse to a hard stop and Alex was out of the hansom in a blink. Standing on the sidewalk, he flipped a coin to the man in a black greatcoat and turned to face the storefront.

Mrs. Talbot's dress shop on Bond Street was a small, squat building that looked as though it had been forced between its neighbors as an afterthought by a giant, untidy hand.

Except for the proprietress's name, done in small, precise black lettering on the door, there was nothing to distinguish the faded brick building as one of the most fashionable dress shops in England. Its front windows were discreetly blinded by hangings of the sheerest rose-colored linen. The flimsy draperies served, as they were no doubt meant to, to stir curiosity in passersby; some of whom were even now trying to peer through the linen at the shop beyond.

Alex ignored them, stepped up to the front door, and pushed it open. A bell overhead jumped and clattered, announcing his arrival.

Walls of mirrors flanked the tiny front room. Except for two dainty armchairs, apparently designed to hold no one bigger than a child, and a glass cabinet containing feathers, beads, and assorted other pieces of trim, the shop was empty.

Silence blanketed the room and when he cleared his throat restlessly, Alex felt as though he'd shouted in church. Suddenly uneasy, he tugged his watch free of its fob, flipped the case open, and studied the clock face. Anything was better than meeting his reflected gaze in the mirror facing him. "A fine pass this woman's brought you to, MacGregor," he muttered to himself.

He'd carefully avoided actually setting foot in a dress shop for years. Usually, Mrs. Talbot or her competitors were more than happy to call on him either at home or the shipping office, where he spent an unfortunate amount of time lately.

Where he should be *now* instead of cooling his heels in a lady's shop.

Alex shifted position, stretched his neck against his too tight collar, and frowned. There was something about a lady's dressmaker that put a man at a disadvantage. Even the smell of the place worked against him.

Warm and perfumed, the air of Mrs. Talbot's establishment, like so many of her competitors, seemed designed to keep a man off his guard. The sense of the place was quiet, intimate, as though any man who walked inside was being given the rare privilege of peeking into the world of women—only to discover that he didn't understand a bit of it.

Grumbling under his breath, Alex had almost talked himself into leaving when the deep burgundy curtains at the back of the room parted and a woman joined him.

Mrs. Talbot herself. He'd only seen her once or twice over the years, but she wasn't an easy woman to forget. A tall, angular woman with sharp black eyes and a royal carriage, she wore her midnight-black hair high on her head. Diamonds and sapphires shone on her earlobes and complemented perfectly her vivid blue satin gown. She swept into the showroom carrying an emerald-green and white dress over her arm.

Surprised, she said, "Mr. MacGregor!" then glanced down at the dress in her arms. "I'm sorry, I thought you were Miss Hesselthwaite, here to collect her gown."

Feeling more out of place than ever, Alex wanted only to complete his business and get out of there. Before some other woman wandered in off the street. He waited until the dressmaker had hung the unclaimed gown carefully on a brass hook before speaking.

"I'm sorry to disturb you, Mrs. Talbot," he said.

"Nonsense, always happy to see a customer," she answered.

He'd no doubt about that. Not only his mother did her shopping here . . . but every one of his mistresses had been gifted at one time or another with one of Mrs. Talbot's creations. Oh, he was a *very* good customer, indeed. It was more than likely that his account alone had paid for the earrings she wore.

"I've come about the order placed by the guest in my house—Miss Simmons?"

"Oh, yes." Wary, she pointed out, "The order isn't quite ready though, Mr. MacGregor. Even with the rush your mother requested, I told her it would be a few days." She spread her hands eloquently and shook her head slowly as if addressing a slow child. "I *do* have other customers."

"I understand," Alex assured her. "Actually, what I wanted to say was, you may have a few extra days time."

"I beg your pardon?"

He couldn't blame her for being surprised. No doubt most people who patronized her shop were always clamoring for her to hurry. But then, his was rather a special case.

It had occurred to Alex that if her wardrobe were delayed, Kit Simmons would be forced to remain in London—with him. After all, hadn't his own mother insisted that she not travel to the country without her new wardrobe?

And while she was in London, Alex was determined that he would find a way to coerce Kit into his bed. Since she apparently needed to be "in love" . . . Alex needed a little more time. At least a few more days. It shouldn't take longer than that, he thought with an inner smile. By heaven, if she could fall in love with *Ian*, she could bloody well fall in love with *him*, as well. At least temporarily.

Then, finally, he would have some peace and be able to put her from his mind.

However, he could hardly give Mrs. Talbot *that* explanation.

"I have . . . *business* in town for several days yet and as I promised my mother to personally escort Miss Simmons to the country house—" He shrugged.

"I see." The woman nodded.

Alex had the distinct impression she saw more than he particularly cared for her to.

But there was nothing he could do about that.

"Well," she added, "thank you so much for having the goodness to inform me. The extra time will come in very handy. We're always busy at this time of year, you know."

"Yes, I can imagine." Visions of the hundreds of balls and dinner parties given during the Season, each demanding a new gown, rushed through Alex's mind. Every female in England would be attending each event, parading about for the sole purpose of attracting a male, be it husband or lover.

For the first time in years, Alex wasn't the least bit interested.

"And too," Mrs. Talbot was saying, "I'm afraid my seamstresses show little interest in working on the fabrics Miss Simmons chose."

"What?"

She shrugged. "When my employees have the choice of working on brocade or silk ball gowns, it is difficult to make them give their best to"—she shuddered delicately—*"brown* muslin."

"Brown?" Alex echoed. "She selected *brown*? Only brown?"

"No." Mrs. Talbot frowned. "She also requested three frocks in gray."

Damn. Brown and gray. Hell, why not black? Alex

thought furiously. He didn't understand Kit at all. In fact, every time he thought he'd puzzled her out, she surprised him again.

Oh, he'd known that she'd tried to refuse the new wardrobe. But when his mother informed him that she'd finally accepted, Alex had told himself that her refusal had all been an act. She'd simply wanted to play the part of overwhelmed country miss long enough to ensure that they wouldn't think her mercenary.

Now this? His brain moved quickly, trying to figure out her latest maneuver. Was the drab wardrobe part of a bigger plan? Or was she really trying to keep from being indebted to him?

Shaking his head, he realized that it didn't matter. At least, not this minute. He would have all the time he needed to discover exactly what it was that Kit Simmons was about. For now, he had other, more immediate concerns.

Like easing the continuous ache in his body, for one.

"Disregard her selections please, Mrs. Talbot." He continued before she could protest, "Instead, I'd like you to choose appropriate colors and fabrics. Anything you think she will need."

"Anything?"

He saw the flash of greed in her eyes but ignored it. "Anything. From the inside out, include whatever you think necessary."

"Certainly, Mr. MacGregor," she said quietly, a pleased smile curving her rouged lips.

Idly his gaze shifted to the dress hanging behind its creator. Mrs. Talbot noticed.

"Do you like it?" she asked and lifted it from the

hook. "The overskirt is green and white striped lawn drawn over emerald-green silk taffeta." She turned it around and waved her hand over the fabric. "As you can see, the green silk is pulled up high to accentuate the extravagant bustle. A lovely dress, if I do say so."

A sudden, clear image of Kit wearing the gown shot through his brain. He didn't know much about silks or taffetas or bustles for that matter. But he did know what he liked. And Alex was certain that dress was made to be worn by Kit.

"You say the woman who ordered it is supposed to be picking it up today?"

The dressmaker looked embarrassed for a moment. "Ordinarily, we do of course deliver. But in this case . . . well, there have been *problems*." She lifted her hands as if reluctant to say more.

Immediately he understood. Problems with payment, she meant. As his gaze skimmed over the elegant-looking day gown, he heard himself asking, "If you don't mind my asking, the dress appears to be about the size worn by my houseguest. Am I correct?"

"Well," she said thoughtfully, giving the gown a brief glance, "yes, as a matter of fact. It's quite near. Why?"

Alex reached into his inside pocket and pulled out his leather purse. Taking out several large bank notes, he held them out toward Mrs. Talbot. "I should like to purchase the gown. Now."

She eyed the money hungrily. Alex watched her as she mentally weighed the offer of ready cash against her promise to a faceless young woman who'd already proven herself to be less than eager to pay her debts. After several long minutes, Mrs. Talbot slipped the notes from his fingers and muttered, "Very generous, Mr. MacGregor."

"Not at all." He tucked his purse back into his jacket and added, "However, I do have one request."

"Yes?" Her eyes narrowed slightly.

"You say the gown is a near-perfect fit. Could you make the alterations say in the next hour?"

"I don't know . . ."

"For an extra twenty pounds?"

"One hour, sir. It will be ready."

"Excellent." He nodded and turned for the door. "And the wardrobe she ordered? No sooner than the first of next week?"

"Not a moment sooner, sir."

"Good morning, Mrs. Talbot."

"Good morning, Mr. MacGregor."

The bell over the door sounded out once more as Alex left the shop, already making his plans for the seduction of Kit Simmons.

Kit walked aimlessly for over an hour before the rain started.

Groaning, she paused under an ancient oak tree only long enough to untie her cape and pull it up over her head. Glancing up at the leaden sky, she cursed herself for not snatching up her umbrella and purse when she went into the house to get her cape.

But in all fairness to herself, she'd hardly been in a rational frame of mind. At the time, she hadn't been able to think further than getting out of the house. She needed time to think. She needed to be outside, in the air.

For the week she'd been in London, Kit had hardly left the MacGregor house. And the forced inactivity was beginning to wear on her. She was used to long walks in the countryside. She was accustomed to passing the time of day with the neighbors who'd remained friendly to her after Rose's birth. And most importantly, she was accustomed to being in control of herself.

Lately, it seemed that she had no more control than a feather in a high wind. She was blown this way and that by Alex, his mother, the housekeeper, Rose . . . Kit sighed, brushed raindrops out of her eyes, and stepped out from under the tree.

Hunching down beneath her cape, Kit kept a wary eye out for the other people caught up in the surprise rainstorm. Muffled curses and short barks of laughter crowded in with the sound of the storm as all around her passersby were hurrying to the safety of their homes.

Rain pelted against the street, danced in the puddles, and kept up a steady chatter to accompany her hurried walk. Kit slipped, skidded, then righted herself again and went on.

She had to go back to the MacGregors'. There was nowhere else to go. A trickle of envy filled her as she watched the others fleeing the rain. They, no doubt, had warm homes and families awaiting them. They would sit by a fire, comforted by their loved ones. They would laugh over how silly it was to be caught unprepared by a London storm.

Kit's lips pressed together tightly and she told herself to stop. But she couldn't help thinking that only a few months ago, she too had a place to belong. People who loved her.

Now, she had only shelter.

A huddled figure off to her right caught Kit's attention and she half turned for a better look. Straining to see through the falling rain, Kit finally managed to make out the form of an old woman, crouched down against a half wall. Unkempt, gray-streaked hair lay in sodden streamers along the woman's cheeks as she curled in on herself in a futile effort to keep dry.

A flash of shame swept through her and she told herself that no matter her circumstances, she had much to be grateful for.

Instinctively Kit hurried to the woman's side, pulling at her cape as she went. Quickly she draped it across the woman's hunched shoulders and head, knowing even as she did so that it would be poor protection against the weather. Still, it was better than nothing.

The woman looked up, smiled her thanks, and, nodding, burrowed even deeper into the false security of the cape.

In seconds Kit was soaked to the skin. Her dress clung to her body like cold fingers and she felt long tendrils of wet hair plastered against her face and neck. Pushing her hair out of her eyes, Kit determinedly started walking again.

Burdened by her clinging skirt, now heavy with rain, each step seemed a challenge. Still blocks from her goal, her mental image of the house seemed more welcoming than it had before. She imagined the front door swinging wide and Harris's usually calm demeanor shaken as he pulled her into the warmth.

Mentally, she saw herself huddled under the quilts on her bed, her fingers cradling a hot cup of tea, a cheerful fire in the grate. Silently she promised to be mindful of her blessings more often. Kit lifted her sodden skirts clear of the streets and immediately stepped into a mud hole at least a foot deep.

Cold, dirty, and bedraggled, she lifted her eyes to heaven and said a quick prayer that whatever test she was being given was now over.

She pulled her left leg free of the muck and trudged on.

"Is it ready?"

"Yes, sir," Mrs. Talbot answered and handed Alex a wide, flat box tied in string. "Your order will be delivered next week, Mr. MacGregor," she said briskly. "Now if you'll excuse me"—she waved one hand at the burgundy curtain behind her—"I have customers to see to . . ."

"Of course."

She left him and he stood for a moment, staring down at the box in his hand. It would look well on Kit, he knew. And he would insist she wear it tomorrow night. He'd already decided that after their trip to the museum, they would go to the Gaiety Theatre. Something told Alex that Kit would thoroughly enjoy Gilbert and Sullivan's latest play, *The Mikado*.

In fact, he mused, tomorrow morning they would stop by Miss Michele's shop for the hat his mother had promised Kit.

A straw, he told himself, would complete her outfit

perfectly. Then Alex smiled at the idea that *he* was actually planning a lady's costume.

"Alex?"

A too familiar voice called out and Alex's smile slowly died. He groaned quietly before he looked up.

Elizabeth Beckwith.

Damn.

She moved up to him in a swirl of silk and taffeta. Her skirts rustled and whispered with her every movement and her eyes shone with amusement.

"Alex!" Elizabeth stepped in close, laid one hand on his arm, and reached up for a kiss. When he didn't respond, she clucked her tongue at him and kissed him instead. "Are you still angry with me?"

"I wasn't angry, Elizabeth," he answered, surprised to find that her perfume now seemed rather cloying. He seemed to remember it being more . . . *alluring* somehow.

"I'm so glad," she breathed up at him and smiled a mischievous smile that used to send chills of anticipation racing along his spine.

Now, Alex noticed that one of her front teeth was crooked.

Elizabeth ran the flat of her hand over his shirtfront. "I've missed you, you know. It's been nearly a week, Alex, and I'm so . . ." She inhaled sharply, breathed it out in a rush, and rubbed her breasts against him gently. *"Lonely."*

"Is Richard not in town then?" he asked, knowing very well that Richard Beckwith was certainly in London, doing everything humanly possible to stay away from his beloved wife.

She pouted prettily. The same pout that used to have Alex tripping over his own feet to get her whatever it was she wanted. Now, he simply wanted her to say what she felt necessary so he could be on his way.

"Oh, Alex." Elizabeth smoothed her fingers up his arm. "Richard and I don't get along, you know that . . ."

"Well," he said offhandedly, "perhaps you'll be able to work things out together now that I'm out of the way." He couldn't resist asking, "Or is there someone else already?"

"You're so heartless!" she said and skimmed one long fingernail along his jaw.

Strange, Alex thought. It was the first time he noticed that those nails of hers were sharp as daggers.

"There'll never be anyone but you, Alex." She sighed and rose up to press her mouth against his.

Her lips were smooth, practiced. She knew just what to do to make a man hungry. Or at least, she *had* known. But this time, Alex didn't feel a thing. Instead, he found himself remembering Kit's mouth. Warm, pliant, almost reluctantly eager.

Deliberately he pulled back and took a step away.

She pretended not to notice and reached for the package. "Alex, you didn't have to buy me another gown. I would have taken you back with a simple apology."

Amazing.

Alex stared down at the woman who'd ruled his bed for the last six months and couldn't understand what it was he'd seen in her. Not only was he not aroused by her playacting, he was a bit sickened by the thought of just how many men had lain where he'd been. How many men she'd touched and spoken to and kissed just as she had him.

Suddenly he wanted nothing more than to be far away from Elizabeth Beckwith.

Kit's image rose up before him and he savored it. Yes, she'd been with another man. His own brother. But . . . she'd lain with Ian for love. Elizabeth Beckwith and others like her knew only greed.

"I'm afraid this is not for you, Elizabeth," he said calmly.

Immediately her manner changed. Her dewy eyes narrowed and hardened and her full mouth flattened into a grim, unyielding line.

"So," she accused, "it's *you* who've found someone else already. Or were you with her while you were coming to *my* bed?"

A sharp bark of a laugh shot from his throat. He couldn't keep it back. She sounded like a jealous wife, for God's sake!

"Elizabeth," he said, choking back another laugh, "thank you."

"For what?"

She was furious. Every inch of her screamed with anger. And yet, he knew she wouldn't dare throw a repeat of her last tantrum. Not here. Not where Mrs. Talbot could—and would—report it to every one of her customers.

"For making me see clearly at last."

"What are you talking about?"

"Even if I explained, I doubt you would understand," he answered and gave her a half bow.

"Alex, if you leave now . . ." She drew herself up to her full height, arched her back, and pushed her large, heavy breasts forward temptingly.

He looked at her and all he could think of was Kit's smaller, firm bosom and how she continually tried to hide it behind her crossed arms.

"I won't have you back," she warned and ran her hands down her hips in a motion that used to be as a siren's call to him . . . and, no doubt, others. "It will be over."

It had been over for quite a while, he now realized. Only Elizabeth would never accept that a man would willingly leave her bed. In her mind, the end came only when *she* wished it.

Fine, he told himself. He could give her that much.

Alex inhaled slowly and frowned as he got yet another sample of her overpowering scent. Strange that it had never bothered him before.

But then, he was noticing quite a bit lately that he'd never bothered with before. Say, for example . . . children. He'd never been able to bear most children. And yet, Rose was quite a becoming child . . . He shook his head to clear his wandering thoughts.

The woman in front of him was still waiting and he could tell by her posture that she was very sure of herself.

Ah well.

"If you think it best, Elizabeth . . ." He started to say more, then thought better of it. Tucking the box under his arm, he gave her a brief nod and said only, "Good-bye."

When the door closed behind him, Elizabeth kicked it and winced with pain.

10

"**M**iss Simmons!"
Kit trudged on. She heard the man shouting, but paid no attention. Oblivious to all but her need to reach a dry, warm haven, she didn't even raise her head.

"Miss Simmons!" the man's voice called again and when she still didn't look, she heard him shout, "Cabby! Stop!"

A mud-spattered hansom drew to a halt on the street beside her and the cab door flew open. Kit pushed her hair out of her eyes, blinked blindly at the raindrops on her lashes, and looked up into John Tremayne's astonished features.

He held a huge umbrella over the two of them and she was grateful for the respite from the pounding rain. Drops of water pelted at their black fabric shelter, the drumming noise making it necessary for him to shout.

"Miss Simmons?" His blond eyebrows rose almost to his hairline and she saw how she must look reflected in his horrified expression. "You're soaked through!"

Kit glared at him and sluiced water from her face with one hand. Had he stopped merely to get a better look at her? Hadn't her humiliation the day before been enough? Her gaze ran over his dapper attire, still miraculously neat despite the weather. A groan started deep in her throat but she managed to squelch it.

Certainly he remained dry and well groomed. *He* had an umbrella! *He* had the fare for a cab! And apparently he had nothing better to do than point out to her just how disreputable her own appearance was.

"Sorry," he said quickly, giving her a lopsided grin. "Suppose you already know that, eh?" Not waiting for an answer, he hurried on, "Got caught outside without your umbrella then?"

She didn't bother to answer him, since she felt it was quite apparent that he was correct. Kit had never been so miserable. Cold down to her bones, she thought she could *hear* her own teeth chattering over the raging storm. All she wanted was to be dry again. Warm.

"Stupid question," he said as if reading her mind. "Come on"—John held her upper arm firmly—"I'll take you home."

Home. If only she could go home. But since that was impossible, she would be grateful to reach the Mac-Gregor house. "Thank you," she managed to say though she was sure he couldn't hear her over the rain.

"C'mon then, Guv!" the driver shouted. "I'm bloody well drownin' up 'ere!"

"Just coming!" John called back.

She felt as though she had boulders tied to her legs. Mud clung to her feet as though reluctant to let her escape. Each time she pulled one foot free, the other sunk even lower into the muck.

"Lean on me," John urged.

Her fingers dug into his forearm and she clenched her jaw tight as she struggled to move. Soaking wet fabric slapped against her legs, pushing her back for every step she took. Kit's right foot came down on what felt like a large, half-buried stone and she lurched to one side. The mire suddenly shifted beneath her feet. Gasping, eyes opened wide, she swung her free hand wildly in a desperate attempt to stay upright. But it was no use. Despite her every effort—despite even John's help—she felt her balance dissolving.

And John knew it too.

"Miss Simmons!" he shouted.

Kit's head fell back on her neck and she watched the umbrella above her sway in a wide arc as John Tremayne began a slow drop to the mud.

His umbrella speared the muddy ground and snapped like a dry twig. John hit the sludge facedown. Arms and legs spread wide, face in the muck, his breath left him in a rush when Kit landed across his back.

As if from a distance, she heard the cabby laughing and immediately closed her ears to the sound. Somehow, she'd managed to keep her face out of the mud, but that was the only bright spot, she told herself. Ribs aching from her fall, Kit muttered under her breath and briefly wished that she knew a few colorful curse words. Unfortunately, her education had been sorely lacking on that point.

Grimacing, Kit planted her hands in the mud and straightened her arms, lifting herself off of her would-be rescuer.

When she moved, his head rose and she heard him spit out a mouthful of mud. Groaning, Kit asked herself silently if there was *any* way this day could get worse.

Pushing herself to her knees, she sat on her heels and watched John do the same.

He used his now filthy sleeve to wipe his face before looking up at her. His Adam's apple wobbled uncertainly in his throat, then he swallowed and his face screwed up in disgust.

Rain continued to fall, leaving tiny streaks of clean flesh on his features like white stripes on dark fabric. His pale blue eyes stood out in sharp relief against the grime and when he gave her a wry smile, she saw that even his teeth were coated in mud.

Slowly, silently, he reached around for his ruined umbrella. He stared for a long moment at the ripped fabric, flapping madly in a sudden gust of wind. Then solemnly he lifted the umbrella's almost bare, bent frame directly over his head.

A bubble of amusement formed in Kit's chest and she didn't even try to hold it in. After such a miserable morning, it felt good to laugh. And when John's laughter joined hers, she laughed even harder.

"It's all well and good to laugh, y'know," the cabby called down to them, "but you'll not be ridin' in *my* cab covered with that muck!"

John tossed his ruined umbrella over one shoulder and pushed himself to his feet. Holding out one grimy hand to Kit, he looked up at the driver and asked, "Would an extra fiver change your mind?"

The man's eyes gleamed under the brim of his worn derby. "Guv', for a fiver, I'll wash ye down meself!"

"That won't be necessary, thanks," John answered, grinning. Then turning to Kit, he asked, "Shall we go, Miss Simmons?"

"Kit." She struggled to her feet, still clasping his hand.

"Kit it is, then." He swept her an elegant half bow and a clump of mud fell from his head. Tucking her arm through his, he guided her to the waiting hansom with the aplomb of a man being presented at court.

Once settled inside, John closed the cab's doors over their legs and tapped on the roof with his knuckles. "All right, cabby. Twenty-three Mayfair."

"Where the hell did she go?"

Harris swallowed a sigh, lifted his chin, and answered his employer for the third time.

"As I have already said, sir. She didn't say."

"Didn't say? Why on earth did you let her go?"

"I didn't realize that she was to be confined to the house, sir."

"Confined?" Alexander's eyebrows shot straight up. "Bloody hell, Harris. She's not a prisoner, you know!"

"No, sir."

"And stop 'sirring' me, Harris! We're alone here." Alex scowled ferociously at the man opposite him. "You sound like a damned parrot! Yes, sir. No, sir."

Harris watched Alex MacGregor pace the length of his study and told himself that perhaps Tess was right. He hadn't given her speculation much credence when she'd first suggested that there was something going on between her son and their guest. But after watching Alex for the last twenty minutes, Michael Harris was willing to admit that perhaps he wasn't as astute as he once was.

He'd served the MacGregor family for over twenty-five years. He'd watched Ian and Alexander grow into men and had always prided himself on the fact that he knew them better than they knew themselves.

Ian had been a spoiled child and had grown into a willful adult. Interested only in his own gratification, he'd cared for no one but himself.

Alex too, Harris admitted silently, had been spoiled by his doting mother. But beneath the sometimes selfish manner, there was an honorable, giving core that Ian had lacked.

Until, of course, the year Alex had reached his majority. The butler frowned slightly as he recalled that year and the changes in Alexander MacGregor since then.

"When did she say she'd return?"

"She didn't, sir," Harris told him again, banishing his idle thoughts. It seemed the older one became, the more one's mind tended to wander. "She left soon after you, sir. I assumed she was going for a walk, since she left her purse behind."

"A *walk*? There's a river of water and mud flowing down the streets, Harris! Even a *duck* couldn't take a walk in that!"

"But it wasn't raining when she left, sir."

"Damn!" Alex plopped down into the chair behind his desk and frowned at the white box he'd brought home with him. "Even when she isn't *trying*," he muttered, "the woman thwarts me."

"Sir?"

"Nothing." Alex shot back and then added, "You're doing it again, Harris."

"You *are* my employer, sir."

"Yes, yes, and as you used to be quite fond of telling me, you've known me since I was in nappies!"

Harris's lips quirked.

"So," Alex demanded, "why don't you tell me what I'm doing wrong?"

"I don't understand what you mean."

The younger man snorted derisively. "You understand perfectly well, Harris, and we both know it! What I want to know is why the woman found *Ian* so damned fascinating and can't stand to be around *me* for more than a few minutes!"

Harris didn't know what to say to that. Truthfully, that same question had bothered him once or twice. Kit Simmons just did not seem the type of woman who would believe in any of Ian's promises.

A frantic pounding on the front door startled both men and saved Harris from having to come up with a credible answer to Alex's question. The older man turned toward the hall but before he had taken more than a few steps, Alex passed him, crossed the marble floor, and threw open the front door.

John Tremayne and Kit, hands clasped tightly together, stumbled into the entry, both of them laughing like fools.

Alex's gaze locked on the couple's joined hands and Harris watched his employer's features harden. He wasn't the least bit surprised to hear an all-too-familiar icy tone in Alex's voice when he spoke.

"Good afternoon." Ignoring Kit completely, Alex looked at his old friend. "John, you're almost late for our business meeting."

John pulled his watch free, but didn't bother to flip

open the dirt-encrusted lid. Grinning, he shrugged and answered, "Hardly afternoon, Alex. It's not eleven yet."

"Still . . ."

"And almost late—" He glanced at Kit, then looked back to Alex. "Doesn't that mean *on time*?"

Alex inhaled sharply, frowned, and turned to glare at Kit. "And you, madam," he said brusquely, "would you mind telling me where you've been?"

"Yes."

Taken aback, Alex opened and closed his mouth several times before asking, "I beg your pardon?"

"I said yes. I *would* mind telling you."

Harris cleared his throat uneasily.

John took a single step to one side.

Kit and Alex stared at each other silently until the room fairly crackled with expectation. The hall clock marked the passage of each second with an inordinately loud tick. Even the whisper of their breathing seemed to echo in the silence.

"Very well!" Alex said suddenly and John jumped at the explosion of sound. "John," he continued, "take yourself to my room and . . . freshen up. You're dripping all over the hall."

"Oh!" As if he'd momentarily forgotten what state he was in, John looked down at the puddle forming around his feet and immediately moved for the stairs. After a few steps, he turned back and asked, "Kit? Shall I see you to your room?"

"No thank you," Kit and Alex answered at the same time.

Before she could speak again, he went on, "I'll see to Kit myself, John."

"There's really no need," she said firmly.

Alex ignored her. He nodded at John and only paused long enough to see the other man hurrying up the stairs before snapping, "Harris!"

"Yes, sir?"

His gaze locked with Kit's, Alex ordered brusquely, "See that one of the maids cleans this mess right away, will you?"

"Of course, sir."

"I can see myself upstairs," Kit said quietly, *"if* you don't mind."

"I do," Alex countered as he walked to her side, bent down, and swung her up into his arms.

"You do what?" she demanded.

"Mind."

"Put me down this instant!"

"I think not." He started for the stairs, ignoring her attempts to get free.

"This is ridiculous," Kit nearly shouted as she pushed at the strong arms wrapped around her. She looked over his shoulder and saw Harris hide a smile. Apparently refusing to put on a show, she stopped her futile efforts to escape but continued to protest. "I am perfectly capable of walking!"

"Madam, you have already been the cause of extra work for the maids." He frowned down at her. "If you were to attempt walking, you would only succeed in spreading the grime you're covered in from one end of this house to the other!"

"What about John?" she argued. "Why aren't you carrying *him* as well?"

He snorted a laugh and flicked a quick glance at her.

"I have *never* harbored the desire to clutch John Tremayne close against me, thank you very much." His hands tightened their hold on her as he added in an undertone, *"You* on the other hand are a different matter entirely."

She flushed beneath the mud.

"Besides," Alex went on, *"he* isn't hampered by sodden skirts!"

Finally realizing that nothing she could do or say would prevent him from doing just as he pleased, Kit lapsed into a mutinous silence. She looked up at him from beneath her lashes and saw that despite his light, bantering tone, his features looked as though they'd been carved of stone.

A wave of cold washed over her and she shivered, instinctively huddling closer to his broad chest for warmth. His arms tightened perceptibly, but he said nothing.

When they reached the first-floor landing, John was already out of sight. Alex's long legs made short work of the lengthy hall and almost before she knew it, he was carrying her into her bedroom.

He set her down on the threshold of the adjoining bath and ordered, "Get out of those wet things." Without another glance at her, he turned and walked toward the hearth on the far wall.

She thought about arguing, but quickly dismissed the idea. What was the point? He was right. Even as she reached around to the buttons at the back of her neck, another series of tremors shook through her. Kit felt as though she'd never be warm again. She was cold to the bone. Her fingers felt stiff, wooden.

Plucking uselessly at the collar of her gown, Kit's frustration mounted. No matter how she tried, she couldn't reach around far enough to be able to undo the tiny buttons marching down her spine. Kit chewed at her bottom lip and shook her hands frantically, trying to warm them up enough to cooperate.

"Stand still," a deep voice commanded from right behind her.

She hadn't heard him approach. There was something disconcerting about a man as big as Alex MacGregor being able to walk without making a sound. If she had any sense at all, she would insist that he leave her and send a maid. The very idea of a *man* helping her to undress should have shocked her to her soul.

As his fingers deftly slid down the row of buttons though, Kit found she didn't even mind the impropriety of the situation. All she wanted was to be out of the clinging, cold material hugging her body.

When the last button was freed, Kit's gown slipped off her shoulders. Instinctively she clutched the icy garment to her chest to keep it from falling off completely.

"Do you want me to run your bath?" he asked gruffly. "Or would you prefer that I send a maid?"

"Neither," she whispered, suddenly aware of his proximity in the too-small washroom. "Thank you for your help, but I can manage now."

She held her breath, praying he would leave, yet— God help her—hoping he would stay.

His fingertips slid down the length of her spine and even through the frigid damp of her chemise, frissons of heat danced through her bloodstream. She sucked in a desperate gulp of air. A tumult of emotions raced through Kit and she frantically tried to tell herself that this was wrong. That she meant no more to him than Marian had to Ian. She was simply there. Accessible.

Hesitantly she took a small step forward, out of his reach.

But he too stepped forward, unwilling, it seemed, to let her go just yet.

"Where did you meet John?"

Surprised, and somewhat relieved that he hadn't said anything more . . . *dangerous*, Kit slowly turned to face him. Tilting her head back, she looked up and met his gaze. Shadows darkened his clear blue eyes and she wondered briefly why it was so important to him. She knew it was. She'd known it from the moment they'd entered the house to be met by Alex's grim features.

She could have explained everything then. But her own stubbornness had goaded her into keeping silent in the face of his demands. But now, he wasn't demanding. In fact, he looked almost as if he'd rather not hear her answer.

Maybe it was for that reason alone that she began to talk. Kit took a long, deep breath and heard herself telling him exactly what had happened. She told him why she'd left the house. She told him about trying to avoid seeing him. She told him about the rain and how John had tried to rescue her only to fall victim to the same mud hole that had caught her.

And as she talked, Kit saw the shadows in his eyes lift. Strangely enough, she realized that she was pleased.

"I was w—" he started at the conclusion of her story, then finished lamely, "*concerned* that you might have gotten lost."

Worried, he meant. Alexander MacGregor was worried? About her?

"After all, you're new to London"—he nodded as if approving of what he was saying—"it's a big city."

"Yes," she said and began to feel the cold again.

"Well then," he spoke quickly, loudly, "have your bath. I'll send one of the maids up with tea."

"Thank you." Kit tugged the sleeves of her gown higher on her shoulders.

"I'll light the fire, shall I?" Without waiting for her agreement, he strode across her room and knelt beside the hearth.

Thoughtfully Kit watched him as she closed the washroom door. Something was . . . *different* about him. Decidedly different.

Alex held a match to the kindling in the grate until the flames caught and began to consume the fresh fuel. Pushing himself upright, Alex leaned his forearm on the mantel and stared into the fire. He couldn't remember the last time he'd laid a fire himself. Strange how completing such a small task could be so satisfying.

Hmmph! His lips quirked slightly at the obvious lie. His sense of self-satisfaction had nothing to do with a well-laid fire. No. It was much more to do with Kit Simmons. How she looked. How she felt in his arms.

But mostly, Alex thought, the satisfaction rippling through him was brought about by what Kit had told him about how she'd come to be with John.

Briefly he recalled the stab of jealousy that had sliced through him when they'd arrived, laughing together like old friends. Companionably. Intimately. And when Alex saw that John had Kit's hand firmly clasped in his own, Alex had had to fight down the incredible urge to break his oldest friend's arm.

His fingers curled around the edge of the mantel. Nothing had gone the way he'd planned all day.

First, missing John at the office, then running into Elizabeth at Mrs. Talbot's, and then Kit being gone when he'd arrived home. And he hadn't been at all prepared for the concern that had shot through him when he'd learned that no one knew where she'd gone!

For God's sake! A week ago he hadn't even known her!

And today he was pacing the floor, worried because she was wandering through the streets of London during a rainstorm!

Alex turned his head toward the closed door across the room. From behind it came the sound of running water, and in his mind's eye, he saw Kit, stripping off the rest of her muddy clothes.

He tried to push the mental image away, but it was useless. Ever since seeing her in her drawers, his imagination had taken free rein. To his horror, he'd even caught himself once or twice imagining what she must have looked like when her belly was round and full with child.

Good God, what had happened to him?

No woman had ever affected him so. At the mere thought of her, his body tightened eagerly. He'd *never* been so eaten up with desire that he could think of nothing except the woman in question.

Alex MacGregor prided himself on his ability to keep his emotions separate from his body's demands. And yet

. . . his gaze bored into the door separating him from Kit. Inside the small room, she'd shut off the water. He strained to listen and was rewarded by the gentle slap of water against flesh as she stepped into the tub.

"Dear God," he muttered thickly and closed his eyes against the image rising in his mind. If he had half a brain, he told himself, he would march right into that damned washroom, climb into the tub with her, and *demand* that she deliver him from the torment she'd caused.

Instinctively he took a half step forward, then stopped abruptly. He couldn't do that. Rubbing one hand over his eyes, Alex told himself that she would no doubt scream the house down and every one of his servants would know him for the undisciplined bounder he no doubt was!

No. No, he had to remember his plan. If he was to survive this insanity, he would have to take his time with her. Woo her. Seduce her. Make her love him. Then, by God, he'd get her into bed so fast, her heels would catch fire!

A timid knock on the open bedroom door demanded his attention. He frowned at the young kitchen maid standing hesitantly in the hall. She held a tray nearly as big as she was, loaded down with a teapot, cup, saucer, and a plate of sandwiches.

"Cook says the lady might be wantin' somethin', sir," she mumbled uneasily.

With a profound effort, Alex banished his frown and nodded at the girl. "That's very kind of cook. Bring it in please and set it there." He waved one hand at the small round table near the fire.

"Yessir." She bobbed a half curtsy and hurried across the room, keeping a watchful eye on the rattling teacup.

"Will the lady be wantin' anythin' else, sir?" she asked as she set her burden down.

"No," Alex answered, "not for now. Thank you."

She jerked him a nod, spun about, and almost ran from the room.

Alex watched her go, a half smile on his face. He knew he didn't intimidate Kit in the least—but it appeared that *other* women had more sense.

Idly he picked up one of the sandwiches and took a bite. From across the room came the distinct sounds of splashing and he knew she was scrubbing the dirt from her body. How he ached to do it for her.

Frowning again, he ate the last of the sandwich and stomped across the room. He stepped into the hall and firmly shut her bedroom door behind him.

Grumbling to himself, Alex headed for his study downstairs. He would be *damned* if she'd catch him standing in her room waiting for her like some love-struck bull in a pasture. He stopped suddenly, one foot poised in the air above the step. *Love-struck?*

Love had nothing to do with it, he assured himself. *Lust*-struck was more like the truth. And once that lust was fed . . . once he'd feasted on that luscious body, that would be the end of it.

His life could return to normal. And he would be able to put all thoughts of the too-tempting Miss Kit Simmons out of his mind entirely!

That settled, he continued on to the study, never noticing that he was humming.

11

"**S**he was a bloody good sport about the whole thing, I can tell you!"

So you have, Alex thought and leaned back in his desk chair. He watched John Tremayne through slitted eyes and was still able to see the flush of excitement on the man's face.

"Imagine, Alex! Covered in mud, lying about on the ground where all of London could see her, and she *laughs*!" John tossed his hands wide and shook his head delightedly. "And did I tell you what an infectious laugh she has?"

At least a dozen times, Alex countered silently.

"And the *cabby*!" John spun about to face his friend. "I haven't even *told* you about the cabby! Rude fellow, really. But Kit didn't let him bother *her*!" Chuckling softly, John continued on his aimless stroll about the study. "Magnificent woman!"

Truly a paragon among women. Alex frowned, lifted one booted foot to the edge of his desk, and studied the highly polished toe. It wasn't necessary to answer John. The man had been doing a soliloquy for over an hour and showed no signs of slowing down.

He was completely smitten. Grumbling softly, Alex's gaze followed his friend around the room.

"Do you know, Alex?" John stopped suddenly and looked at him. "I believe it was Providence sent Kit Simmons here, to this house."

"Providence?" Good Lord.

"Certainly." Pushing his hands through his still damp blond hair, John went on, talking more to himself than to Alex. "Why else would she come to London now? Why would I have met her? And just look at what happened today! Do you think it was mere *chance* that I happened upon her today in the rain?"

"No."

"No?" Eagerly John turned toward him. "Really?"

Alex set his feet back firmly on the floor, leaned his elbows on his desktop, and glared at his friend. "Really."

"Then you think it was destined for us to meet too?"

"Destiny had nothing to do with it, John!"

"What?"

"Think, man!" His temper frayed and his patience sorely tested, Alex had had enough. By thunder, if John wanted to go and fancy himself in love—why now? Why *this* woman? Could *nothing* go along as it should? Well, he wouldn't stand for it, Alex told himself. "You really believe it was the hand of Providence that brought her to London?"

"Why else?" John's chin lifted defiantly, as if daring Alex to disprove him.

"Because she needed money for her illegitimate child, of course!"

John blanched.

"For God's sake, John! You're behaving like a schoolboy. She was Ian's *mistress*." Alex heard himself shouting and lowered his voice. "Have you forgotten?"

"Of course not," he mumbled unconvincingly.

"And it wasn't happenstance that you met her! You're my business manager! We grew up together!" Alex jumped up from his chair, suddenly too tightly strung to sit still. "Of *course* you would meet a woman who was a guest in *my* home!"

"Yes, but . . ." John's voice was much more subdued, though he appeared to be clinging to his own fantasies.

"And you came upon her today because she was fool enough to go for a walk in the rain and *you* missed a business appointment." Coming around the edge of his desk, Alex stomped across the floor and stopped within inches of John. "You were both heading for *this* house. *Certainly* you would meet!"

"But it all seems so . . . fortuitous . . ." John's lips twisted into a frown.

Alex's hands came down on the other man's shoulders briefly. "It could seem that way I suppose, to *most* men." He inhaled sharply and added, "But you're not a romantic fool, John. Think about this for heaven's sake!"

Long, silent minutes passed and Alex held his breath. Lord knew, he'd always felt closer to John than he had to his own brother. But by God, he wasn't going to share Kit Simmons with him—and he had no intention whatsoever of gallantly stepping aside to make way for his friend. Only a blindly generous idiot would do that! Well, Alex was no idiot and he wasn't feeling particularly generous at the moment, either!

The best he could hope for was that John would come to his senses.

Finally, after what seemed forever, John sighed and admitted, "I suppose you're right, Alex." He looked up and gave the other man a sheepish grin. "Still, even if destiny had nothing to do with our meeting . . . shouldn't I make the most of it now that it's happened?"

"Ordinarily, John," Alex said and turned back toward his desk, "that's just what I'd advise. But in this case . . . I don't know."

"Well, I *do* know," John said softly. "I think I could become quite . . . *fond* of the girl, Alex."

Fond? Fond? Good God. He could become *fond* of the girl? If the situation wasn't so ridiculous, Alex would laugh. His best friend in the world was spouting roses and poetry over the woman that *he* wanted to toss on a bed and bury himself in!

Something had to be done. Alex couldn't very well go about seducing Kit if John was forever trailing about sighing and looking moonstruck!

"In fact," John said firmly, "as soon as she comes down to dinner, I shall ask her to accompany me on a ride through Hyde Park tomorrow."

"Tomorrow?" Quickly Alex's brain raced for a solution.

"There's really no point in waiting for a better time, is there?" John countered, clearly pleased with himself. "I'm telling you, Alex. This woman is . . . is . . ."

Becoming more trouble by the moment, Alex finished silently. There must be *something*, he told himself. *Some* way to get John out of London. Quickly. Absently he noted that John was talking again. Listing still more of

Kit's many attributes. Alex shut the sound out—concentrating instead on the various notions presenting themselves in his mind. Just when he was convinced that nothing believable would occur to him, the answer leapt into his brain.

"I'm afraid you won't be able to escort her to the park, John. I'm sorry."

"What? Why not?"

"I, uh . . ." Alex walked behind his desk and dropped down into the chair. Keeping his gaze steady, he looked John straight in the eye and said, "I forgot to mention that I wanted you to go to the shipyards for me."

"The shipyards?" John stepped up to the desk, leaned his palms on the polished wood surface, and said, "That's *hours* away by train! Whatever for?"

"The new ship we're having built. I want a complete report on it."

"But it won't be finished for another month yet, Alex." John shook his head. "There's no reason for a report now, man."

"Well, that's it, y'see." The lie was beginning to come easier and even Alex was amazed at the smoothness of it. "I've decided I want the ship ready in two weeks."

"Two weeks?" The blond man looked at Alex as though he were crazy. "Impossible!"

"Not really. All it will take is you. At the yards yourself to direct the workers." That part was certainly true. John had the uncanny ability to spark employees into a veritable frenzy of work. Alex had seen him do it any number of times and still had no idea how he managed it.

"You want me to *stay* there?" John's jaw dropped.

"I can't trust anyone else to do it, John." Another truth. Alex was beginning to feel much better about the whole thing.

"Why in the hell is this so damned important?" John straightened up and frowned down at the other man. "What possible difference can two weeks make in the completion time?"

Without hesitation, the answer rolled off his lips. "Two weeks will ensure that we have another ship sailing for the Argentines before the Lansard yard can do it. We'll be bringing back twice as much chilled beef as they can." By thunder! Yet *another* truth! And heaven knew, John couldn't very well dispute *that* argument.

Much to his own dismay, after having the family business foisted on him at Ian's death, Alex had had to learn more than he'd ever *cared* to know about the meat business. Of course, he'd never dreamed that knowledge would be useful in a situation like this one. Now, he studied John's reaction and just managed to hide a satisfied smile.

If there was one thing John Tremayne enjoyed as much if not more than he did women . . . it was business. The man was born to be in charge of a balance ledger. He could add more figures in his head than Alex could on a piece of paper, if given a week to do it.

"Yes," Alex said softly, expanding on his story, "if we beat the Lansard ship out of dock, our profits should climb through the roof." He leaned back in his chair and waited.

"You know, you could be right," John answered thoughtfully. Rubbing his chin, he continued, "I hadn't really considered it before. But it would be a stroke of genius to beat the new Lansard ship out of dock." He chuckled to himself before saying, "The old bastard's heart will probably give out when he hears . . ."

"Then you think it's possible?" Alex asked, knowing damn well that now the idea was fixed in John's mind, it was as good as done.

"Just." John grinned suddenly. "By heaven, Alex! Your father would be proud of you!"

"What?"

"Douglas didn't think you gave a damn about the business, y'know. Wouldn't he be surprised to hear you today?"

Alex shifted uncomfortably.

"Why, he always hoped that you'd come around. Take an interest."

The conversation had taken a decidedly unpleasant turn.

"Maybe your mother was right after all."

"Mother? Right? About what?"

"Tess tried to tell your father that all you and Ian needed was responsibility. Work. That once begun, the task itself would become a reward." He shook his head and beamed at his friend. "She always said that the blood of the MacGregors would show itself one day. And damn me if it didn't!"

Alex cleared his throat and let his gaze slide away from John's.

"Well, I'd best be getting off then, hadn't I?" John stuck his hand out and when Alex clasped it in a firm shake, the blond said, "You'll tell Kit I'm sorry I couldn't say good-bye?"

"Of course."

"And tell her that when I get back, I'll . . ." He shook his head and grinned again. "Never mind. I'll tell her myself when I return."

Alex nodded.

John turned to leave, then stopped. Looking back over his shoulder, he asked, "Take good care of her?"

"I will."

Satisfied, John left the room, a smile still firmly fixed on his features.

Alex stared at the empty doorway and told himself that it was for the best. John's infatuation wouldn't have lasted and would, no doubt, only have made for an uncomfortable situation. This way was better for all concerned. He was doing John a favor, really. Sparing the man Kit's refusal.

As for his promise to take good care of Kit . . . well, Alex had every intention of taking *excellent* care of her.

Then why did he feel so . . .

Unwillingly Alex's gaze slipped to the portrait of his father, hanging over the blazing hearth. Douglas stared down at his younger son and the frown on the old man's face appeared to be more distinct than usual.

"What are you glaring at, Father? I've taken care of the business. Mother is happy. The grandchild *you* dismissed is alive and well." Getting up from behind his desk, Alex walked across the room to the tray of liquor decanters on a sideboard. Deliberately he kept his back to the portrait. He poured himself a strong drink, then took a quick gulp of the whiskey.

It didn't help. He set the unfinished drink down,

shoved his hands in his pockets, and walked to the nearest window.

What had happened to his well-ordered life? It seemed he couldn't plan on anything anymore. Too much was changing. Hell, he hardly recognized himself these days.

When Ian died, Alex had fought like an unbroken horse against the ropes of duty and business. At the time, he'd considered it a cruel joke of fate, leaving *him* in charge of the MacGregor fortunes.

He was the second son! It was supposed to be *Ian* having to muck about with tally sheets, imports, exports, and the endless list of repairs to the country estate. It was *Ian* who was supposed to be mired up to his neck in the boring details of the shipping business.

Alex had spent the greater part of his life training himself for absolutely *nothing*. And that was as it should be. As it was supposed to be. As the younger son, he'd been destined since birth for a life of card-playing, whoring, and learning the latest dance steps. For the love of heaven, *work* had never entered his mind!

All of that changed the moment Ian was swept overboard on a voyage to the Argentines. Alex snorted and stared blankly at the street outside. And ever since Ian died, Alex had been accosted from all sides by customers, clients, shipping agents, his mother, and John Tremayne—all of them demanding that he take charge.

And he'd tried. Hell, he was even willing to admit that sometimes he enjoyed the challenges involved in keeping on top of the business. There was a certain thrill in outbidding or outwitting the competition. He didn't even mind missing some of the balls and parties he normally attended during the Season.

In fact, if he were to be completely honest, he would have to admit that the same old affairs with the same people saying the same foolish things had become something of a bore.

But dammit! A man could only change so much!

And Alexander MacGregor wasn't yet ready to give up women and take up the cloth! He tossed an uneasy glance at his father's stern features, then looked back at the busy street.

Though his gaze was fixed on the passersby, Alex's mind was fixed on the woman upstairs. He'd never wanted a woman as badly as he wanted Kit Simmons. Not even when he was twenty-one and believed himself in love.

Strange, he told himself. Usually, when that particular memory rose up to taunt him, he pushed it aside rather than look at it. This time, though, he even allowed his brain to draw up the image of that long-ago woman.

Althea Castlemain.

Her memory, strangely enough, was indistinct. He found that he couldn't quite recall if her eyes were blue or green. The mental image of her wavered and grew dim and the harder he tried to focus, the more blurry her features became.

But it didn't matter. It wasn't her face he needed to remember.

It was the lesson she'd taught him so thoroughly.

Because of Althea, Alex now knew that when a woman said "love," it was because she wanted something. And generally, that something was money.

His hands curled into fists inside his pockets as he recalled the humiliation of overhearing Althea talk to her friends just weeks before their wedding.

It was in the garden of her parents' somewhat shabby country home. The familiar walls of his study slipped away and became the towering shrubbery surrounding the rosebed at Castlemain Hall. The scene was so sharp, so fresh in his mind, he could almost smell the damp earth and the heavy fragrance of spring roses.

Eager to see the woman he was about to marry, Alex had ridden out to her home on an impulse. One he was eventually thankful for.

He'd been wandering around the estate looking for her for nearly a quarter of an hour when he heard voices. Thinking to surprise Althea with his unexpected arrival, Alex slipped up on her and two of her friends and positioned himself behind a nearby oak tree.

"How can you marry him?" Charity Baker had asked. "He's so . . . *common*."

"Common perhaps," his beloved answered, "but his money spends as well as anyone's." She giggled. "Better than most!"

Alex's heartbeat stopped and he wanted to leave before he heard more. But the next question kept him frozen in his hiding place.

"Yes, but, Althea," Martha Hendricks asked on a breathless laugh, "what about Arthur?"

Arthur Bingham? Alex wondered. Wasn't that the man Althea had been seeing before they met? Something cold settled in his chest and it was a battle just to breathe. Dreading her response yet unable to leave, he waited.

"Oh, Martha." Althea giggled. "Arthur understands completely. Besides, it's not as though we have to say good-bye forever. Once I'm married," she hesitated shyly before hinting, "well, the rules change, you know, for a married woman."

"Oh, Althea," Martha squealed delightedly, "you *are* wicked! But you will at least wait until after the honeymoon to contact Arthur again. Won't you?"

Grinding his teeth together in an effort to keep from shouting, Alex stood his ground, determined to hear it all.

"Of course I will." Althea sighed her disgust. "Actually, Mother says I must wait until after I've given MacGregor a child. Then Arthur and I will be free to do exactly as we please."

"Will he stand for it do you think? MacGregor, I mean?"

"He won't have much choice, will he?" Althea laughed and the sound of it began to echo in his ears. "Even the prince . . . *dallies*. As long as one is discreet, of course."

"Oh, of course!" Charity spoke again. "And heaven knows you're discreet! Why I don't believe anyone outside of our little group knows that Arthur still comes to visit you, despite MacGregor."

"Shh!" Althea warned the woman. "My father is about here somewhere."

"What are you worried about? Oh, Althea! You haven't let Arthur . . . *have* you?"

Pain lanced through Alex when he heard Althea's answer.

"Certainly I did!" At her friends' gasps, she rushed on, "I wanted my first time to be for true love. Heavens! You don't imagine for one minute that I wanted *MacGregor* to be the first, do you?"

"But," Martha asked, "won't MacGregor be able to tell? I've heard it said that a man *knows* when a woman is no longer a virgin."

"Pooh!" Althea dismissed the notion. "MacGregor is so totally captivated that I shall simply moan at the appropriate time and he will be all concern for my welfare."

"Moan?" Charity whispered. "Then it *does* . . . hurt?"

"It's really quite a disgusting procedure," Althea pronounced in a worldly tone, "but Arthur seemed to enjoy himself immensely. Heaven knows why. It was most uncomfortable and very . . . *messy*."

There was more but the roaring in his ears prevented Alex hearing anything else. He struggled to breathe and fought to rid his brain of the image of Althea's legs spread for Arthur Bingham's bony body.

A film of water covered his eyes and he angrily brushed it away. For months he'd treated Althea Castlemain like a queen. He'd hardly dared touch her, for fear of offending her delicate sensibilities. Rage choked him. Delicate. Virginal.

Whore.

The pounding in his head faded to a miserable ache and Alex heard Althea's mother call her from a distance. He waited, rooted to the spot, for the group of young women to stroll toward the house. Only when he

was sure they were gone, did he finally leave the safety
of the oak. Thankfully, he'd had his coachman park on
the lane beyond the estate. He'd wanted to surprise his
soon-to-be bride. Carefully, quietly, he skirted the edges
of the property, determined to avoid meeting Althea or
her family.

It wasn't until he was seated in his coach again that he
noticed the pieces of tree bark clenched in his fingers.
His fingers were cut and bloodied and he didn't even
remember injuring himself. Slowly Alex dropped the
fragments of wood to the coach floor and brushed his
palms together.

The very next day he sent his regrets to Althea by
messenger. He had no doubt that she would have
caused a scandal if he also hadn't induced his father to
include a handsome check to compensate her for her
"loss."

A shout from a cabby on the street brought Alex back
to the present. In the window glass he caught a glimpse
of his own reflection and smiled grimly.

No thank you, he said silently. He'd had more than
enough of "love" already in his life. He would take his
pleasure where he could. And never again would he
allow a woman close enough to destroy him.

"I beg your pardon," Kit said softly from the doorway, "am I disturbing you?"

Alex spun about quickly. The memories of Althea's
features faded even further into the past. How could he
ever have thought her lovely?

In the gaslit hall, Kit's soft brown hair shone like polished mahogany. She studied him through blue eyes that

seemed to reach inside him, delving for secrets. Even her well-worn ivory gown, clinging to her figure like a lover, seemed designed to torment him.

His body tightened uncomfortably and he had the almost overwhelming urge to grab her, hold her. To bury himself so deeply inside her that nothing else would matter. Not the past. Not the future. Nothing but the two of them and the pleasure they would find together.

"Alex?" she asked, taking a half step into the study. "Are you all right?"

He forced what he hoped was a pleasant smile to his lips and held out one hand toward her. "Of course. And you aren't interrupting. On the contrary, you've saved me from my own thoughts."

She didn't look convinced, but at least she was walking toward him.

When her palm slipped into his, he guided her to one of two chairs on either side of a readied chessboard.

"Do you play?"

"Yes, I do," she replied, "my father taught me."

"Excellent! Would you care for a game before dinner?"

Kit nodded and took the seat he proffered. When he was settled, she looked around the room and asked, "Where is John? Mr. Tremayne, I mean. Has he gone?"

"Yes." Alex smiled again, easier this time, and leaned his elbows on his knees. "He said to tell you good-bye, but he was called away on business."

"Oh."

To Alex's relief, she looked only mildly disappointed. At least, he told himself, he didn't have to worry about confronting *her* infatuation with John!

"That is a shame," she said and began to study the chessboard in preparation for the start of the game.

"Yes, it is." Alex nodded. Then he added softly, "It's your move, I believe."

12

Mrs. Beedle pushed at the unappetizing mess in her bowl and wrinkled her nose. Mutton stew, indeed. She'd be very much surprised if a sheep had even walked past the kitchen where the meal was prepared! Her spoon uncovered a small bit of carrot and she hesitantly lifted it to her mouth.

One taste was enough to finish off what remained of her appetite. She resolutely pushed the wooden bowl to the opposite side of the table and reached instead for the chunk of still-warm bread on the plate to her right.

So far, the village of Oxgate had little to recommend it. The houses were poorer than most villages. The road was pockmarked and narrow and the people were, generally speaking, unintelligent and crude. In fact, Mrs. Beedle could almost understand why a woman like Kit Simmons would do close to anything to escape the place.

Understand. Not forgive. Especially Mrs. Beedle couldn't forgive the fact that in escaping her own misery, the slut had created trouble for Theodora Beedle.

Smoke from the cooking fire drifted into the public room and mingled with the stale, sweaty odor of the men clustered around the bar. Mrs. Beedle's formidable nose wrinkled again and she sniffed audibly. She could only hope that the rooms above the inn were more habitable than the rest of the place.

She pulled off a small piece of the fresh bread and popped it into her mouth. Grainy but acceptable. Mentally she began to plan her strategy for the coming day. It would be best, she supposed, to speak to the village parson. If anyone would have information on the people hereabouts, it would be the shepherd of the flock.

A roaring snort of laughter from one of the ill-dressed men nearby brought her thoughts up short and she glared at his back as he started talking to his friends.

"This new parson's so full of piss and vinegar, you'll not be sleepin' through *his* sermons, Bob!"

Another man, Bob she supposed, frowned guiltily.

"The reverend give me a bleedin' 'eadache last week, 'e did," Bob whined pitifully. "All that shoutin' and carryin' on! Why, ol' Preacher Simmons never went on like that about the devil and such."

"Well now, that wouldn'ta been easy, would it?" the barkeeper tossed in. "Not with what went on in 'is own 'ouse, I mean."

"True, true. Course, he were a good man, the rev."

"Good, sure. But *'ow* good, I asks ya? 'E couldn't even keep 'is own girl outta some toff's bed!"

Mrs. Beedle's ears pricked.

"A man can't 'elp what 'is girl does, can 'e?"

" 'E bloody well better if 'e's preachin' at ever'body else!"

"True—'ard to preach the straight and narrow path when one of yer own's breedin'."

Mrs. Beedle sat back on the settle and leaned closer to the conversation. She didn't want to miss a word.

"She din't do it on 'er own, y'know," the barmaid argued hotly. "You bunch're all alike. The girl gets caught and the fella scarpers."

"Now, Daisy," the barkeeper soothed, "nobody's sayin' that 'e ain't guilty too. But she shoulda known better! She was educated!"

"Educated!" Daisy snorted. "As if book learnin' can keep a poor girl from believin' some no good man's lies!"

"Well," one of the men observed, "wot's a father to do? Rich fella comes to town . . . sweet-talks a girl out of her shimmy . . . And she always was a trustin' little thing."

"Aye, not like her sister, that's fer sure!"

Sister? In her excitement, Mrs. Beedle leaned too far forward and caught the eye of the barkeeper. The big man immediately shushed his companions. "Pardon, missus. We didn't mean no offense."

Inwardly seething at the halt of information, Mrs. Beedle nonetheless smiled at the man behind the bar.

"It's quite all right," she assured the men who looked shamefaced for speaking so freely in front of a woman. "I, well . . . I know all about the Simmons girl."

"Y'do? 'Ow?"

"I met her in London. She told me the whole story," she confided, hoping they'd continue talking. "In fact, I've only come to Oxgate because dear Kit told me how lovely it was." She almost choked on the lie, but it was in a righteous cause, after all.

"Ah well, that was good of 'er," the innkeeper said.

"Kit's a good lass, in't she?" the barmaid shot back.

"Always was. Not many would do what she did, takin' on Marian's kid that way."

"Marian?" Mrs. Beedle prodded, barely able to contain her excitement. If she heard enough from this group, perhaps a visit to the local reverend wouldn't be necessary.

"Aye," one of the men said quickly, "her sister. Shameful creature, really. But she 'ad a lovely baby girl!"

"I thought you said Kit told you about it?" the barmaid asked, eyeing Mrs. Beedle warily.

"So she did," the older woman answered quickly. Inwardly she berated herself for showing her ignorance about Kit's sister. Mrs. Beedle knew she'd be getting no more information out of that lot. One look at the frowsy woman opposite her told her as much. Still, she tried to cover her error. "I'd just forgotten her sister's name, is all."

"Uh-huh." Daisy noticed the smug smile on the stranger's face and immediately distrusted her. Whatever the old bat was up to, it boded no good for Kit. Well, she thought, Kit Simmons had always been kind to her, and Daisy wasn't about to stand still for some hatchet-faced woman to do her dirt.

Sidling up to the nearest man, Daisy rubbed her generous breasts against him and leered at the man beside him. One sure way to keep the men's minds off gossiping was to give 'em something else to think about.

When Bob's hand settled on her breast and he began to tug and pull at her nipple eagerly, Daisy smiled at him, then glanced at the stranger. The old woman was paying no attention to the others in the room now. Lost in her own thoughts, a twisted simper settled on her features, and Daisy felt a chill crawl up her spine in sympathy for Kit.

Despite her misgivings, Kit was having a wonderful time. She sat at a small table on the museum patio, enjoying the sunshine while she waited for Alex to arrange for tea to be served.

When Alex had first suggested this visit to the British Museum, her instincts had screamed at her to refuse. But then she'd recalled how much she'd enjoyed herself the night before.

Their chess game had turned out to be a protracted one. They'd had to return to it after dinner and hadn't finished until quite late. She knew she'd surprised him with her skill at the game, but surely he'd been no more surprised than she was by his casual, relaxed manner.

For the first time since arriving in London, Kit had felt at ease. It almost seemed as though he was going out of his way to make her comfortable. And unlike his usual behavior, he'd been a perfect gentleman.

In fact, his manners had been so impeccable, Kit had found herself forgetting that he was Ian MacGregor's brother. She discovered that she *enjoyed* talking with him. And when he'd escorted her to her room when it was time for bed, she'd caught herself hoping that he would attempt to kiss her.

But he hadn't.

"It appears there won't be any tea," he said and Kit jumped, startled at the sound of his voice. Really, she would have to tell him to stop sneaking up on her like that.

Alex grinned. "Did I frighten you?"

"No. Not *frightened*. Just startled me, really. I didn't hear you come up." The promise of tea forgotten, she took the hand he offered to help her stand. "You move so . . . quietly."

He tucked her arm through the crook of his and patted her hand. "Habit, I suppose."

As they left the patio for yet another of the museum's long halls, Kit asked quietly, "And how did you come to develop such a habit?"

His head fell back on his neck and he laughed unexpectedly. "It's a bit embarrassing to admit now . . . but when I was a boy, I was determined to become an Indian."

"An Indian?"

"Oh, yes." Alex smiled down at her. "An *American* Indian, if you please."

"Oh!"

They passed by a huge room devoted to the history of the British glassworks. Kit barely glanced inside, noting absently the walls of glass-fronted cabinets containing varied shapes and colors of blown glass through the ages. "And how did you come to learn about American Indians?" she asked.

"Ian and I had a tutor when we were boys . . ." He paused and frowned momentarily. "Good Lord, I can't even remember the man's name now. He wasn't with us very long, I'm afraid."

"Why not?"

"It seems that my father was not as enamored as I was with the man's obsession."

"Obsession?"

Grinning again, Alex confided, "Now, there are only a handful of people in all of England who know what I'm about to tell you. You'll have to swear yourself to secrecy."

Appropriately solemn, she held up her right hand. "I do so vow."

"Very good." Alex nodded and went on. "The tutor's obsession revolved around taking his clothes off and crawling about in the shrubbery at night, after the household was abed, looking for 'tracks.' "

"What?" A bubble of laughter shot from her throat before she could hold it in. The silent, tomblike halls echoed with the delicate sound. An elderly matron frowned at her and Kit tried to swallow back the rest of her amusement.

"Oh, it's safe enough for you to laugh," Alex teased. "But you haven't heard the part that convinced my father to discharge the man."

"There's more?"

"Oh, yes!" Alex nodded blithely at the matron as they passed, then said softly, "One summer night, while my tutor and I were 'tracking . . .' "

"*You* were tracking at night too?"

"Of course!" He stretched his neck and lifted his chin proudly. "A *true* Indian never travels alone, my child."

"Dressed in your . . ." Her voice faded off.

"In my altogether, as it were," Alex confided with a wink. "Of course, I insisted on a towel, strategically placed, for modesty's sake."

"Oh, of course."

"Hmmm . . ." He pulled back and studied her for a moment. Apparently satisfied with what he saw, he went on. "Well, there we were, my tutor and I, communing with nature, hunting for wolves and coyotes . . ."

She clapped one hand across her mouth to stifle a giggle.

Alex ignored her response and dropped his voice a bit dramatically. "When a sharp, sudden noise sounded out in the night."

Kit's eyes opened wide.

He nodded at her. "Exactly *our* reaction. In all the nights we'd been crawling across the grounds, we'd never been disturbed. Imagine our surprise to at last *hear* an animal nearby."

"What did you do?" Kit's mind whirled with the images he was creating. She saw it all so clearly. A near-naked little boy and his tutor moving silently through the darkness of rural England hunting adventure. She could imagine their surprise and delight at finally encountering the quarry they'd searched so diligently for.

And even now, on Alex's animated features, Kit saw a glimmer of remembered excitement.

"I am ashamed to admit it to you"—Alex's lips quirked a bit—"but my first reaction was to go running for the safety of my room."

"It would have been my first thought too."

"Kind of you to say so." He nodded gratefully.

"But you didn't?" she prodded, now completely caught up in the story.

"Oh, no. My tutor wouldn't hear of it." Alex shook his head fondly. "He whispered that *this* was the moment he'd trained me for. That generations of Indians were, at that very moment, looking down from the heavens, waiting to see how I would perform."

"Gracious!"

"Indeed." Alex smiled and winked at her again. "I ask you. How could a ten-year-old be expected to turn from a challenge such as that?"

"Impossible."

"Quite."

They wandered on, down hallway after hallway. Past the exhibition on medieval armor, past the documents rooms, past even the Egyptological displays that they'd examined earlier. And as they walked, Alex talked, re-creating that long ago night.

"We circled around the garden and came up quietly on the spot where the noise had originated."

"Yes . . ."

"We had to wait then. Sniff the air, listen carefully."

"I see . . ." Her lips curved, but she nodded seriously.

"Then, when the noise came again—closer, louder—we were ready."

"And?"

"*And*, because *he* was the brave in charge of the expedition, my tutor took the first shot."

"Shot?" Kit stopped short. "You were *armed*?"

Alex stopped too and looked down into her eyes. "What self-respecting Indian goes unarmed on a hunt?" he asked, pretending to be insulted.

"What kind of weapons?" she asked, narrowing her eyes thoughtfully.

"Oh"—he shrugged—"the usual. Bows and arrows. Knives. Tomahawks."

"Good heavens."

"As I was saying," he went on, a wicked gleam in his

eye, "my tutor took the first shot. He carefully notched his arrow in the bow, pulled it back—and let it fly. Immediately the quiet night was rent by the most horrible scream I had ever heard."

"He hit it?"

"Oh my, yes."

"Did he kill it?"

"Thankfully, no."

"Thankfully?" Kit asked, suddenly wary of his answer.

"Well, I daresay, if my tutor had killed my father outright, there would have been any number of awkward questions to answer."

"Your *father*?"

A low, throaty chuckle rumbled through Alex's chest. His eyebrows wiggled and danced over his eyes and he squeezed her hand companionably before he finished his tale.

"Yes. It seems that Father had left his spectacles on one of the benches in the yard." Alex's lips twitched despite his serious tone. "The old man had stumbled around in the dark, nearly blind, to look for them."

Alex's laughter began to roll out around her and Kit grinned in response. She realized that it was the first time she'd heard him really laugh and told herself that he should do it more often.

"It was mere chance," he was saying between gasps for air, "that Father bent over when he did."

"Bent over?" she cried. "You mean he was hit in the . . ."

"Precisely."

"Oh, my . . ."

"Well naturally the tutor was fired on the spot."

"Naturally."

"As for me . . . It was nearly two weeks before I could sit again in comfort."

"Oh, poor Alex . . ."

"Of course"—he flashed her a crooked smile—"it was a small consolation at the time that it was very nearly a *month* before Father could sit down without wincing."

Kit's laughter spilled out and joined his as they stepped out of the museum into the afternoon sunshine. Arm in arm, they began walking down the steps to the busy street below.

"Your poor father," she said in sympathy.

"I like that!" He drew her closer against his side. "I was hoping you'd take *my* part!"

Kit looked up at him and her breath caught in her throat. A genuine smile creased his face and his deep blue eyes twinkled with good humor. In that moment she realized she'd never seen a more handsome man. Or a more appealing one.

Warmth blossomed in her chest and Kit found herself *liking* him. It was disconcerting to find that there was much more to Alex MacGregor than she'd thought. The day spent with him had been a revelation in more ways than one. This—*playful*—attitude was one she hadn't been prepared for and it touched a responsive chord in her that was nearly overwhelming in its strength.

Tilting her head back she took a moment to study him. In his features she could see the remnants of a ten-year-old adventurer and briefly she wished she could have known him then. Judging by his story, the rich man's daring son and the preacher's stubborn daughter would have made a good match. What fun they might have had together. What times they could have shared.

If they'd only met years ago, Kit knew that as children, they would have been friends.

All at once, she remembered something. Not once in his story had he mentioned his older brother. Strange. In the next moment she heard herself asking, "And Ian? Wasn't he part of your adventure?"

Alex's smile slipped a bit as he shook his head. "No. Ian and I . . ." He took in a gulp of air and exhaled on a rush. "We never agreed on much of anything, I'm afraid. But for living in the same house, we had nothing in common."

"I'm glad," she whispered.

Kit realized she'd spoken aloud when he asked, "Why does that make you happy?"

"Oh . . ." She tried to think. She couldn't very well tell him how pleased she was to know that he'd never been like Ian. That she was glad that even from the time they were children Alex had been different. Instead, she offered lamely, "Well, I'm glad to know *he* didn't get into trouble too."

"Uh-huh."

Kit lowered her gaze quickly. She felt his curious stare on her and didn't dare meet his eyes. Surely he would be able to see the truth written plainly on her features.

And what, she asked herself, *was* the truth? Risking a quick, sidelong glance at him, Kit grudgingly admitted that she was beginning to care for him. A nagging voice in the back of her mind laughed at that. She was well beyond "beginning" to care.

If she were to be honest, at least with herself, Kit knew she cared for him very much. Despite her best intentions. Despite the fact that she *knew* he didn't care for her. At least not in the way she might have liked him to. Oh, he desired her. She knew that every time she caught him looking at her.

But he didn't . . . and *wouldn't* . . . *love* her.

Stunned at her own imaginings, Kit shook herself mentally. It was ridiculous to fancy yourself in love with a man based on a silly story about his youth and a few kind gestures. But, she corrected herself, it was more than that.

It was a combination really of so many little things. His protectiveness toward his mother. His growing affection for Rose. Even the way he stubbornly held on to his own opinions after being proven he was wrong was beginning to seem almost endearing. But was that *love*?

And . . . if it wasn't love she was feeling—why did her body seem to burst into little flames of life whenever he touched her?

Why were her dreams haunted by the memories of his kisses? And why did she awaken every morning trembling with a need she couldn't even fully understand?

A silent groan reverberated through her brain.

Oh, Lord help her. Like her sister before her, she'd fallen in love with a MacGregor.

Whatever was running through that mind of hers wasn't very pleasant, Alex thought grimly. He watched her features change with lightninglike flashes of emotion and found himself wishing that her smile would return.

He couldn't understand what was happening. Every-thing had gone nicely. Quite according to plan. She'd accepted his invitation to visit the museum with much less fuss than he'd expected. And she'd even seemed to enjoy herself thoroughly.

The most surprising aspect of the whole day was that *he* hadn't had so much fun in years! Who would have thought that a *museum* of all places could be so enter-taining? But then, he told himself a split second later, it wasn't just the museum.

It was Kit.

He'd received such pleasure just watching her perus-ing the exhibits! Her interest in the artifacts from Egypt had especially pleased him, since his own interest in mummies and whatnot was so keen. He couldn't re-member the last time he'd had an intellectual discussion with anyone on the merits of Petrie's archaeological findings. And though her conclusions were, naturally, all wrong . . . Alex had thoroughly enjoyed arguing against her position.

Something terribly odd was happening and he wasn't quite sure what to do about it. Ever since nearly beating him at chess the night before, Kit had been a constant surprise. He'd had no idea that a parson's daughter would be so learned.

Why, he was willing to wager that there weren't many *men* in England who could read Latin and Greek. But Kit could. He smiled to himself as he recalled their little confrontation over a Latin manuscript. Of course, her translation was a bit muddied—not that *she'd* admitted she was wrong. Alex frowned slightly. She *was* wrong . . . wasn't she? He shook his head firmly.

As they walked down the last of the steps to the busy sidewalk, Alex told himself that he was making far too much of all this. Did it really matter if he and Kit could actually *converse* on a number of subjects? Did it matter if he found her laughter delightful? Or her company engaging?

No. It didn't. And yet . . .

"Are we going home, now?" she asked, interrupting his line of thought.

"Eh?" He looked down at her upturned face and couldn't stop the smile that crept to his lips. He wasn't ready for their day to end and he certainly didn't want to examine his reasons for *that* at the moment. Alex had the distinct feeling that he wouldn't care overly much for his conclusions. But he had to say *something*. "No, not just yet, I think."

The conflicting emotions gone from her face, she smiled up at him. "Then where to, sir?"

Strange, he thought absently, how her eyes seemed to shine more brightly when she smiled. Why hadn't he noticed that before? And more to the point, why was he noticing it *now*?

He gave himself a mental shake and tried to ignore the warmth of her hand on his arm.

"Miss Michele's, I think," he said, suddenly remembering his secondary mission for the day.

"Miss Michele's?"

"Yes." He patted her hand as it rested on his forearm and Alex realized just how much he liked the feeling of her holding on to him. "We're going to get that hat Mother promised you."

"Alex," she protested feebly, "I don't *need* a hat."

"Ah, but you do!" He lifted one hand and stroked the line of her cheek unthinkingly. When he realized what he was doing, he reluctantly let his hand fall back to his side once more. Forcing a brisk note into his voice, he said, "All ladies of good breeding wear hats to the theater."

"The theater?"

"All in good time, Kit." He grinned and shook his head. Not wanting to entirely divulge the surprise he had planned for her, he repeated, "All in good time. Stay right here. I'll hail a cab."

She grabbed his arm to keep him from moving off. When he turned back to look at her, she said, "Couldn't we walk? It's a lovely day."

"Walk?" He frowned momentarily and stared off down the sidewalk as if looking for the milliner's shop. "It's at least two miles."

"But I'm a country girl, sir. And two miles is merely a good stretch of the le . . . *limbs*."

"It is, eh?" Alex knew a challenge when he heard one. And frankly if walking had had the least bit to do with the shapely curve of her legs . . . then he was all for it. Besides, he thought with a smile, walking would take much more time than a cab ride. "Very well. We walk."

As they started off together, he didn't bother to hide his smile. If anyone he knew saw him strolling down the street, they probably wouldn't believe it. But then, who would have thought that Alex MacGregor—well known for his scoundrellike ways—would prefer a walk in the sunshine with a country miss to anything else he could think of?

He shook his head slowly.

There was definitely something strange happening.

13

Mrs. Beedle ran her hand over the cold glass of the train window and stared silently out at the passing landscape. Her own reflection smiled back at her.

Her little trip to Oxgate had turned out to be a very profitable one. Or, she mentally corrected, it *would* be as soon as she spoke to Alexander MacGregor.

She hadn't gotten one more piece of information out of the group in the public house, thanks in large part to that slovenly barmaid. Mrs. Beedle frowned momentarily, then smiled again as she admitted that it had all worked out for the best anyway. If she'd learned all she'd wanted to, she wouldn't have gone to see the village preacher.

And heaven knew that if Alex MacGregor wanted witnesses to verify what she planned to tell him . . . a *reverend* would be far more impressive than drunken louts in a bar.

The steady clack of the train wheels faded into the distance as she recalled her meeting with Reverend Falden only that morning.

"I understand you're a friend of Kit Simmons?" he'd asked as she was escorted into his small study.

"Yes," Theodora lied, slipping into a straight-backed

chair opposite his cluttered desk. "When Kit heard that I was going to be passing through your lovely little village, she asked me to stop in and give you her best."

He answered her with a noncommittal humming sound and Theodora used the few moments time of silence to briefly study the man.

About sixty-five, with sharp black eyes, thinning, iron-gray hair, and a skeletal face, the Reverend Falden had the look of a man who'd peered into hell and seen a place reserved for himself.

"Then she is well?" he finally asked.

"Oh, yes," Theodora answered in a fluttery tone she'd always found impressed older men. "She's living with the MacGregors now in London."

"Followed the sin and clutched it to her bosom, eh?" He nodded as if hearing exactly what he'd expected. "All to the good. Her presence in Oxgate was a slap in the face to God-fearing people and a bad example for the other young women."

"But I understand the child isn't hers." She *had* to be certain on that point.

"Not physically, of course." He straightened even more rigidly in his chair. "But morally, yes. As I understand it, from the moment the . . . *child* was born, Katherine Simmons refused to hide it away. Insisted on walking about the village with it. As though it were a source of pride, not shame."

"Ah . . ."

"Certainly, with her father being the rector here, she wasn't overly chastised for her lack of contrition."

Mrs. Beedle got the distinct impression that the "chastisement" he would have preferred would have been a public flogging. She didn't bother to examine her sudden distaste for the man. Instead, she asked another question.

"But I believe she told me her parents died some months back?"

"Yes." He bit off the word. "My good wife and I came to Oxgate directly following the tragic accident."

He didn't appear moved in the slightest, but Theodora didn't really care.

"And I must say," he continued, "I was appalled at her infamy!"

"Infamy?"

"Every Sunday, without fail, she would appear in church for service, the child on her hip." His lips tightened into a thin, flat line. "Marched straight up the center aisle to a front row pew, bold as brass."

"Ah . . ."

"It was a relief to every righteous soul in the village when the shameless female took away the seed of her sister's sin."

"And her sister?" Theodora asked quietly.

"Dead." His long, thin fingers reached spasmodically for a stack of papers to his right. Shuffling them importantly, he added, "Willed herself to death from what I understand. No doubt she suffered guilt from the disgrace she'd brought down on her family."

"I see."

"Now, if you will excuse me, madam, I must be about the Lord's work."

He didn't even look up when Theodora Beedle left the room. She saw herself out of the tiny parsonage and before she knew what she was doing had walked into the adjacent graveyard. Walking amid the stones, some tilted, some covered over with weeds, she searched for the familiar names.

Finally, she found what she was looking for. In the far corner of the cemetery, as if placed there purposefully in the hopes of making them invisible, were the graves of the Simmons family.

Marian's marker said simply, "Beloved Daughter, Sister, and Mother." The woman's parents lay on either side of her. Obviously, at Marian's death, her body had been laid to rest as far away from the upstanding members of the community as was possible.

Despite her own antipathy for Kit Simmons and the child, Theodora felt a small stirring of pity for the woman lying below, who'd ended life so young and so alone.

The train lurched to one side and Theodora's forehead smacked against the window glass. Rubbing the sore spot, she told herself that she had no room for pity. Besides, it would be wasted on Marian, now. And Kit Simmons certainly had no need for it.

Hadn't she displaced her, Theodora? No. She ground her teeth together and clasped her hands tightly in her lap. Pity wasn't called for . . . but *justice* was demanded. If she was forced to lose her position . . . then she would see to it that Kit too landed in the street.

Theodora Beedle knew that she herself wouldn't have a bit of trouble finding a new position as housekeeper. There were any number of wealthy people who'd pleaded for her services over the years. All she need do was choose one.

But Kit Simmons was a different matter entirely.

If Theodora had her way, Kit would soon see that the hardships she'd faced in her village were nothing compared to what a woman alone would suffer in London.

Smiling pleasantly, Mrs. Beedle leaned her head back against the leather seat and closed her eyes. In a few short hours she would be back in the city.

The gentle rocking of the coach and the hypnotic clack of the iron wheels on their rails soon lulled the woman into a fitful sleep.

"You look lovely."

Kit looked into the full-length mirror and saw Alex standing in the doorway of her room. She didn't know how long he'd been there and couldn't imagine why she hadn't noticed him before. Probably, she told herself, because she'd been too caught up with her own reflection.

"Thank you," she whispered and shifted her gaze back to her own image. Never in her life had she owned such a beautiful dress. The vivid green silk complemented her, she knew, and the workmanship was exquisite. The woman in the mirror looked so elegant, so . . . *pretty*, it was hard to believe she was looking at herself.

"You see," Alex said softly as he stepped into the room, "I was right about the hat."

"Yes." She nodded and smiled into the mirror. The white straw, tipped at a devilish angle over her right ear, was decorated with what seemed yards of green ribbon, interspersed with tiny, artificial white daisies. It looked and made her *feel* like a breath of spring.

And though she'd protested against the extravagance

at the time, Kit loved her new hat. Tess MacGregor was right. The milliner *was* a marvel. In less time than Kit would have taken to describe it, Miss Michele had designed and created the new bonnet.

Alexander stepped up behind her and gingerly touched the back of her upswept hair. "I take it Harris managed to find you a maid to assist with your hair?"

"No." She smiled and shook her head.

He frowned slightly. "But I specifically told him . . ."

"Oh," she cut in quickly, "he *did* send someone, but I'd already finished." Turning around to face him, Kit was startled to see just how closely he stood to her. Licking her lips nervously, she added, "I've been arranging my own hair all my life, Alex. Parsons' daughters learn to do without maids."

"Hmmm . . ." His gaze moved over her face and hair slowly, thoroughly, before he said, "It seems that parsons' daughters do very well on their own."

"Thank you again." She swallowed heavily, lowered her gaze, and stepped around him. Quickly she walked to her dressing table and picked up her matching green silk bag. Though her hands were shaking and her heartbeat thudded painfully against her ribs, she managed to make her voice at least appear steady. "Are you ready to tell me yet where we're going?"

He didn't say anything for the longest time. Instead, he studied her in the silence that stretched out between them. Kit felt his eyes on her as surely as if he'd touched her. The butterflies she was becoming so familiar with took up residence in her stomach again and began to turn her knees to water. She didn't realize she was hold-

ing her breath until it burst from her in a rush when
Alex finally said, "No."

"But, Alex . . ."

He shook his head, walked to her side, and took her
hand in his. The fine fabric of her gloves couldn't protect her from feeling his warmth. Alex's thumb moved
across her knuckles in a slow caress and when he tucked
her hand through the crook of his arm, he covered it
firmly with one of his own. Smiling down at her, he
whispered, "Allow me to surprise you."

"Surprise?" she echoed as she stared up into his eyes
and tried to remember how to breathe.

Alex nodded, then bent and placed a quick, gentle
kiss on her cheek. Awareness rocketed through her and
she had to fight to keep her balance.

"All I will say," he added teasingly, "is that I am taking you where everyone in London will be able to see
how lovely you look."

Where they went didn't matter, Kit thought to herself. As he led her from her room, down the stairs, and
out into the soft night, she knew that at that moment
she would have gone with him *anywhere*.

Harris stood in the shadows of the hall, unnoticed by
the couple walking out the front door. Thoughtfully the
butler stared at the doorway long after the footman had
closed it and gone about his other duties.

Really, Harris told himself, evidently he *was* getting
old. He wouldn't have thought that any kind of a "com-
munion" could be built between the two younger people. But Tess . . . he smiled softly, Tess had had a
feeling about this all along.

Michael Harris couldn't remember the last time he'd seen Alex looking quite so . . . *happy*. And it seemed that Tess's one worry—that Alex might coerce Kit into something she would regret—was groundless. Kit Simmons looked every bit as pleased with the world as Alex did.

Yes, the butler told himself as he walked back to the kitchen for a cup of tea, he owed Tess an apology. And frankly, he could hardly wait to get to the country to deliver it.

Of course, until they *left* for the country house, he would continue to keep watch on Kit, just as he'd promised Tess he would. As he stepped through the servants' hall into the huge kitchen, Harris couldn't help wondering just where Alex had taken the young woman.

He wanted to take her *everywhere*. Alex leaned back in his seat, propped one elbow on the balcony railing, and watched Kit—as he had all evening.

She was on the edge of her seat, her fingers curled around the rail in front of her, her eyes fixed on the stage below. Totally engrossed in the play, Kit had only occasionally glanced at him long enough to grin companionably.

As far as Alex was concerned though, they might have been in an empty theater. He didn't notice anyone or anything but Kit. Amused with the absurdities of the situation, Alex stretched his legs out along the floor of the box seat and told himself he was behaving like a fool. And what was more, he'd been doing it all bloody day long!

Even worse . . . he couldn't remember another day in his life that he'd enjoyed half as much.

Good God, he'd even told her about the tutor and shooting his father with an Indian arrow. He hadn't thought about that incident in *years*. Much less told anyone about it. And yet, telling her had seemed so . . . right.

Oh, he was doing a marvelous job of seduction. The only problem was, he was seducing himself into believing all manner of nonsense about the woman sitting beside him.

But then again, perhaps it wasn't nonsense.

Maybe she wasn't like every other female he'd ever come across. Maybe she had only bedded Ian for love. Maybe she hadn't come to the MacGregors for anything save keeping Rose safe.

And maybe he was beginning to care far too much about the answers to those questions.

"Alex?"

Startled, he blinked and looked directly into Kit's concerned eyes.

"Alex, are you feeling well?"

"What?" He straightened abruptly and gave himself a mental shake. "Quite well, thank you," he whispered. "What's wrong? Aren't you enjoying the play?"

Her lips curved into a smile that left him breathless before she said, "Nothing is wrong. But the play ended five minutes ago."

What? His gaze slipped from hers and he saw the velvet curtains drawn across the wide stage. For the first time he heard the sounds of the audience taking their leave. A distant murmuring hovered in the air as the patrons of the Gaiety discussed the merits of *The Mikado*. Glancing down to the floor level, he saw that the theater was more than half empty already.

"Well"—he turned back to face a still smiling Kit—"it seems I've missed the ending." And the beginning, he added silently. As well as the middle. Strange thing was, he didn't care in the slightest. "Did you enjoy it?"

"Oh, yes," she sighed and clasped her hands tightly together in her lap, "it was wonderful."

"I'm glad." Standing, he held out his hand until she slipped one of hers into his palm. "Shall we go?"

They left the box, descended the impressive staircase, and threaded their way through the crowd. Perfume assailed him and an occasional high-pitched tittering soared over the noise of the crowd and for the first time in years, Alex wasn't scrutinizing the well-dressed women. In fact, he couldn't take his mind off the woman at his side. His only goal at the moment was to get them out of the lobby to where he could have her to himself once more.

Once on the well-lit sidewalk, he glanced down at the long line of carriages, waiting for their owners to appear. Vapor clouds encircled the horses' heads and the coachmen all wore the same uniform of heavy greatcoats, scarves, and hats. Alex felt Kit's hand slide through the crook of his arm and he was suddenly filled with a need to be moving. Quickly he strode past the milling crowd and happily noted that Kit had no trouble at all keeping up with him.

When he finally spied their carriage, James, the driver, appeared stunned to see his master coming toward him. Alex could hardly blame the man, since normally he wouldn't have willingly walked farther than the curb.

Hopping down from his perch, James flung open the carriage door.

"No, thank you, James," Alex said quickly. "Miss Simmons and I thought we might walk a bit. Didn't we?" He looked down at her belatedly and could only hope she shared his need for movement.

She looked him square in the eye and answered without even a glance at the coachman, "That's right."

He could've kissed her right there.

"But, sir . . ."

"I tell you, James," Alex said quickly, "why don't you go ahead five or six blocks and wait for us there. All right?"

The coachman couldn't have looked more stunned if one of his beloved horses had spoken to him. But he quickly recovered the proper mask of blank features. "Yes, sir," he muttered and slowly closed the door.

As they walked away, Alex felt the man's bemused stare on them.

A soft humming drifted up to him and Alex looked down at Kit, the coachman forgotten. "You *did* enjoy yourself, didn't you?"

The humming stopped.

Hugging his arm tightly, she nodded. "It was all so beautiful. The costumes, the theater . . . the people. And the music! Oh, it was wonderful, didn't you think?" Then, in a light, playful voice she sang the line "Three little maids from school."

He was quite sure the play must have been everything she said it was. Still, he acknowledged, it could've been the screeching of love-starved cats for all Alex knew. But he was reluctant to spoil her enjoyment. "Yes," he said, "I've always been partial to Gilbert and Sullivan myself."

They walked on, wrapped in the sounds of street life in London. Gaslight flickered, casting uneven shadows dancing across the faces of the people they passed. Children darted in and out of traffic, raced down sidewalks, and screamed curses at the vendors they crashed into. Chilly night air, laced with damp, swirled around them and when they passed a meat pie vendor, Alex stopped suddenly.

"Pastie, sir?" the weather-beaten man asked hopefully.

"I believe we will," Alex answered quickly, caught by the tantalizing smells drifting up from the man's cart.

The man leapt into action, lest his customer slip away. Carefully he set the small pies down on square sections of newspaper, wrapped them, and handed them to Kit and Alex.

Alex folded the paper back, looked down at the flaky brown crust, and inhaled the delicious, familiar scent. Glancing down at Kit, he said thoughtfully, "When we were boys, Mother used to make meat pasties for Ian and I. Now, though, I don't even remember the last time I had one."

She smiled and bit into the pie. Catching crumbs with her forefinger, Kit nodded at the vendor. After a moment she said, "It's delicious."

"Ta, miss," the older man said and let his gaze slip to Alex.

As if performing a ritual, Alex ran one finger over the

pie slowly, inhaled the tempting aroma again, and then reverently took a bite. His eyes closed as he chewed and a blissful smile creased his face. After he'd swallowed, Alex looked at the pieman. "Even better than I remembered."

The other man sighed as though he'd just passed an important test. "I'll tell me missus. She'll be that pleased, she will. Makes 'em fresh ev'ry night." Holding out one hand, he added, "That's sixpence, sir."

Alex reached into his pocket and pulled out two shillings. Handing them over to the surprised vendor, he shook his head. "You underestimate your goods, sir."

The pieman quickly stuffed the coins into his jacket pocket and grinned widely at them. "Thank *you*, sir!"

As they walked away, they both heard him shout, "Mind now! Tell your friends!"

Alex shook his head, took another bite, and admitted silently that his "friends" would be appalled at the idea of eating something sold from a cart. He snorted derisively at their snobbery. They had no idea what they were missing.

"Vi'lets for the lady, sir?"

A small voice to his right accosted him and Alex turned to the little girl huddled beside a box filled with flowers.

She looked to be no more than ten or eleven, with huge, dark eyes at least a hundred years older. Her clothes were ill-fitting and patched and her hair looked as though she hadn't brushed it in months. Her fingers, blue from the cold, were wrapped around the stems of a small cluster of violets she held out for his inspection.

Staring into those fathomless black eyes, Alex felt—

guilty, somehow. There he stood in his formal wear, a lovely woman on his arm, strolling briefly down the street where the child had to eke out a living. Unexpectedly the meat pastie he'd been enjoying turned to dust on his tongue.

The street seemed dirtier, noisier. The child's eyes seemed to get larger, darker.

He glanced down at the bit of pie left in his hand and curled his fingers around it. Looking back up the street, he mumbled to Kit, "Wait here for me."

"Alex?" she called after him, but he didn't stop until he reached the pieman.

In seconds, he was back, holding a grease-stained sack. Dropping to a squat, he got down on eye level with the child and spoke in a hushed whisper. The little girl hurriedly nodded, reached into her flower box, pulled out four neatly tied bunches of flowers, and handed them to Alex. In exchange, she took the proffered sack and clutched it to her chest as if afraid someone would come along and snatch it.

Alex stood up, gave the violets to Kit, and reached into his coat pocket for his wallet.

Kit's hand on his arm stopped him. "If you're thinking to give her money, Alex . . . don't."

"What?" He couldn't believe it. She was the *last* one he would have expected such a reaction from.

"I *mean*, don't give her notes." She glanced at the girl, smiled, then looked back up at Alex. "She would have a much easier time of it with coins. Small ones."

Of course, he thought and cursed himself for a stupid fool. Certainly a child like this would be questioned as to how she came to possess bank notes. Someone bigger and stronger than she might also take them from her before she had a chance to use them. Properly chastened, he reached into his pants pocket, pulled out several shillings and coppers, then bent down and poured them into the child's cupped palms.

When she looked up at him, her tired eyes now filled with astonishment, Alex felt his chest swell and an unfamiliar warmth wind its way through his body. Thoughtfully he took Kit's free hand in his and began to walk again.

They continued on in silence, oblivious to the noise around them until tinkling, slightly out of tune music brought them up short.

"Alex," Kit cried, *"look!"*

He followed her lead and saw an old man busily turning the crank on an ancient-looking hand organ while his partner danced and jumped to the jerky music issuing from the machine.

The partner, a tiny monkey with a wizened face and wearing a preposterously small red derby, pranced about at the end of its leather lead. Whenever one of the people crowding around him held out a copper penny, the little animal would trot right over, pluck up the coin, then tip its hat. Each coin was then carried to its master and deposited in a battered tin cup at the old man's feet.

"Could I have a penny, Alex?" Kit asked, her delight in the monkey clearly etched on her features.

As he handed her the coin, he stood back and watched the little beast scamper to Kit's side. Its incredibly tiny, fast fingers grabbed the coin, then reached for its derby to offer its silent salute. This time though, before running to the old man, the monkey buried its nose in the bouquets Kit held.

"Isn't he sweet?" Kit glanced up at the tall man behind her. "Come on, Alex. You give him a coin!"

The monkey darted in and out of the small group of people clustered around the organ grinder and it was another minute or two before it returned to collect the copper Alex held out to it.

Little fingers grasped the coin, snaking across Alex's knuckles. He smiled when the animal threw its head back and grinned. In appreciation for the extra attention, Alex reached for another coin and inadvertently produced a shilling. A heartbeat later, the animal had the coin clasped firmly in hand and was scampering up Alex's chest to his shoulders.

The crowd around him burst into laughter and even Kit was giggling helplessly.

Apparently, he told himself, a tip of the derby wasn't near sufficient thanks for a shilling! The monkey marched across Alex's broad shoulders as effortlessly as if strolling down Bond Street. Alex felt his hair being tugged and pulled by tiny hands but before he could think what to do, the little beast had crawled down Alex's stiff shirtfront, jumped to the street, scurried back to its master and deposited its treasure in the tin cup.

Kit reached up to smooth his hair back into place. A grin on her face, she said, "You should have seen yourself, Alex!"

A low, throaty chuckle started at the base of his throat. The absurdity of the whole situation suddenly struck him as too funny for words. Two weeks ago, if anyone had told him he would be walking down the Strand, buying meat pies for little girls and playing with monkeys . . . he would have reserved them a cell at Bedlam.

"Alex?" she asked, her hand lingering on his cheek. "Are you all right?"

He covered that hand with his own, then turned his lips into the palm. Alex heard her sharp intake of breath and before he could think better of it, his arms snaked around her waist and pulled her tight against him. Dipping his head, he claimed her mouth in a kiss he'd been dying for for days.

A moment later she kissed him back, leaning into his embrace and cupping the back of his head with her hand. He might have stayed there all night had not the appreciative clapping from the people around him finally penetrated his brain. As it was, he came to himself slowly, reluctantly. With a last tender brush of his lips on hers, Alex pulled his head back and stared down into the eyes that had haunted him for nearly two weeks.

Kit trembled slightly and gasped for air through parted lips. Alex traced the outline of her mouth gently with his thumb and was almost unmanned completely when she kissed it.

With the ending of their embrace, the crowd soon lost interest in them entirely. But Alex and Kit hadn't moved. Staring into each other's eyes, it was as if they were alone in a garden—not surrounded by strangers on a busy street corner.

Alex's entire body ached with the need to have her and he knew that desperation was shining in his eyes when he asked, "Are you ready to go . . . *home*?"

He was asking far more than that and he knew that she was well aware of that fact. It felt like an eternity before she swallowed heavily and whispered, "Yes, Alex. I'm ready."

Thank God, he said silently. If she'd said no, he was quite sure he would have died.

Carefully, tenderly, Alex slipped one arm around her shoulders and began the interminable walk to where the carriage waited.

If James noticed anything amiss, he was far too well trained to let on.

Her heartbeat thudding in her ears, Kit turned into Alex's arms the moment he seated himself beside her. There would be no more lying. Not to herself. Not to him.

She wanted his arms about her. She wanted to feel what Marian had once described in such glowing terms. Kit wanted—no—*needed* to become one with the man she'd once thought she hated.

The carriage pulled away from the curb but she was spared the usual jostling. Cradled in Alex's arms, she felt only his warmth.

"My God, Kit," he whispered thickly, "I've wanted you so."

Then his lips came down on hers again and Kit closed her mind to everything but the wonder of him. The gentle slide of his mouth across hers became an insistent demand. His tongue traced an outline of her mouth, then prodded at her lips until she parted them for his entry.

She gasped at the intimate invasion, then pressed herself to him, opening herself for him. His hands moved over her and she knew she would never be able to feel him enough. When he cupped her breast and rubbed his thumb over her already hard nipple, Kit groaned and felt a warm tingling begin at the juncture of her thighs.

She scooted higher on his lap and the hard strength of him beneath her was the final proof of his need. Instinctively she wiggled her hips, enjoying the groan she elicited from him with her movements.

Alex's hand left her breast and moved to her calf. Sliding up the length of her leg, he brushed aside petticoats and coaxed her into relaxing when she clamped her thighs together.

Raising his head, he looked down at her and she was just able to make out his features in a shadowy haze of darkness.

"I won't hurt you, Kit."

She knew he wouldn't hurt her purposely, but at the same time she was sure that if he touched the spot he was seeking—she would shatter.

Slowly though, she yielded to the pressure of his hand and when he cupped her, Kit's body jumped in response. She clutched at his shoulders, her fingers digging into the fabric of his coat . . . while *his* fingers created magic.

Then all at once, he stopped. Removing his hand, he straightened the fall of her skirt and tenderly sat her back on the seat. Struggling for air, Kit stared at her surroundings blankly.

They were back at the house. Embarrassed, Kit felt herself flush to the roots of her hair. And even then she couldn't be sorry. No, she admitted silently, she was only sorry the ride home had been such a short one.

"Kit?"

She blinked and looked at Alex.

"You go on upstairs," he whispered and stroked one finger along her throat. "I'll bring you some tea in . . . a half hour?"

Thirty minutes. She swallowed heavily and nodded. Tea. Tea had nothing to do with what Alex would be bringing her, but perhaps the excuse would be enough to fool the servants.

Once inside the house, Kit kept her eyes averted from Harris, who stood waiting to greet them in the hall. Hurriedly she climbed the stairs to the upper floors and didn't even glance behind her.

Michael Harris watched the young woman thoughtfully. Turning a slow eye on Alexander, the butler noted the other man's ruffled hair and the tilt in his once perfect cravat.

"What is it, Harris?" Alex asked. "Haven't we been through this often enough? I've told you repeatedly that you needn't wait up for me."

Though reluctant to be the bearer of ill tidings, Harris saw no other hope for it but to be blatantly honest.

"There's someone here to see you, sir," he said.

"What? Now? At this hour?" Alex pulled his watch free and flipped open the lid. "It's nearly ten-thirty, man! I don't receive callers at this time of night!" He flicked a quick glance at the empty staircase.

Harris saw the look but disregarded it. "I'm afraid she

refused to leave, sir, and short of throwing her out bodily—"

"She?" the other man asked warily. "She who?"

"Mrs. Beedle, sir."

"Good God!"

"Yes, sir. She's in your study, sir, and as I said, refuses to leave until she's spoken with you."

"What does the bloody woman want now?"

"She didn't say, sir." But privately Harris thought the woman was up to no good.

"Oh . . ." Alex gave the staircase another lingering look before saying resignedly, "Very well. I'll give her fifteen minutes." He turned for his study, clearly in a hurry. "Oh." He stopped and looked over his shoulder at the butler. "As long as you're up, Harris . . . would you bring me tea for two in twenty minutes time, please?"

"For you and Mrs. Beedle?" His astonishment was hard to hide.

"Certainly not!" Alex's eyebrows shot up into his hairline. "Really, Harris, sometimes I think you're not quite right in the head!" He walked on to the study, but before entering the room, he reminded the butler, "Twenty minutes."

14

"Lord knows I can't *force* you to believe me," Mrs. Beedle droned on. "But if you don't, you have only to travel to Oxgate yourself to see I'm right."

Alex heard her voice as no more than a hive of bees buzzing. In fact, he was hardly aware of the hawk-nosed woman sitting opposite him. His surroundings, likewise, had faded into nothingness. From the moment he'd heard Mrs. Beedle's eagerly told story, everything in him had come to a shuddering halt.

Oh, certainly Mrs. Beedle had every reason to invent disparaging stories about Kit. But *this* story was too easily checked. And he would check it. First thing in the morning, he would send someone to Oxgate to corroborate Mrs. Beedle's facts.

But for now, all he could rely on were his instincts.

And his instincts told him Mrs. Beedle was telling the truth. The memory of the night Kit had defended herself for "bedding" Ian came rushing back. Alex remembered distinctly when Kit had slipped and begun talking about Ian's mistress as if she'd been someone else.

He'd thought at the time that it was merely because she was overwrought. Apparently, he told himself wryly, it required a certain amount of distress for the *truth* to leave the woman's lips.

Strange. Only ten minutes ago, he'd been a happy man. Happy and eager to bed the woman who even now was upstairs readying herself for him. Odd how quickly things could change.

The sense of enjoyment, the peace that had filled him throughout the day, was gone. In its place was the cold, hard knowledge that once again a woman had found a way to use him. And he'd been *that* close to believing in her!

The seemingly ceaseless chatter spewing from Mrs. Beedle's mouth came to an abrupt halt. Blinking, Alex responded to the sudden silence in the room, banishing his thoughts until he was alone again. Unwillingly he turned his gaze on the victorious woman seated opposite him.

Once she had his attention, she began to speak again. "So, as you can see . . . I was right about the slut."

His throat tightened on the knot of anger choking him. Trust the vicious harridan to bask in her moment of triumph. Still, somehow he managed to answer her in a cool, detached manner.

"It would seem that she is hardly the slut you insist on naming her, madam." He forced a negligent shrug. "She is *not* the mother of the child."

"True, but didn't she come here, pretending to be such?" Spittle formed at the edges of her narrow mouth. "Didn't she upset this household and throw herself at you in a way that no decent woman would consider righteous?"

He declined to give her satisfaction. "Whatever her reasons for pretense," Alex said calmly, "they are no concern of yours."

"But I . . ."

Alex smiled grimly. At least he'd had the pleasure of taking the wind from her sails. He stood up, signaling the end of the interview. "Now, if you'll excuse me . . ."

Her fingers clenched and unclenched on the clasp of her bag. He watched her mouth rapidly open and close like a landed fish and was too angry to enjoy the sight.

"But what about my position?" she finally managed to say.

Alex's eyes narrowed as he looked down at her. "Your *position*, madam?"

"As housekeeper," she countered, jumping to her feet. "I was wrongly dismissed and I demand justice!"

"*Justice?*" His voice dropped and every ounce of his distaste for her was clear in that single word. "You are in no position to demand anything."

"But I went to Oxgate! I found out the truth!" She glared at him and Alex had to fight down the uncivilized urge to slap her. "You owe me for that!"

Inhaling slowly, Alex thought a moment, then said, "Very well. See Harris on your way out. He will recompense you for your train ticket."

"My train ticket?" she gasped, clearly stunned. "But what about my job?"

"Your job, madam, will soon be filled by someone else." He turned his back on her deliberately. "Frankly, by *anyone* else! I suggest you look elsewhere for employment. And I might also advise that you not seek a position among my acquaintances." He gave her a quick, disgusted glance before turning back to stare into the fire. "Because I will not hesitate to tell them precisely *why* I discharged you."

It was several long minutes before the woman moved. Alex could almost *hear* her thinking, weighing her options. When she finally left, the air in the room suddenly seemed much fresher.

And still, her departure solved nothing. He was left to deal with the problem of Kit Simmons. His fingers tightened over the edge of the mantelpiece and he watched his knuckles turn white.

Why? he asked himself. Why the elaborate lies? Why not simply identify herself as the child's aunt the night she arrived?

Alex snorted at the naive question. The explanation was a simple one. She'd obviously hoped to dupe *him* as easily as Ian had duped her sister. Kit Simmons, by pretending to be Ian's mistress, had clearly hoped that Alex would desire her enough to keep her on at his house. In that way she would have a fairly easy life. The child would be cared for and she herself would never want for anything.

And the only price she had to pay was her "virtue." Apparently a commodity not very highly valued by either Kit or her sister.

Alex muttered viciously under his breath. It had very nearly worked too. All because he was no better than that rutting idiot of a brother of his.

But didn't the fool woman know that he would realize she was a virgin the moment he entered her? Or was she counting on the fact that he would be so dazzled by her person he would notice nothing?

Every thought that flew through his brain fanned the

flames of Alex's anger. He felt like a perfect idiot. All day long, she'd probably been laughing at him. Secretly sneering at his compliments . . . his confidences. God! When he told her that story about him and his tutor, she must have been hard put not to laugh in his face!

All because his swollen manhood had taken precedence over his brain! And even knowing what he did now, his body didn't have the decency to become flaccid. No. Alex's groin ached stronger than ever with the desire that had clouded his thinking of late.

True to MacGregor form . . . not even a woman's outright manipulation was enough to quell the rampant need holding him in its grip.

He drew in a long, shaky breath in a futile effort to calm himself. Releasing his hold on the mantel, his right hand slid along the polished wood until it reached a small china figurine.

An angel. An angel with dark hair and blue eyes. Smiling.

Scowling down into china-blue eyes, Alex saw instead Kit's eyes, filled with delight. He remembered every look she'd given him that day. Delight, amusement, desire. Lies. All of them. His fingers curled around the delicate piece and tightened until he felt the edges of the angel's robes dig into his palm. Then in a swift movement, Alex drew his arm back and hurled the angel into the fire. The fine porcelain shattered on impact. Tiny, fragile shards scattered over the flames.

The study door swung open, but he didn't turn around.

"Your tea, sir," Harris said softly.

"Tea?"

"The tea you requested?"

"Oh, yes." Of course. Tea. His excuse for mounting the stairs and marching boldly to Kit's room. Another lie. Lord. The house seemed filled to the rafters with them.

"Would you prefer that *I* deliver the tea to Miss Simmons, sir?" Harris asked quietly.

Alex thought that he would prefer it if everyone in the world suddenly fell off the face of the planet. At least then he could be assured of privacy. But instead he heard himself say, "No, thank you. Set it on the desk please."

A moment later Alex heard the butler do as he'd asked.

"Will there be anything else?"

"No, Harris. Thank you. Go on to bed."

A long, silent pause elapsed before the butler said, "Very well, sir."

Alex heard the man walk across the floor, but still didn't turn around.

"Mrs. Beedle has left, sir," Harris offered. "I gave her the money she said you promised her."

"Fine, fine." Just go away, Alex thought desperately. Then, as the study door creaked in closing, he asked quickly, "Did Mrs. Beedle tell you why she'd come?"

"No, sir. Was she supposed to have?"

"No." At least there was that. The woman had been so intent on delivering her news to Alex, she'd obviously clasped her secret tightly to her. And he wasn't overly concerned that she would start flapping her vicious tongue now, either. She knew very well that a word or two in the right places could prevent her from ever receiving another decent position. "Thank you, Harris. Good night."

"Good night, Alexander."

Alex almost smiled as the door closed behind the butler. How did the man know when to stop "sirring" him? Alone again, he turned and looked at the silver tea tray. Along with the elaborate serving pot and two china cups and saucers was a small plate of sandwiches.

Just the thought of eating right now was enough to make Alex's stomach churn. And yet . . . he walked toward his desk. After such a full day, he'd be willing to wager that Kit could eat one or two of the dainty bread and butter sandwiches. He knew from experience that lying could be a draining exercise.

His fingers trailed along the scalloped edge of the silver tray. Anger still raged in his brain and desire still wracked his body. What better time to go upstairs and demand a confrontation with the woman who'd set his life in turmoil? Before he could think twice about what he was doing, Alex lifted the tray, crossed the room, opened the door, and started for the staircase.

A single gaslight, burning dimly, was the only sign of life in the great house as Alex slowly mounted the stairs to Kit's room. It might be very interesting to find out just how far the woman was willing to go to continue her charade.

Kit fidgeted nervously in front of the mirror. The gas in the wall sconces had been turned up and the light in the room flickered with its bright, yet soft glow.

Behind her, the wide four-poster bed awaited. Its blankets turned back invitingly to reveal clean, fresh sheets; a mountain of plumped pillows lay stacked against the headboard.

Kit forced her gaze away from the cozy-looking bed and looked instead into the mirror. She threw her long, loose hair back over her shoulders and studied herself thoughtfully. The voluminous, white, lace-trimmed nightgown she wore covered her completely from head to foot and yet she'd never felt more exposed in her life.

What was she doing? She, a parson's daughter, had *invited* a man to her bed! And not just any man. The brother of the man who'd destroyed her family. Her reflected image stared back at her openmouthed. Kit's hands flew to either side of her face and she felt the heat of the flush that stained her cheeks.

Why was she doing this? To protect Rose? No, she admitted silently. She knew very well that Rose's position in this house was safe. Tess MacGregor would do *anything* to keep from being separated from her granddaughter.

Then, to keep her *own* position in the MacGregor household? Was that all this was? Had she been reduced to trading her virtue for shelter? If she had, was she any better than the women on the streets who traded their favors for money?

"No," she said aloud and her hands dropped to her sides. It wasn't like that. She hadn't allowed Alex liberties in an effort to protect herself.

It was worse than that.

Kit reached out and held on to the sides of the full-length mirror. The cold brass was a tenuous grasp on reality, but she clung to it desperately as the truth asserted itself in her mind.

She loved Alex MacGregor.

Good heavens.

How had this happened? Heaven knew he wasn't exceptionally lovable. He could be bossy, arrogant, demanding.

But, her traitorous mind argued, he could also be sweet, funny, and kind. And as long as she was being honest, she may as well admit that there was something else, as well.

There were the incredible feelings he generated in her body and soul with his every touch. It wasn't just pleasure, though Lord knew that was a formidable part of it. But his touch was more than that. It seemed to reach deeply inside her. Every stroke of his hand or caress of his lips seemed to extend into the tiny corner of her soul where she'd hidden her loneliness. And once there, Alex's attentions banished the sensation of isolation she'd carried with her for what seemed forever.

Slowly she released her grip on the mirror and straightened up, staring once more at her reflection. Beneath the white linen fabric, she could see the outlines of her breasts. Her dark, distended nipples appeared to be no more than shadows, yet every time her nightgown rubbed against the sensitive flesh, Kit felt an answering ripple of sensation between her thighs.

What if he didn't like her? she wondered. What if he thought her body ugly?

She chewed at her bottom lip as thought after thought chipped away at her already faltering self-confidence. Kit had no idea if her body would be considered attractive to a man. She'd never even seen *herself* naked. Not completely.

Even when afforded the luxury of a tub bath, Kit had resolutely kept her eyes averted from her own nudity. And now it was too late. Even if she dared peek at herself, the invitation had been clearly issued and soon Alex would be appearing at her door.

Kit inhaled sharply, deeply, and the fine linen scraped across her nipples again. Without conscious thought, she lifted her hands and covered her breasts with her palms. Hoping to still the trembling need coursing through her, she held the fabric tightly against herself. But instead of halting the tingling, her actions only served to heighten the prickly sensation.

Eyes opened wide, she stared at her reflection and a curl of forbidden desire began to snake throughout her limbs. Slowly, hesitantly, Kit's fingers moved on her own hardened flesh and she gasped at the sudden damp warmth flooding the triangle of curls between her legs. Remembering Alex's actions earlier, Kit rubbed her nipples with the edges of her thumbs. Her eyes half closed with pleasure, she concentrated on the feel of the fabric being dragged across her too sensitive flesh.

She moved slightly, shifting her bare feet on the carpet, trying to answer the throbbing need between her legs. But her swaying movements only intensified that mysterious ache. Slowly she opened her eyes fully, looked into the mirror again—and saw Alex, standing in the now open doorway.

Alex couldn't think. He couldn't speak. In fact, he wasn't sure he'd be able to draw another breath.

All thoughts of confrontation had ended the moment he'd opened Kit's bedroom door. He'd watched her silently as she'd tentatively explored her own body and he'd felt himself harden until he'd thought he might explode with want.

Now that she'd seen him though, the spell she'd been under was broken. Her hands dropped to her sides, leaving the luscious peaks of her breasts to strain against her nightgown, futilely begging for attention.

His own mouth dry, Alex stepped into her room and slowly pushed the door shut again with his foot. Hardly daring to tear his gaze from her reflected stare, he bent, set the tray he carried on the floor, then turned and locked her door.

In that moment he didn't care what she'd done. He didn't care about the lies, the pretense. In truth, everything but the overpowering desire rocketing through him was forgotten. Keeping his gaze locked with hers, Alex crossed the room and stopped when he was directly behind her.

Her lips parted, Kit's breath came in ragged gasps. He watched as her breasts rose and fell with her uneven breathing and his palms itched to cover them. Instead, he lifted each of her hands and placed them back on her breasts. Then, Alex covered her hands with his own.

Kit's head fell back against his chest and her eyes drifted closed.

He, though, looked into the mirror at their joined hands cupping her full breasts. Tenderly he urged her palms to move. To stroke her own flesh with his more than willing assistance. She shuddered in his arms and Alex's knees buckled. Still keeping a watchful eye on the mirror, he dipped his head and began to nibble at her throat.

She moaned softly and beneath his hands her own began to move again. Together, they caressed her nipples, bringing the already sensitive dark buds to hard, rigid peaks. Kit sighed and tilted her head to one side, silently asking for more of his kisses.

Eager to oblige, Alex began to move along the length of her throat, stroking her heated flesh with his tongue, his teeth nibbling at her. Kit's every breath inflamed him and still he wanted more.

Sliding his hands from hers, he moved his palms down over her rib cage, along her waist, and down the curve of her hips. He splayed one hand against her abdomen and smiled to himself when her hips moved instinctively. With his free hand, he began to draw up the length of white linen covering her.

Drawing his head up, he stared directly into the mirror and whispered, "Open your eyes, Kit."

"I can't." She sounded breathless.

"Open your eyes, Kit," he said again, "watch me love you."

At his words, her blue eyes slowly opened and met his in the reflected room.

He continued to draw her nightgown higher. Inch by slow inch, he exposed the length of her legs to their view. Just before the fabric would clear the juncture of her thighs, Kit's hands dropped from her breasts and she closed her eyes again.

Lowering his head to her throat once more, Alex teased her and lavished warm, damp kisses along her flesh until she groaned with pleasure.

His hands moved to her hips. Beneath the nightgown, his palms caressed her skin gently, pushing the linen material even higher. When he'd taken the nightgown up to her waist, Alex sucked in a gulp of air and stared at the treasures she'd been hiding from him.

His gaze traveled up the length of her long, lean legs until coming to rest on the dark, tight curls guarding her center. Alex moved one hand over her flat abdomen and felt her body jump at the contact. Against his chest, Kit's head swung back and forth as if she didn't know what to do.

Keeping his hand firmly placed just inches above the spot he so wanted to explore, Alex caught her mouth with his. Her arms went up and back to encircle his neck and she leaned into his kiss hungrily, desperately. When he finally pulled back, he whispered, "Look in the mirror, Kit. Look at *us*."

For a moment he thought she wouldn't, then slowly she turned to stare at the two people in the mirror. She gasped and he knew she was torn between shock and desire. When her gaze locked on the sight of his hand pressed so closely to the intimate secrets of her body, her hips moved gently. Alex smiled and began to smooth both palms over every inch of her. With each movement, he pushed her nightgown higher and higher. Finally, he took a moment, undid the collar button on the back of her neck, and pulled the distracting gown off completely. Casting it aside, he looked his fill of the delectable body pressed so closely to him.

He felt her shiver and didn't know if it was from shame or desire. But he wanted it to be desire. He wanted her to be as crazy mad with want as he was. And when he lifted his hand to tug gently at one of her nipples, he had his answer.

Kit's head fell back on her neck and she moved instinctively, trying to push her breast into his hand. Her arms reached back again to wrap themselves about his neck. And as she stretched, she arched her back with a languid movement. His jaw clenched tightly, Alex struggled to control the waves of passion crashing through him.

While his right hand toyed with her dark, rigid nipple, he lifted her left hand and placed it on her other breast. Not a word was spoken, yet she seemed to understand. Watching him in the mirror, Kit's fingers teased her left nipple, in imitation of his actions. Alex groaned at the sight of her hand at her breast and his left hand slipped down to her abdomen. Briefly he pulled her buttocks against his hips, letting her feel the evidence of his response to her.

Then quickly he allowed his hand to roam downward, to the damp, warm center of her. To the spot that he'd waited so long to caress.

She watched the two of them in the reflection and somewhere in the back of her mind Kit was amazed at what she was doing. But she hadn't the time to explore her own shock. There was simply too much happening.

Alex's fingers toyed with her nipple and each tug sent spirals of need spinning throughout her body. When he pulled her back against his hardness, Kit felt the unmistakable urge to rub herself against that strength. She shifted her buttocks a bit and was rewarded with a rush of his warm breath against her neck.

Merely glancing at the sight of her own hand pressed to her naked skin, Kit's gaze darted away to watch breathlessly as Alex's left hand skimmed through her dark triangle of curls.

The instant his fingers touched that most intimate spot, she gasped as if she had been shot. Her left hand dropped and held his still. She was afraid to let him touch her again and yet terrified he would stop.

But Alex wouldn't be stopped. With an unintelligible whisper of encouragement, his hand moved again, taking hers with him. Slowly, lazily, he stroked her body until she thought she might scream. And when she thought he could do no more to her, his hand slipped farther back and his fingers dipped inside her warmth.

Kit gulped in air and instinctively parted her thighs. She leaned back into him and luxuriated in the rough feel of his clothes against her nudity. Alex pulled his fingers free of her body and Kit wanted to weep at the absence. Instead, she bit down on her lip and tried to stifle the moans of distress clogging her throat.

"Come with me, Kit," he whispered into her ear and Kit knew that she would go with him anywhere.

He turned for the bed, and once there laid her gently down on the mattress. Kit stretched her body and realized for the first time how deliciously cool fresh sheets felt against her skin. She looked up at Alex and saw that he too was now naked.

His clothes lay strewn about the room as if he'd yanked them from his body and thrown them in the air. He knelt on the mattress, then slowly lowered himself to her side. When she reached for him, Alex moved into her embrace.

His mouth came down on hers in a frenzy and Kit met him with an eagerness she hadn't known she possessed.

She parted her lips for his entry and when his tongue slipped inside her mouth, she met his every touch with a caress of her own.

And then his fingers moved once more to the juncture of her thighs and her body jumped in response. Alex pulled his head back, looked down at her, and said, "Spread your legs for me, Kit. Let me into your warmth."

She stared at him, unable to speak. But slowly she opened her legs wide. Feet flat on the mattress, knees drawn up, her thighs parted in invitation. Slowly Alex's fingers dipped inside her warmth.

Kit groaned and squeezed her eyes tightly shut. She felt him. His hand. His fingers. She felt his fingertips press against the inside of her body and wondered at the incredible feel of Alex being *inside* her.

Even Marian's vague tales of pleasure hadn't prepared her for the simple, yet amazing feel of the man you love becoming a part of your flesh.

Alex bent his head and kissed her again, all the while continuing his gentle assault on her senses. As his fingers moved in and out of her warmth, his thumb stroked against a sensitive piece of flesh until Kit's hips began to rock and sway in desperate appeal.

When he pulled away from her momentarily, Kit saw her own passion reflected in his eyes. Beads of perspiration dotted his forehead and the dusting of curls on his chest. She reached up and dragged her fingertips along his shoulders and down his arms and felt him flinch, his body obviously as sensitive as her own.

Kit watched him position himself between her legs and to her surprise didn't feel the slightest bit of embarrassment. Rather, she lifted her hips from the bed in a completely wanton manner.

A brief smile crossed Alex's face and he let his fingers smooth over the flesh of her thighs before sliding his hands beneath her buttocks and holding her still. Kit's breath caught as she watched him rise up on his knees and probe at her opening with his swollen flesh.

He entered her slowly, tenderly. With each of his movements, Kit pushed her head back farther into the pillows behind her and curled her fingertips into the sheets.

He filled her. And still she knew he was holding back. That he hadn't driven himself completely inside her. Yet his body seemed to crowd out the last shreds of loneliness hiding in her soul. Kit rocked her hips, silently pleading with him to enter her fully. She wanted to feel nothing but Alex. She didn't want to be able to tell where he ended and she began. She wanted to be a part of him.

Then he answered her silent call and pushed himself home. Kit's body jumped with the unexpected pain but in seconds it had passed, leaving behind only Alex. Always, Alex.

She opened her eyes to look at him and found she couldn't read his expression. There was a mixture of sadness and pleasure etched in his features that hadn't been evident earlier. Kit opened her mouth to speak, but before she could, he pulled his body from hers and slammed it home again.

Kit's breath caught. He lowered himself onto her body and she wrapped her arms about his neck, clinging to him as if he were the only stable thing left in her world. Again and again, Alex plunged in and out of her. She locked her legs around his waist and welcomed every thrust.

Something incredible was building inside Kit and she began to struggle wildly, trying to help it along. Her body was lit from within as if fires licked at her blood.

Alex's ragged breath on her neck sounded accompaniment to her own staggered heartbeat. She rocked her hips, straining against Alex's body, and each time he entered her, she tried to hold him there, deeply inside. And still the feeling built. As if she were climbing a mountain, Kit took step after step, chasing the mysterious sensation that always remained just out of reach.

Then Alex slipped his hand between their bodies and his fingers moved on her damp center. Immediately Kit's eyes widened. She saw the top of the mountain and with a half choked cry raced to her goal.

She held on to him while tremors shook her body and when she felt an identical shuddering through Alex, Kit held him tighter, closer.

He called her name, then lay still in her arms.

15

Jesus! Alex lay perfectly still in Kit's arms and felt himself trembling. He'd never experienced anything like that in his life. Aware that he was probably crushing her beneath his weight, Alex still couldn't muster the energy to roll over. In fact, if the house were afire, he would simply have to lie there and burn to death. Beneath his ear, he heard her heart thudding rapidly in her chest and knew that she too had been shattered by their lovemaking.

Struggling to regulate his breathing, Alex tried to rationalize what had happened. Perhaps it was because he'd waited so long to bed her. Perhaps it was merely a heightened sense of release due to the uncomfortable frustration of the last few days.

One by one, explanations presented themselves in his brain and one by one, he discounted them. It was none of those things. He knew the truth whether he wanted to admit it or not. The simple fact was, he'd experienced what he had because the woman he was with was Kit.

It was her. Everything about her. Her smile. Her voice. The innocent sensuality. The eager way she accepted his touch and craved more. Simply put, he loved her.

And that was unacceptable.

Summoning up every ounce of his depleted strength, he quickly levered himself off Kit's limp body and rolled to the side. Throwing one hand behind his head, he stared up at the ceiling overhead and remembered everything.

Mrs. Beedle's accusations. His anger. His determination to confront Kit with the truth. And then, the dissolving of all his plans at first sight of her. God, somehow, he'd managed to forget everything but the glorious feeling of her in his arms. Until the moment his body had joined hers.

As soon as he'd encountered the unmistakable signs of her virginity, it had all come rushing back at him. *How* had she thought to deceive him? For God's sake, didn't she know the slightest thing about what went on between a man and a woman?

And now what? He'd deflowered her. There was no denying that. Was this the time she'd been waiting for? Would she start making her demands *now* while he was still so sated with passion he wouldn't argue?

His eyes squeezed shut. Even Althea, in her own way, had been more honest than Kit. At least *she* hadn't offered up her virtue on an altar of security.

"Alex?" Kit whispered and he heard the hesitation in her voice. "Alex? What is it? What's wrong?"

He moved his head to look at her and had to force himself to keep from reaching out to her. Dammit, she looked so young. So . . . confused, *innocent.* No, he told himself firmly. Not innocent. Despite her appearance, he knew only too well that Kit was very skilled at deception.

And he would *not* be swayed by more lies. Raising up

on one elbow, Alex looked down at her. His lips curved in a mocking smile, he said flatly, "You really were willing to go to any lengths at all to stay in this house, weren't you?"

Her eyes widened, her jaw dropped, and the rosy flush in her cheeks faded to a milky paleness. Alex ignored the wounded expression and went on.

"Did you really think I wouldn't *notice*?"

"Notice?" Kit said in a small voice. "Notice what?"

"That you were a *virgin*!"

Her jaw dropped and she grabbed at a sheet, drawing it up over her breasts. "I can explain."

For some reason, the sight of her caught in her own lie saddened him. Normally, he would have thought to feel some sense of triumph. Victory. But there was nothing. Watching her now, as she struggled for words, it occurred to him that his taking the offensive had spoiled her plans.

"I'll wager you could," he finally answered softly. Alex jumped off the bed and began to stalk about the room stark naked. He felt as though he might burst if he didn't release some of the anger and betrayal racing through him. As he walked, he started talking. "No doubt, you consider yourself prepared for any eventuality."

"Alex . . ."

"No." He held one hand up and shook his head. "Allow me to furnish your 'explanation,' please." Cocking his head to one side, he gave her a bitter smile. "I have it! Being a parson's daughter, no doubt you became pregnant through some *spiritual* happening! But I must warn you—if that is the story you choose to present"—

he barked out a harsh laugh—"please don't bother trying to convince me that *Ian* was some sort of heavenly messenger!"

"It's nothing like that, Alex. If you would only listen," Kit said and sat up, clutching the sheet to her chest.

For an instant his brain shouted, Yes! Listen, you fool! She can explain. Lord knew, he'd like nothing better than to be able to believe her. To recapture the feelings he'd experienced all too briefly earlier that day.

But that was impossible, knowing what he did now.

"I think not." Alex walked close to the foot of the bed and stood staring down at her. "What could you possibly tell me? That you're *not* Rose's mother? That you never bedded Ian or anyone else for that matter until tonight? That's hardly necessary, do you think?"

"Alex, you must let me explain!"

"Spare me, madam." His tone carried the chill of the ice that had settled around his heart. "Your explanations would surely be every bit as creative as your other lies, but I find that I'm not much interested."

"But how did you . . ."

"How did I find out?" He grabbed hold of one of the bedposts and leaned in close to her. "It might interest you to know that Mrs. Beedle took a short trip to Oxgate today."

"Oh, God." Kit groaned and covered her mouth with one hand.

"Indeed. She came back to London chock-full of information and came trotting right along to me in the hope that I would throw you out on the street and welcome her back with open arms!"

"Oh, Alex . . ."

"Not to worry," he assured her. "I haven't the slightest intention of allowing that woman back into my home." Turning away, he didn't watch her face as he added, "As for you, my dear. Frankly, I haven't quite decided *what* to do about you."

"Alex, if you would only listen, I might be able to explain all of this. You owe me that much at least."

"Owe you?" He spun around again. "I owe you? For what? The lies you've spouted since first coming here? For welcoming me into your bed? I don't think so. We both know that you had your own reasons for making such a grand sacrifice."

Kit came up on her knees. Still holding the sheet tightly to her, she pushed her hair out of her eyes and glared at him. All traces of the humble country girl were gone. This was the very image of a woman in the grips of a mounting fury.

"I made no 'sacrifice' here tonight," she said. "And you owe me *nothing* for what I gave willingly." Her lips curled into a sneer on that last word. "But by God, you do owe me the courtesy of hearing me out. I've told you repeatedly that I can explain. If you would only be silent long enough to listen!"

He cut her off. "No." Suddenly Alex didn't think he had the stomach to watch her invent plausible excuses for her deception. "I've finished listening to you, madam. As I said, I've no interest in your *explanations*. At least not now. Frankly, I've heard quite enough tonight and I find I'm very tired, suddenly."

"If you knew the truth," she snapped at him, "why did you come to me? Was this whole"—Kit waved one hand at the rumpled bedclothes—*"episode* meaningless?"

"Why did I come?" Alex snorted. "That should be patently obvious, even to a virgin!" His lips curled slightly. "I wanted you. You wanted me." He drew in a long, deep breath. "Meaningless? Certainly not. This 'episode,' as you call it, served a purpose for us both. I think you will have to admit that you enjoyed yourself every bit as much as I did." He crossed his arms over his broad chest and added, "As for all that nonsense you spouted a few days ago about having to *love* someone to willingly go to his bed . . . I believe we just shattered that illusion. Quite nicely too."

"You don't understand."

"Nor do I want to," he shot back. Moving about the room quickly, he snatched up his clothes, then stopped at the side of the bed. "I know all I need to know. Whatever else you are, madam—you are the most *gratifying* bed partner I've had in quite a while."

She tried to slap him, but he was too quick for her and caught her wrist in a hard grasp.

"Let's not play the game any further tonight, if you don't mind." Alex heard all the anger and viciousness spewing from him and couldn't seem to stop the flow of words. Even when he saw her face blanch from his verbal attacks, he went right on as if goaded by some devil inside.

Now, he leaned down, cupped the back of her head with his hand, and pulled her mouth to his. He ground his lips against hers in a hard kiss that left them both gasping for air when it ended.

Clutching his clothes to him, he stalked across the room to the door. After he'd opened it though, he paused, looked back at her, and heard himself say, "I must say I'm beginning to tire of this game." At her blank look, he said, "You know, 'Outraged Virgin and Irresponsible Scoundrel.' Of course, if you're still of a mind to play your part again tomorrow night, I shall do my best to accommodate you." Thoughtfully he added, stroking his chin, "Although we might like to try something different tomorrow. Variety, as they say . . . perhaps, 'Pirate and Slave Girl'?"

She clamped her lips tightly together and lifted her chin defiantly.

"No?" he asked and shook his head. "Well, why don't you think of one, eh? I won't disappoint you. I promise."

Then he left the room and quietly closed the door behind him.

Kit stared at the closed door for a long minute, then slowly let herself drop back on her heels. Damn him anyway, she thought furiously. She hadn't even been allowed a moment to savor the incredible things he'd done to her before having to listen to him destroy it all.

Reaching behind her, she grabbed one of the innumerable pillows and hurled it at the door. There was no satisfaction in it though, and she was too mindful of her precarious position in that house to throw anything breakable.

Besides, what she really wanted to do was follow Alex down the hall to his room and have *her* say. She'd been forced to hear him out, hadn't she? The more she thought about it, the more she liked the idea. After all, what more could he do to her?

For one, her brain reminded her, he could throw her out in the street.

"No," she said aloud, "he wouldn't do that."

He could prevent her from seeing Rose.

"Not unless he killed me," she vowed to the empty room.

Then what more was there to fear?

"Nothing."

As soon as she'd made her decision, she climbed off the high four-poster and walked to the door. Not even bothering to get dressed, she simply pulled her sheet tightly about her body and set off down the hall. Her furious steps slapped against the bedsheet, entangling her legs and inhibiting her progress. The long, dark hall seemed to stretch on forever and the eerie silence echoed with the sounds of her passage. But she went on, determined that he listen to her now, while her anger was still white-hot.

At his door she hesitated only a moment before throwing it open. When the heavy panel slammed back against the wall, Alex spun around to face her.

He'd taken the time to throw on a robe of some sort, but the burgundy fabric hung open in the front. She swallowed heavily and tried to ignore the sight of the naked flesh she'd only just been caressing. Deliberately it seemed, he took his time about drawing the edges together and tying the matching belt. Crossing his arms, he braced his legs wide apart and glared at her.

"I might have known you wouldn't have the good grace to knock."

"As I recall," Kit shot back, "you didn't bother

knocking at my door earlier." She refused to be cowed by his arrogant manner.

"Touché."

"I heard you out, Alex, and now I require the same courtesy from you."

His arms fell to his sides. He inhaled deeply, then let the air rush out of his lungs with a sigh. "I don't give a good damn what you require, Miss Simmons. I've told you I'm tired."

"Fine! Climb into your bed, Mr. MacGregor. I'll talk while you lay there." She took a half step closer. "Think of it as a bedtime story."

He laughed, but the sound held no humor. His features were cast in shadows, owing to the single, dimly lit gas lamp in the room. Perhaps, she thought, it was better that way. She'd be able to talk more openly if she wasn't forced to watch the contempt on his face. Briefly Kit wished that she'd waited until morning. Maybe it would have been wiser to give them both a chance to let their tempers cool.

But it was too late now to back down.

And she'd waited too long already to speak the truth. Perhaps if she'd been honest from the first night, this would never have happened.

"When I came to this house," she started, "I had every intention of telling you that Rose was my niece."

"I'm sure," he said, a sarcastic edge to his voice.

"I know you won't believe me," Kit stated firmly, "but you *will* listen."

"You may speak for as long as you want to, my dear. It doesn't mean I will listen."

"I'll just have to take that chance, won't I?" she said, sounding far more confident than she felt.

"Suit yourself." He shrugged and moved to his bed. Ignoring her completely, he sat down on the mattress, swung his legs up, and pulled the heavy silk coverlet over him. He lay against the pillows like some impossible potentate and she'd never seen him look more uninterested. Kit knew that he'd already made up his mind about her.

Stubbornly, though, she refused to leave. If he was going to think the worst, then he might as well have the truth. "The night I arrived, I was furious."

"Why doesn't that surprise me?" he murmured, one eyebrow lifting in a high arch.

"I blamed you, your parents, Ian mostly . . . *everyone* for what had happened to my sister Marian."

"Ah"—he nodded sagely—"the virtuous Marian."

"Ian seduced her, promised her marriage, used her, then discarded her as if she were no more important to him than an old pair of shoes."

"It is hardly my fault if your sister deluded herself."

Anger shot through her, but she swallowed it back. For the moment. There would be time later, she hoped, for her to defend her sister. Presently, though, she was far more interested in telling him the truth at last. For her own sake, if not for his.

"So when Rose and I arrived at your doorstep, I began thinking of just what might happen once we'd entered your house." Kit started walking about the room, slowly, thoughtfully. "I knew you were wealthy . . ."

"Oh"—he snorted a laugh—"I'm quite sure of that!"

She flicked him an irritated glance. "I knew that you'd

shown no decency whatever in your dealings with my sister."

He grumbled something but she ignored it.

"And I also knew that it was quite possible that you would simply take Rose from me and order me off." She looked at him briefly, but the shadows in the room successfully masked his features. "As her aunt, I had no right to demand that I stay with her. But it occurred to me that even the MacGregors would hesitate about separating a mother and her child."

"How did you know that we wouldn't know the truth?"

She hid a triumphant smile. At the very least, he *was* listening. "I knew Ian was dead. And I very much doubted that he'd bothered to discuss my sister at any length with his family." Kit grimaced. "I would have been surprised indeed to learn he had remembered her name."

Alex said nothing.

"It was a risk, but one I decided to take. When your mother accepted Rose and me immediately, I knew I'd done the right thing. Even though," she added, more to herself than Alex, "as I came to know her, it bothered me to lie to Tess."

"Oh, certainly . . ."

"Believe what you will, I am not in the habit of lying to all and sundry!" Challenging him with a direct stare, she said, "Perhaps if I was, I might have done a better job of it."

He frowned.

"Then, as the days passed, I felt helpless to undo the

lies I'd told. I simply couldn't risk being separated from Rose!"

"And what about tonight?" he whispered, his voice scraping against her soul. "Was that part of your plan?"

"Hardly! Do you really believe I would have *planned* to lie with the brother of the man who ruined my sister?"

"Then why did you bloody well *do* it?"

Even unable to see him clearly, she could judge his expression from the tone of his voice. It was an odd mixture of hurt fury and curiosity. That curiosity gave her hope.

Resolutely she plunged ahead. "Because of *you*!"

"Me?" He tossed the quilt back, leapt from the bed, and crossed the floor to stand directly in front of her. Kit held onto her sheet more tightly. "Are you trying to say that I *forced* you in some way?"

"Not 'force' exactly . . ."

"Hah!" He jerked her a nod. "I should say not! You wanted me every damned bit as much as I did you!"

"I can admit that . . . But you certainly made it clear that you expected me to become to you what I'd supposedly been to Ian."

He opened his mouth, then snapped it shut again.

Kit took advantage of the momentary silence to demand, "What was I supposed to do?"

"Tell me to go to hell!" He threw his hands wide. "God knows you had no trouble at all avoiding me the first few days of your stay here. In more ways than I can name, you made it painfully obvious that your distaste for me knew no bounds!" He leaned in to hover over her. Hands on his narrow hips, he finished, "Why did you suddenly change direction?"

"You still had the power to separate me from Rose."

"That's ridiculous." He shook his head at her, clearly disappointed in her reasoning. "You know as well as I that my mother would never permit you being tossed out." Alex shoved his hands through his hair as if needing something to occupy him. "She would have made my life a living hell!"

"Perhaps," Kit granted him. "But it is still *your* house. My presence here was tenuous at best."

"So you made the ultimate sacrifice?" His sarcasm left no doubt at all as to his thoughts.

"No." She stared up into his cold, hard features and was silently amazed at the difference between the man before her and the man who only minutes ago had taken her to heights she'd never dreamed existed.

Kit knew that he would never believe her when she told him why she'd allowed him into her bed. But she was tired of lying. Tired of trying to remember which lie she'd told when. So she pulled in a deep breath and told him the rest of it. Told him what she'd only recently discovered herself.

And damn the consequences.

"It wasn't a sacrifice," she whispered, deliberately looking into his eyes.

"Then why?" His voice was hushed, but every inch of his body was taut with tightly reined emotion.

"Because, I've come to . . . *care* for you."

There was a minor shift in the sharp planes of his face and Kit hoped it was a good sign.

"Over the last few days," she went on hurriedly, hoping to say all she needed to before he cut her off, "I discovered, much to my own surprise, I might add, that I —*love* you, Alex."

The silence in the room was deafening. She heard each breath she took and imagined she could even hear his heartbeat. He held himself perfectly still. In the soft glow of the lamplight, he might have been a statue, carved to represent some angry god.

Kit stared at him, waiting. A small muscle in his jaw began to twitch. Finally, when she didn't think she'd be able to bear the silence a moment longer, he spoke.

"You disappoint me, Kit."

"What?" Though she'd expected something of the kind, the reality of it was hard to bear.

Shaking his head, he smiled at her. It was the same bitter smile she'd seen so often in her first days in this house.

"And you were doing so nicely until then too."

"Alex, I don't know what you mean by this, but I swear—"

"Please, have the goodness not to swear any undying oaths. It's quite tiresome."

"Alex." She offered her love and he thought her *tiresome*? Kit blinked. He was speaking again and she had to force herself to stand still and listen.

"I will admit, you very nearly succeeded again." He held up one hand, his thumb and forefinger only a hairbreadth apart. "You came this close to convincing me of your story. Until that last part. Really, my dear. You must learn not to overplay your hand."

Kit stared at him, momentarily speechless. She'd

known from the first that he wouldn't believe her—but she hadn't expected such bitter derision.

"Shall we agree on something right now, Kit?" he said, stepping closer to her.

She couldn't answer, her throat felt as though it were in a vise. A knot of rejection and anger had formed, threatening to choke her.

He held her upper arms in a firm but gentle grip. "Let us right now make a pact. We shall continue to enjoy each other's 'company' without burdening each other with any false protestations of 'love.' "

Bending down, Alex covered her mouth with his.

For the first time, Kit felt no answering warmth. Instead, she was aware of her ready temper beginning to boil.

Perhaps in reaction to her lack of response, he pulled back quickly.

"Well?" he asked and she saw a brief flash of pain dazzle his eyes. "What do you say?"

Kit inhaled sharply. He'd made himself perfectly clear. He wanted a mistress. A quiet, subservient mistress. One with no feelings or emotions to dirty up the bed.

A tiny voice in the back of her mind laughed at her surprise. What had she expected? Forgiving arms? A *marriage* proposal for God's sake? No. Alex MacGregor wasn't the kind of man to marry. *That* act required faith —and the ability to love. Both qualities, she realized now, Alex was sadly lacking in.

She ground her teeth together helplessly. She'd told him that she loved him and he'd thrown it back in her face. And still he expected her to warm his bed? A silent groan shuddered through her as she recalled all the things she'd done with this man. Her own brazen behavior rose up in her memory and crashed over her like an icy cascade of water.

How could she have been such a fool?

"Kit?" He released her and stood waiting for her answer.

Kit's gaze locked with his. A strained quiet stretched out between them. The hurt, the anger simmering deep inside her, shone in her eyes, and the harsh planes of Alex's face shifted, softened, then froze again.

Slowly Kit turned her back on him and left the room without another word.

She felt his stare as she walked away.

Michael Harris sighed and looked down at the bedsheet. Alone in the butler's pantry, he told himself that it was a fine thing for a man of his years to be playing "spy." And if Alexander were to discover what he was doing . . . well, they *shot* spies, didn't they?

Shaking his head, he held the sheet up to the bright shaft of morning sunlight pouring in through the small room's solitary window. Frowning, he realized that there was no mistaking the obvious. He would have been far happier to have remained blissfully ignorant of this new development.

But Tess had given him explicit instructions, and he would have agreed to anything for her.

Now, he would do as she'd further requested and send a message to her at once. Though what she hoped to accomplish from a distance was beyond him. Harris shrugged and told himself he would probably be much happier if he didn't find out what she was planning. Instead, he would concentrate on his instructions.

James could take the message, he supposed. If the coachman hurried, he should be able to make the early train to the country and still be able to get back to London by nightfall.

"Tess, my dear," Michael whispered to himself, "I hope you know what it is you're doing."

Then with a resigned sigh, he tucked the bloodstained sheet into a corner of the closet and closed the door. He must find James at once.

16

The air in his study was thick with smoke and the heavy odor of whiskey. Alex slouched in a blood-red leather chair, his legs stretched out in front of him. Groaning, he propped one bare foot on the brick hearth, leaned his elbow on his upraised knee, and tiredly rested his head in the palm of his hand.

He felt hideous. And what was worse, he knew it was nothing more than he deserved.

The moment Kit left his room the night before, he'd marched downstairs, still wearing nothing more than his robe, went directly to his study, and locked himself in. Alex had then proceeded to drink himself into a stupor. He'd emptied one bottle and whittled away at half of another before blessed oblivion crashed down on him.

But any solace he'd hoped to find had eluded him even in his dreams.

Whichever god was in charge of doling out punishment to drunken fools had certainly fulfilled his job. In the grip of an alcoholic mist, Alex had been forced to listen to himself, time and again, saying the vicious, cold-blooded words he'd hurled at Kit. Over and over again, he watched her wounded expression and heard her try to defend herself against his outraged accusations.

And repeatedly he'd heard the echo of Kit's voice saying, "I love you."

Alex groaned and massaged his temples, hoping for a reprieve from the pain. The hangover he'd earned was a massive one but even *that* discomfort was small in comparison to the pain he felt every time he remembered how he'd practically spit at her declaration of love.

But surely, he thought, she didn't expect him to *believe* it! Surely she could see how that declaration lacked conviction, coming as it did directly after she'd been informed that he knew about her lies.

Briefly, though, he wondered what it might have been like to be able to believe her.

He snorted and winced as his head pounded in response. How had he come to this? he puzzled and stared about the empty room.

Draperies closed against the late afternoon sun, a blue haze of cigar smoke streaked across the room like horizontal bolts of lightning in the still air. An empty whiskey bottle lay on the floor beside the too short settee where he'd slept the few fitful hours granted to him. The half-full bottle still stood sentinel by his side. And a tray laden with food rested on the edge of his cluttered desk. As yet untouched, it was evidence of Harris's one successful entrée into the study.

After the butler had been chased out, everyone in the house had since avoided the study and he hadn't been disturbed.

Disgusted, Alex turned back to the fire and stared into the flames as if hoping to find an answer to his situation. But it was futile. There *was* no solution. Hadn't he come to that very conclusion hours ago?

He shook his head slowly, carefully. Who would have guessed that Alex MacGregor would find himself in love again? Certainly not he. Heaven knew, he'd done everything possible to steer a wide path around the very idea of love. He'd vowed to avoid that emotion like the very plague and by damn, he'd made a good job of it. Until recently.

Alex's fingers curled over the arms of the chair. Bloody hell! How was he to know that the little parson's daughter would be the woman to sneak past his defenses? He'd thought himself invulnerable. Certainly, he hadn't been prepared for *her*. Who *would* have been?

And by the time he realized what was happening, it was too late.

Damn her! Alex leapt up from his chair and caught his forehead between his hands to keep it from exploding. The pounding seemed to last a lifetime before at last fading into a dull throbbing ache behind his eyes. Cautiously he opened his eyes and began to walk about the confines of his study.

"If she'd only been in reality what she was pretending to be!" he muttered thickly to no one. Alex stopped a moment, then asked himself if he really meant that. Did he really wish she *had* been Ian's mistress?

No. No, God help him, he was glad she'd never been with his damned brother. But if she had, his mind argued, then he wouldn't feel like such a fool. As it was, she wasn't a woman demanding security for her child . . . she was an *aunt* looking for a rich idiot to take care of her.

"And she very nearly found one, didn't she?" He snorted to himself. He was only thankful he hadn't done anything stupid like actually confessing his love for her. Lord knew what she'd have made of him then!

Why hadn't she told him the truth before? And why, when confronted with it, did she have to sink to professing undying love? More importantly, why couldn't it have been true?

Raking his hands through his unkempt hair, Alex closed his eyes and told himself to forget it. All of it. It was no good at all to wish for things that just weren't so. And still, his mind conjured up the phantom image of him and Kit, strolling arm in arm across the wide lawn at the country house. She was smiling up at him and even in the dream vision, he could *feel* how happy he was.

What must it be like to be loved like that? he asked himself absently. He opened his eyes again and stared up at the portrait of his father. Even with all of the old man's faults, Alex knew that his parents had loved each other deeply. And secretly he'd always hoped to find a love like that someday.

Until Althea.

And now, Kit.

He shook his head and welcomed the resulting pain. It was pointless to go over and over this. He would eventually recover from these ridiculous notions of love and when he did, all would be as it was.

His life hadn't been all that terrible before she'd entered it, had it? He frowned suddenly, not wanting to answer that question . . . even to himself.

Standing beside his desk, Alex lifted the corner of the cloth napkin covering the food tray and stared down at the dried-out plate of sandwiches. Curling his lip, he inhaled sharply and ordered his roiling stomach to straighten itself. He dropped the cloth again, picked up the tray, and carried it to the door.

He didn't want a bloody thing to eat, but he could certainly use some coffee.

It was past time for him to stop behaving like some injured schoolboy.

Throwing open the door, he shouted, "Harris," before he saw the butler hovering nearby. Alex jumped, then scowled at him. "Still waiting up for me, Harris?"

To his surprise, the butler frowned. "I was on my way to tell you that your mother has arrived from the country, sir."

"My *mother*?"

"I thought perhaps"—Harris's steady gaze swept over Alex's rumpled, barely dressed appearance—"you might care to 'freshen up' before speaking with her."

Self-consciously Alex straightened his shoulders, tucked one edge of his robe under the other, and tightened the belt. In his best "Lord of the Manor" voice, he told the other man, "I'm not seeing anyone today, Harris. Tell my mother I'll speak with her tomorrow."

The butler's lips curled. "I'll tell her, *sir.*"

Alex ignored the man's obvious disdain. "Fine. And please take this away." He handed the tray over. "I'd like some coffee too, please. *Black.*"

"Right away, *sir.*"

Alex's eyebrows lifted slightly, but he ignored the man's derogatory emphasis on the word "sir." He was simply too tired to care very much one way or the other. And besides, the longer he held the door open, the greater the chance his mother might intercept him.

Quickly Alex jumped back into the study, closed the door, and turned the lock.

Kit had packed, unpacked, and packed again three times during the long night.

Staring down at her stuffed carpetbag, she sighed and once more emptied it of its contents. As she pulled her dresses free and laid them out on the mattress again, she told herself that she was behaving like a fool.

She was willing to bet that Alex hadn't lost a minute's sleep the night before. But she hadn't been able to close her eyes. Every time she tried, his features rose up before her. Sometimes his face wore the hateful expression she'd seen last and sometimes she saw him as he'd been at the Gaiety. Or the museum.

But worst of all . . . sometimes she saw him as he'd looked leaning over her, his eyes glazed with passion, calling out her name as he emptied himself inside her.

Over and over, she tortured herself with recollections. Repeatedly she heard everything they'd said to each other.

Her temper rose and fell so often during the night, she hardly knew from one minute to the next how she was feeling. Rage and disappointment waged a fierce battle for supremacy in her mind. As always, though, her rage, quick to inflame, was also a shortlived thing. Usually, once her temper had passed, she was able to think clearly. Make plans.

Not this time. Now, with her anger gone, she was left with the pain.

Keeping to her room all day hadn't helped any, either. But for the maid who came in early to clean, Kit had talked to no one. Left to her own devices, she'd only tormented herself with more of the fruitless rehashing of all that was said the night before.

And it didn't make any sense! Great heavens, she thought, Alex had acted like he'd been poisoned the moment she'd confessed her love. Didn't the man have an ounce of brains? Couldn't he *see* that she'd had to lie before . . . but that she was telling the truth *now*?

What on earth was wrong with the man? How could he do such incredible things to her . . . *experience* such amazing sensations . . . respond to her every touch— and feel *nothing*?

He couldn't.

Kit shook her head firmly.

It was impossible.

He'd felt everything she had. She was sure of it. But he wasn't admitting it.

For some reason, Alex MacGregor was hiding.

Kit walked to the window seat overlooking the street and dropped down onto its overstuffed cushions.

What a dismal pair they made. Alex was hiding and she was unable to make a decision.

Stay? Or leave?

All night long she'd wrestled with those questions and she'd decided nothing.

Kit sighed, pulled back the lacy curtains, and stared outside at the lowering dusk.

If she stayed, she would only be asking for trouble with Alex. She flushed and felt the heat of it rise up into her hairline. Whether he was going to admit to caring for her or not, he'd made it plain that he planned to continue visiting her in the night. And, much to her own mortification, Kit didn't know if she'd have the will to refuse him.

Even as angry as he made her, she still loved him. Ached to be with him, feel his arms around her. Of course, with her next breath, she wanted to break something over that thick head of his.

If she left the Mayfair house, she would never see Alex again and she didn't know if she could stand that. Added to that, there was Rose to consider.

Oh, she knew the little girl would be well cared for and loved. But if Kit left the MacGregor house, she would be forfeiting the right to watch Rose grow up. And just the *thought* of missing those years was enough to bring tears to her eyes.

Kit picked up a peach satin pillow and clutched it to her chest. She drew her knees up, buried her face in the pillow's smooth surface, and told herself that she really only had one option open to her.

Somehow, she had to make Alex MacGregor see that she really did love him. At the same time, Kit had to convince him to acknowledge the fact that he loved her.

Grimacing slightly, she turned her head to stare through the lace curtains at the outside world again. The only problem was, she thought bleakly, she hadn't the slightest notion of just how she would accomplish her goals.

"This will work, Michael," Tess assured her old friend. "I'm *sure* of it!"

"I don't know, ma'am," Harris worried, "you haven't seen him today. He looks like the very devil, if you'll pardon me."

Glancing down at the bloodstained sheet in her hand, Tess said sharply, "It serves him right." She lifted her chin and looked up into the butler's soft blue eyes. "I hope my son spent a perfectly *dreadful* night!"

"I don't know about his night, Tess. But I'm quite sure the day after was abominable."

"And it's about to get worse," she said with a definitive jerk of her head. "Michael . . . the keys!"

Solemnly Harris handed over the ring of keys usually kept in a housekeeper's possession. Apparently Tess would not allow her mission to be halted by a locked door.

"Thank you," she said and curled her fingers around the ring tightly.

That said, she spun about and marched through the open door of the butler's pantry. Harris listened to the sharp click of her heels on the oak floor as she swept down the passage toward her son's lair.

Harris should have known that she would accompany James back to the city. Tess wasn't the kind of woman to sit about thinking on a problem when she could be acting. Still, he couldn't quite ignore the small curl of apprehension sliding through his brain. He wasn't at all sure she was doing the right thing this time.

Sighing softly, Michael Harris told himself that had he spent the last twenty years with any other family, he might have lived longer. But, he added with a quirk to his lips, life wouldn't have been half so interesting.

The door was locked. Frowning but undeterred, Tess slid one key after another into the lock until at last she heard the satisfying smack of tumblers turning.

She opened the door and stepped inside, closing the heavy panel behind her. What she'd come to say was meant only for Alex to hear.

"Hello, Mother."

She strained through the gloom of darkness and smoke until she located her son, seated behind his desk.

"You might have opened the door, Alexander."

"I didn't want it opened, Mother. That is precisely why it was locked."

Fanning her hand in front of her face, Tess stomped across the room toward the far window. "How in the name of all that's holy can you breathe in this atmosphere?" Quickly she slapped the draperies aside, allowing late afternoon sun to creep into the room. Then opening the window, she took a deep breath of the fresh, cool air. Finally, she turned around to face her son.

Michael was right, she told herself. Alex looked as near death as she'd ever seen anyone. Her lips flattened into a firm, unyielding line. Good, she thought. He'll be in no condition to argue.

"What brings you back to London, Mother?" he asked, wincing at the feeble sunshine.

"This, Alexander," she snapped, and hurriedly walked to his desk. Tess threw the soiled bedsheet on the desktop and waited for his explanation to begin.

"Laundry?" he asked, his eyebrows lifting. "Really, Mother, I'm sure the maids would have been able to handle that without your assistance."

"This is no time for your nonsense, Alex," she said. "Haven't you anything to say for yourself?"

He groaned quietly. "Please, Mother. There's really no need to shout, is there?"

"There certainly is." Waving one hand at the sheet, Tess went on in a rush. "I was concerned about Kit and rightly so, it appears."

"Concerned?"

"About leaving her here. In this house. With *you*." Actually, she admitted silently, she'd hoped for the first stirrings of romance to spring up between the two young people. She hadn't, however, planned on seeing the girl ruined! "As I said, apparently my fears were well founded."

"Lord, Mother"—Alex leaned his elbows on the sheet and let his head drop into his hands—"say whatever it is you've come to say and let me die in peace."

"You're not going to die, Alex," she countered. "On the contrary, you're going to lead a long, full life."

He snorted and groaned.

"As Kit's husband."

"What?" he shouted, then clasped his forehead tightly.

"I'm certain you heard me."

"Oh, I heard you. I just can't believe that you said it."

"I don't know why not. There *is* that sheet."

"Laundry again?"

"A specific sheet. From Kit's bed." Tess waited until he dropped his hands from his eyes and looked up at her warily, a slowly dawning comprehension evident on his features. Then she delivered her demand. "You ruined the girl, Alex. And you *will* marry her."

"Oh, no . . ." He shook his head, glanced at the

sheet, then raised his gaze to his mother's steely green eyes. "There will be no marriage."

"There most certainly will. You shamed me, this house, this family!" She sucked in a deep breath, glared down at her son, and added, "How you could behave in such a terrible manner toward a guest in my home . . . and her practically a member of this family!"

"Ah-hah! Oooooh . . ." His shout was clearly quite painful.

Tess wasn't interested in *his* pain. She was quite sure that right now, *Kit* was suffering a good deal more than the bedraggled man in front of her. Patiently Tess crossed her arms over her ample bosom and waited for the inevitable arguments.

Picking up the soiled sheet, Alex tossed it to the floor in a sweeping gesture. "Perhaps you haven't considered this yet, Mother. But the very fact that those sheets are stained is proof that Kit Simmons is *not* a member of this family in any way! She was a virgin! She is *not* Rose's mother! Her *sister* was!"

Tess shook her head and dismissed that statement with a languid wave of her hand. "Well heavens, Alex. I knew that long ago."

"That's impossible," he muttered and rubbed his temples jerkily.

"Anyone with a brain in their head would have known that immediately," she went on. Of course, she hadn't *known* about Kit's sister, but she'd naturally assumed as much. Tess didn't think it necessary to admit that she hadn't known anything for sure, despite her suspicions, until the day they were leaving for the country. She'd overheard little Rose call her supposed mother "Aunt

Kit." And then she'd listened to Kit cautioning the girl against further mistakes.

That was also the day Tess'd made up her mind that Kit Simmons would make the perfect wife for her only remaining son. Strange how it had all happened so quickly.

And not exactly as she'd thought it would.

Alex still looked as though he didn't believe her. At last, he said, "Then you can see the woman is clearly a liar and out for her own profit."

"I see nothing of the kind," Tess told him hotly. She considered herself an excellent judge of character. And there was absolutely nothing wrong with Kit's. "I see a young woman so afraid of being separated from the child she loves she is willing to say anything to see that that doesn't happen. *And*, I see a young woman deflowered in *my* house, by *my* son!"

At least, she told herself, he had the good grace to look chastened. Now, she only hoped he had enough sense to see that this was his chance for happiness.

Alex jumped up from his chair and began to pace wildly about the room. The pounding in his head momentarily dismissed, he tried to make his mind work. Was he really so stupid? Had it been evident all along that Kit wasn't Rose's mother? Was Tess right in her judgment of Kit? Or was his mother seeing only what she wanted to see?

And what did it matter now anyway?

Lord, he wished his head would clear.

"You can obtain a special license and the two of you can be married within the week." His mother's voice droned on and he only half heard her. "I thought a simple wedding at the village chapel at the country house would be the best solution."

She had it all worked out! For God's sake, Alex told himself, he was thirty-two years old. He didn't need or appreciate his mother picking out a wife for him.

"Mother, this is impossible."

"Alex, it is the only decent thing to do." She pulled a handkerchief from her sleeve and dabbed at the corners of her eyes.

Alex looked at her suspiciously. He'd never known his mother to be much of a weeper and he suspected this sudden brush with tears to be more a ploy than anything else. Suddenly he felt a whole new burst of regard for his father.

The man had, no doubt, been seriously outmatched by his wife.

"You've shamed us all," Tess went on, her voice dropping. "I'll never be able to hold my head up around my friends again."

"They won't know," he pointed out.

"I will know," she sniffed.

He tried a different tack. It was apparent that his arguments were having little, if any, effect. "Kit would never agree to this, Mother."

"Of course she will."

Remembering how they'd left each other the night before, Alex wasn't as sure. If anything, he admitted guiltily, Kit would probably much prefer shooting him.

"Alex," Tess said softly, "it would be best for everyone. You, Kit, *and* Rose. The child would have a real home. A real family." She paused a moment before saying, "I wouldn't have to worry about Kit taking the baby and leaving one day."

"I would never allow that," he assured her.

"And I don't really think she would do it," Tess admitted, "though one can't be sure. But it's not only Rose I'm thinking of here. Kit is a lovely girl. Good-natured, loving. She would be a good wife to you, Alex. And I think you would do well together. Besides, heaven knows it's past time you settled down."

Marriage? Him? And Kit?

Impossible.

He slowed his steps a bit. Why was it impossible? Everything his mother said made perfect sense, actually. If nothing else, it was an answer to some of the problems that had been haunting him all night. After all, he did have to get married *sometime*. He'd always known that he would have a family someday.

Why *not* Kit? he asked himself. At least there would be no surprises with her. He smirked to himself. Alex already knew precisely what it was she wanted from him. There would be no more delusions of love. No more disappointments or sense of betrayal.

Surprised, Alex found that he wasn't nearly as against the plan as he'd been at first. Marrying Kit would ensure that Rose would never be taken away. Of course, that wasn't the main consideration anyway. Deep inside himself, Alex knew that Kit would never use the child as a bargaining chip, no matter what he'd accused her of in the heat of anger.

He'd already discovered that Kit was a delightful bed partner. And when they weren't embroiled in the middle of a disagreement, they'd had many interesting talks together.

Why not marry her?

Deliberately Alex ignored the small flame of pleasure flickering in his chest. He preferred not to examine that feeling too closely. But whether she'd meant to or not, his mother may have done him a tremendous favor.

"All right, Mother," he conceded. "I'll agree. But I assure you, Kit will not."

Tess clapped her hands together and started for the door. "I'll explain the situation to Kit and then bring her downstairs. We shall see you in the sitting room in exactly one half hour. You may propose properly then."

Good God, he thought. She was even arranging the proposal. Still, he wasn't too surprised. After all, he'd been dealing with his mother for years. Kit, on the other hand, was in for quite a shock.

Tess stopped halfway across the room and looked him up and down disparagingly. "For heaven's sake, Alex. Put some clothes on and shave!"

He ignored that and repeated, "She won't agree."

"Yes, she will," Tess assured him.

"I will not," Kit said and jumped up from her spot on the window seat. Horrified, she stared at Alex's mother as if the woman had sprouted another head. "I won't be forced into marrying Alex or anyone else!"

"Don't think of it as forced, my dear," Tess answered, "think of it as 'arranged.' "

Arranged. Not much better than forced, by any means. One word was as cold as the other, Kit told herself. She should have known. Hadn't her father always warned her about the product of sin? Well, she'd lost her virtue and now it seemed that the price was to be a loveless marriage.

But how had Tess found out? And so quickly?

"My dear," the older woman said and rose to stand beside her, "don't you see? It's for the best. Why, even now, you might be carrying the seeds of a child."

A child. She took two faltering steps backward and dropped to the edge of her bed. One hand clapped to her mouth, she stared unseeing at the floor. Heaven help her, Kit hadn't even considered that.

"You don't want to be left in the position your sister found herself in, do you?"

Marian. Kit almost groaned. How could she not have thought about the possibility of becoming pregnant? My Lord, she'd watched her sister slowly fade away from shame. Now, after all of her high and mighty words, Kit might very well be repeating Marian's mistakes.

Oh, Marian, she said silently, forgive me for not understanding more thoroughly. Forgive me for all I said —and more importantly all the things I thought and didn't say.

And if you can, Marian, she added, help me.

"If your sister were here, she'd agree with me."

Kit heard the other woman as if from a great distance. There was too much to take in too quickly. Her mind was a jumble of thoughts, tumbling over each other so hastily that none of them made the slightest sense. She'd thought herself ready to accept the consequences of her actions. She'd told herself that she was a grown woman and able to make her own choices. And never once had it occurred to her that she and Alex might be creating a child.

Now this. Forced to face the woman whose home she'd invaded on the strength of a lie. It still stunned her to realize Tess had guessed that she wasn't Rose's mother. How long had she known?

Quickly Kit dismissed the silent question. What did it matter now?

"It's for the best, dear," Tess said.

"No," Kit whispered.

"This is entirely Alex's fault, you know," the older woman went on, seating herself beside Kit. She laid one hand on Kit's tightly clasped fingers and said softly, "I want you to believe that and accept it."

If she only could, Kit thought. But she knew the truth. She knew that *she* had wanted Alex every bit as much as he'd desired her. Kit had welcomed Alex to her bed with open arms and an eager body. However, she couldn't very well tell the man's *mother* that.

"He's doing the right thing. And so should you."

The right thing.

How was she to know what the right thing was?

Gaslight flickered in the room and Kit's gaze remained fixed on the polished oak floorboards. Strange, she thought, how quickly everything could change.

Kit pulled in a shuddering breath and remembered the decision she'd made such a short time ago. How she'd planned to prove her love for Alex. How he would, one day, admit that he loved her too.

How foolishly simple that sounded now. With the new worry of a possible pregnancy, she didn't have the right to be concerned about herself alone anymore. There was, perhaps, a new life that would depend on her choices.

"This will be good for him," Tess said, "good for you. Good for all of us."

No it wouldn't, Kit sighed. With the best of intentions, Tess MacGregor had just ruined any chance Kit might have had of convincing Alex of her love.

17

"Tess," Michael whispered, unwilling to let the other servants hear him call the mistress by name. "You can't go in there again."

Tess MacGregor let her right hand fall from the sitting-room door. She turned and looked at the butler as he stepped up beside her.

Happiness was stamped on her features and Michael was struck anew with how gently the years had treated "his" Tess. But for the streaks of silver in her mostly black hair and a delicate tracing of fine lines about her eyes, she looked no different to him than the day he'd first met her more than twenty years ago.

Of course, he knew she'd never agree with that assessment. Over the years, he'd heard her complain more than once about the few extra pounds she'd acquired. But privately he approved of her slightly thicker waist and rounded hips. However, he silently acknowledged, he would have loved her if she'd gained three hundred pounds and lost all her hair.

"Michael," she said in a tone as quiet as his own, "I have to get in there with them."

How to argue with her stubborn nature? He'd only just managed to get her *out* of the sitting room, so the two people inside could speak privately.

"No, Tess." Ah, how he enjoyed saying her name. And how he treasured the friendship they'd forged over the years. Now, because of that association, he felt free to tell her the truth. "You don't have to get back to them. You have to go someplace quiet and wait for them to tell you what they've decided."

"What are you saying?"

"I'm saying, Tess, you've done enough now." Following his instincts, Michael laid one hand gingerly on her shoulder. "You've got to let them carry on from here on their own."

"But what if they don't . . ."

"Tess, you can't do it all. They have to *want* this. Don't you see?"

He watched her wide green eyes and could almost *see* her thinking. Several long minutes passed and he was beginning to wonder if she would ignore his advice after all, when she reached up and patted his hand.

"You're right, Michael."

The butler looked at her tiny hand covering his own and a band tightened around his chest. It was such a small gesture and she probably thought nothing of it, for all it meant to him.

Harris found himself wishing, not for the first time, for the courage to tell her how much he loved her. Instead, he pulled his hand away and let it drop back to his side.

He had to stop thinking like that. It was no good to torment himself. Stiffly, to remind himself that she was his employer and he merely the butler, Michael asked, "Would you care for a cup of tea, madam? I can have it served in the dining room."

"No." Tess shook her head. "I'd rather not sit in that huge room all by myself." Glancing up at him through half-shuttered lids, she asked hesitantly, "Would you join me for tea, Michael? We could have it in your pantry, if that's all right."

"In the pantry?" His voice sounded strained even to him.

"That way we wouldn't be a bother to cook in the kitchen and I'd rather like the company, Michael."

His heart hammering in his chest as though it might explode, Harris finally found his voice. "If you say so, madam. I shall see to it."

He stepped aside to allow her to precede him to the butler's pantry at the end of the hall. But before she took a step, Tess rested her hand on his arm and said softly, "Please don't start calling me 'madam' again, Michael. I prefer it when you call me Tess."

Harris stared down at her hand, her fair skin made to look almost translucent against his black jacket. Her warmth seeped into his bones and Michael cautioned himself sternly.

Tess wasn't a stiff, formal woman. She'd never been. And as his "friend," she would naturally urge familiarity. It meant nothing more than that.

Nothing.

"She's right. It *is* for the best."

Kit's gaze flew up to Alex's features and he carefully kept his expression blank, unreadable. Along with the fact that he still wasn't entirely certain how he felt about this whole thing . . . Alex didn't want to tip his hand as to his own confusion before he'd heard what Kit had to say.

Truthfully, he'd have given just about anything to know what she'd said when Tess first proposed the idea. Did she leap at the chance to marry into money? Or was she as torn as he was?

"You don't have to do this," Kit said finally, straightening her shoulders and lifting her chin proudly.

"On the contrary," he countered, "I do." Alex seated himself on the brocade chair directly across from her. Leaning his forearms on his knees, he looked her directly in the eye before saying, "Aside from everything my mother has no doubt pointed out—there is something else as well. A thought *has* occurred to me that perhaps you haven't considered just yet."

"Which is?"

"You might very well have become pregnant last night."

A deep rose color filled her cheeks and she lowered her eyes to her clasped hands.

Alex didn't know why he hadn't thought of it before, but while he was upstairs dressing, the very real possibility of a pregnancy had struck him like a blow. Lord knew, he'd done nothing to prevent a child's conception.

When the thought had first come to him, an image of Rose had sprung immediately to mind. And much to his own surprise, Alex had discovered that the idea of fatherhood no longer repelled him. Actually, the more he considered the notion, the more it appealed to him. As he'd become accustomed to the concept of marriage and fatherhood, Alex had also realized that the main reason that state suddenly sounded appealing . . . was Kit.

"I *have* thought of that eventuality," she whispered, "and there is another choice open to us besides marriage."

"I can't think what that might be," Alex argued, reluctant somehow to let go of the fanciful images in his mind.

"It's quite simple really," she said, her flesh turning a bright crimson. "We have only to wait about three weeks. Then we'll know for sure."

"Oh." His phantom child dissolved and Alex watched it go sadly. However, even if they went along with her idea, there was still the matter of her "ruining." Speaking flatly, he said as much.

She pushed herself to her feet and crossed the room to the hearth. In the soft glow of the fire, Alex watched the play of emotions dance across her features. She held herself regally and even in her tired, pale green gown, Kit Simmons was beautiful.

If only he could trust her.

"Alex," she said, and turned to look at him, "you didn't *ruin* me. I think it would be more fair to say we ruined each other."

"I beg your pardon?" Totally confused now, he got up and walked quietly across the Persian carpet to her side. More negligently than he felt, Alex leaned one arm on the mantelpiece and looked down at her. The delicate scent he'd come to associate with her filled him and Alex welcomed it.

"Last night," she began and took a deep breath, "was

a decision we *both* made. And what followed was surely not something either of us would like to repeat."

He stiffened. No, Alex thought. He wouldn't care for that at all. An angry exchange of hurtful words and accusations was not a pretty scene by any means. One was more than sufficient for any man's lifetime.

"We wouldn't," he said firmly and tried to ignore the sparkle of firelight in her eyes and how the soft glow seemed to shimmer on her flesh.

"How can you know that?"

"Because everything we needed to say was said last night." And more, he told himself with a touch of guilt.

A short, humorless laugh shot from her throat.

"See here, Kit," Alex said quickly, "now that we have all of the venom out in the open, there's nothing more to fear. Each of us knows where we stand with the other . . ."

"Yes," she said and he thought he heard a tinge of sadness creep into her voice.

"You would have what you most desire," he went on, hating to admit that what she most wanted was *not* himself. "Security for yourself and for Rose . . . and I . . ."

"Yes, Alex?" she asked. "What would you have?"

"I . . ." He shook his head. He would have *her*. However she felt about him, Alex could admit—at least to himself—that he wanted her more than anything in the world. Even under these circumstances. But his pride would never allow him to confess that to her. Instead, he finished lamely, "It's time I was married, Kit. And I think that we, understanding each other as we do now, would do as well as anyone would."

"It's not the kind of marriage I'd hoped for." Kit sighed.

"Nor I." Alex shoved his hands into his pants pockets and managed to shut out the little voice inside telling him to hold her, kiss her.

"But I didn't want this," Kit said and silently added, not like this.

"Whether we want it or not"—he shrugged—"the situation has been thrust upon us."

My Lord, she thought hopelessly, they sounded as if they were working out the minor details to a business arrangement. And they were both being so calm about it. So cold-bloodedly *calm.*

At least in their argument the night before there had been fire. Passion. But this . . . and how would she ever convince him that she truly loved him—if she married him for the security he could provide?

"And if I'm not with child, Alex? What then?" She looked up into his shadow-filled gaze and for the first time noticed his pallid complexion and the dark rings of sleeplessness underscoring his blue eyes.

"If not now, you would surely become pregnant in time."

She looked ahead in her mind, down the years stretching out in front of them. Kit saw the two of them, married, living in the same house, sharing the same bed, creating children together, and never reaching each other's hearts.

It seemed a lonely proposition. And yet, did she really have any other option? She could run, she knew. Leave this house and Alex. But she wouldn't, Kit admitted. The memories of Marian's suffering and shame were still too fresh. Too painful. She wouldn't subject herself *or* the child she might be carrying to such a life.

As for her own idea of waiting three weeks—Kit couldn't stand that. Three weeks of misery? She and Alex walking wide circles around each other, nerves strained to the breaking point? No. Neither of them would survive that kind of constant torment.

Decision made, she took a deep, steadying breath and said, "Very well, Alex. I will marry you."

"Splendid." His gaze slipped down to hers and the briefest of smiles touched his lips before fading away. "I'll arrange for the special license immediately."

Before he left the room, Alex leaned down and planted a quick, chaste kiss on her forehead. When she was alone again, Kit couldn't help wondering if the rest of their marriage would become as cold and dispassionate as that first sanctioned kiss.

Within the week, it was done.

Kit scooted back farther on the sun-warmed stone beneath her and tilted her head back to gaze unseeing at the ice-blue sky. With no distractions save for the sound of the sea and gulls, her mind wandered back over the last week or so.

Almost before Kit knew it, they were settled at the MacGregors' country house on the western coast. True to her word, Tess took care of everything. In fact, Kit and Alex hardly spoke to each other in the days following his proposal. There was simply too much to do.

Just three days after their arrival, the simple wedding ceremony took place in the village church. A small stone building, it looked as though it were as old as time.

Huddled at the edge of Cliffton village, it was nearly buried beneath sprawling mounds of ivy and towering hollyhock spires.

A brief service, held in a puddle of rainbow-colored sunshine streaming through the solitary stained-glass window, Alex and Kit's wedding was witnessed by Harris, Tess, and Rose. Once it was done, they'd signed the register, then returned to the MacGregor estate for a wedding breakfast that was as quiet as it was small.

And since that morning, the bride and groom had never once been alone together. Despite what she'd expected, Alex had yet to visit Kit's room in the night and during the day he seemed to do all he could to keep his distance. Truthfully, though she still waited in the darkness, half hoping to hear him at her door, Kit was glad of the reprieve. She needed time to settle in to her new position. To become accustomed to being addressed as "Mrs. MacGregor."

Kit sighed, shifted her gaze from the sky, and stared instead out to sea.

Even after several days of marriage, Kit was wont to come to an abrupt halt when one of the villagers called out a greeting to her. For the most part, they were friendly people, eager to meet her and curious about the new wife in the MacGregor house.

Rose, Kit soon discovered, had paved the way for her warm welcome. The little girl, on her daily walks with her grandmother, had managed to charm most of the township. And Kit had overheard enough people talking to know that the people in Cliffton were convinced that Rose was Alex's child as well as hers. She'd even heard, courtesy of Polly, that the gossips in town were of the opinion that Kit and Alex had been secretly married for years and that the ceremony in the village chapel was held for Tess's sake.

She shook her head and braced her hands behind her on the craggy rock. Kit Simmons MacGregor sat perched on an outcropping of a monstrous boulder resting on the sand not fifty feet from the incoming tide. She watched idly as the water surged for shore, stretched out damp fingers to hug the sand, then retreated again.

The steady roar of the waves filled her and she tilted her head back to watch the gulls do a slow, dipping dance with the wind. A sudden, strong breeze whistled through the rocks, wrapped itself around her for an instant, and then left her as quickly as it had come. Kit lifted one hand, pushed her hair from her eyes, then drew her knees up and stared out at the sea. Cold and tired, she told herself that she should start her walk back to the house. And yet, she was reluctant to leave.

She'd come to think of the half-moon-shaped, sheltered cove as her own secret place. And though she knew she was being fanciful, that undoubtedly any number of the villagers often went there, she'd yet to be disturbed. As she stared out at the horizon, where sea met sky, Kit felt the peace of the place steal over her.

Before her arrival at Cliffton, Kit had never seen the sea. At first sight of the vast, seemingly limitless expanse of water, she was captured by the power of it. Again and again she was drawn to the beach. To her cove, where she would sit for hours in the cold wind, watching the waves in their endless pattern. She drew comfort from the steadiness of the sea. A comfort that was sadly lacking in her new marriage.

Oh, she silently admitted, it was all quite civilized. And she had no doubt that there were probably hundreds of marriages in England that were much like hers. But she'd always hoped for so much more.

And in any other circumstances, this village on the coast could have been the scene of much happiness.

Kit loved the country house. Despite its intimidating size, there was a warm informality about the Tudor-style manor house that welcomed her as the house in Mayfair never had. Even the housekeeper, Mrs. Abbot, was the exact opposite in nature from Mrs. Beedle. Along with her husband, who was the head gardener for the estate, Mrs. Abbot managed to run the household without making everyone else around her miserable.

Of course, Kit smiled to herself, the fact that Mrs. Abbot so clearly adored Rose was another point in the woman's favor.

Images of Rose leapt into her brain and Kit acknowledged that she'd never seen the child happier. With the run of the house and gardens, the little girl wasn't still for a moment. And since Kit and Alex had arrived at the house, Rose had demanded their almost constant attention.

"Rose!"

Kit heard the shouted command first and looked up. As if thinking about her had conjured her up, Kit watched in surprise as the little girl darted past the mouth of the cove. Her delighted giggles spilled out into the sea air and were carried away on the wind.

Kit scrambled down off the boulder and began to run

for the girl. Visions of Rose being tugged out to sea by the relentless tide filled her mind and she willed her feet to move faster across the inhibiting sand.

"Rose!"

The shout came again, and this time Kit recognized Alex's voice. He appeared around the corner of the stone wall and swept Rose up in his arms before Kit had taken more than a few steps in her direction.

"You mustn't run away from me like that, Rose," he told the laughing little girl. "You could be hurt. Especially down here, by the water."

Kit studied him from the safety of the shadows. He was dressed casually in a cream-colored shirt, opened at the throat. His black pants were stuffed into knee-high boots, now covered with sand, and the wind tossed his black hair wildly about his head. Unaware of the woman watching him, he spoke to the girl in his arms and Kit watched his features soften.

Rose, though, was clearly unmoved by his dire warnings. She laid her small hands on his chest and pushed, determined to be free again.

"Down, Papa, down."

"I won't put you down, you naughty girl. You'll go and get yourself soaking wet!"

"Down, Papa!" Rose put both her hands on his cheeks and moved his head in a nod. "Down?"

Kit's breath staggered slightly. Though she was becoming accustomed to hearing the girl refer to Alex as "Papa," seeing them together—and the striking family resemblance—was enough to shake her.

"No." Alex laughed, closed his arms tight around the

child, and turned back in the direction they'd come. It was only then he saw Kit.

He stopped dead and so did his heart. Hungrily Alex let his gaze move over her thoroughly. From her windswept hair to the cold-induced blush of red on her cheeks, she looked lovely. Over the last few days, he'd become used to seeing her in the new, elegant clothes they'd purchased in London. And though they complemented her, they also made her seem more unapproachable for some reason.

Now, seeing her in the peach-flowered muslin she'd worn the first night he'd met her, Alex felt the too long denied, familiar need for her stir to life again.

Lord, he groaned silently, it felt like forever since he'd last held her.

He'd battled his own urges since their marriage and had won a temporary victory. Wanting to give her time to adjust to their new circumstances, he'd distanced himself purposely. And, if he were to be completely honest, Alex had to admit that he'd also stayed away from her in a futile attempt to deny his feelings for her.

If anything though, the distance he'd put between them had only heightened his desire. Every night he had to fight a battle again and again to keep from going to her room and burying himself inside her.

Knowing she was close and yet unreachable was driving him near the edge of madness.

His only answer to the problem had been to keep busy. He'd met with the local farmers, involved himself somewhat in village business, and spent whatever time he had left with Rose. And he'd discovered something surprising. Somehow, over the years, he'd come to believe that life in Cliffton was a bore. That London was the only place to live. But in the last week he'd been happier than he had been in years. Excepting the loneliness of his marriage.

And if his nights were lonely, dark hours spent imagining her, his days were harder. He didn't spend time with her. Didn't even speak to her, really. But he *had* been watching her.

He'd seen her warmth toward the villagers. He'd noticed how she and Mrs. Abbot had struck up a fast friendship and Alex couldn't even remember how many times the local people had stopped him to compliment him on his new wife and wish him well.

In an extraordinarily short time, she seemed to have charmed everyone for miles around. And he had to ask himself if he'd been wrong about her. Why would a woman interested only in her husband's money bother to endear herself to the locals? What could she possibly gain?

His goodwill? That wouldn't be necessary, if Kit were truly as calculating as he'd believed. After all, she already had his name . . . frankly, he could think of no other reason for her actions. Unless he *was* wrong about her.

And as much as he'd like to believe that, he wasn't quite willing to take that risk.

"Hello, Alex," she said and he discovered how he'd missed the sound of her voice.

"I . . . didn't realize you were here," he said and held Rose more tightly.

"I often come here," Kit replied and held out her arms for Rose.

The little girl leaned over and Alex reluctantly let her go. Suddenly unsure of what to do with his hands, he jammed them in his pockets and waited.

"I found this spot the second day we were here," Kit said, "and I've been coming here nearly every day since then."

Ridiculous conversation, he told himself. Standing about in the wind and sand talking about nothing. And yet, it was more than they'd said to each other in days. He was loath to let it end.

Alex let his gaze move over the sheltered area slowly. Ringed on two sides by stones of every size, the back wall of the cove was formed by the sea cliff itself. A half smile curved his lips briefly. He hadn't been to the cove in ages. Memories flooded him.

Almost to himself, he said, "I found this place when I was ten or eleven." He pulled one hand free and pointed at the cliff wall. "Carved my name in that rock with a knife I stole from cook." Alex glanced at Kit, saw her gaze soften, and continued. "Used to imagine that I was a pirate. 'Black Bill' my name was—" His lips quirked in self-mockery. " 'Alex' just didn't have that *bloodthirsty* ring to it, I suppose. I would stare out to sea for hours, waiting for my 'crew' to come ashore and row me out to my ship."

"It would make a good spot for pirates," she said hesitantly and he felt her gaze on his face. "It's tucked away so neatly from the rest of the beach."

"Yes," Alex agreed. He watched her chew at her lower lip nervously. "It's . . . *private*."

Kit nodded slowly and Alex suddenly wished that his delightful little niece was *anywhere* but with them at that moment. He wanted nothing more than to lay Kit down on the sand and in the solitude of the stone shelter make love to her in the sunshine. Looking into her eyes, he fancied that he saw the same desire sparkling in their blue depths.

His body leapt into life. Maybe, he told himself, it was time to stop lying to himself. Keeping away from her wasn't working. The urge to seek her out only grew stronger each day.

Perhaps she'd had enough time to familiarize herself with her new home and status. Perhaps it was time they put aside the reasons for their marriage and went on with their lives. Maybe the time had finally come for them to make their marriage a real one.

"Mama," Rose interrupted his thoughts and shattered the quiet spell when she tugged imperiously at Kit's hair. "Mama, Rose get *down*!"

Kit tore her gaze away from his and crouched in the sand. Setting the little girl on her feet, she said, "All right, you may walk, Rosie. But you must hold on to our hands."

When she stood up again, she had a firm clasp of Rose's pudgy fingers. Dutifully the little girl reached up, snatched two of Alex's much larger fingers, and started moving.

Jumping into the air and swinging her feet free of the earth, Rose became the link that held the two adults at her sides together.

The three of them began their slow walk back down the beach to the cliff path and home.

18

"**G**ood night, you two," Tess said and walked toward the door.

Kit looked up from the book in her lap. Her legs curled beneath her, she sat in an overstuffed wing chair by the fire.

"The game isn't over yet, Mother," Alex called out from across the room.

Glancing at him, Kit saw him toss a brief look her way before turning back to the woman leaving the room.

"Of course it is, dear. We both knew from the minute the game began how it would end." Tess smiled at her son and opened the sitting-room door. "I've never been the slightest bit good at chess and you know it."

"But you still have several moves open to you."

"And I'm much too tired to try to identify them," she countered quickly. Looking to Kit, Tess added, "Kit dear, why don't you take the game over for me?"

"Oh . . ."

"Please do." The older woman's lips quirked as she glanced at her son. "Perhaps you'll even beat him."

"She has before . . ." Alex said softly.

"Really?" Tess grinned. "That's settled, then. Good night, now." She sailed out the sitting-room door, closing it behind her.

Kit looked over at her husband and wasn't sure how to approach him. Since their meeting on the beach that afternoon, the atmosphere between them had changed somehow. It was as if there'd been an undeclared truce.

For the first time since their marriage, dinner hadn't been a trial to be suffered through. The conversation had been awkward, but still better than the silence that had hovered over them all the last few days.

Even Tess, Kit thought, was aware of the difference between her son and his wife. The older woman's smile had never been brighter. She was clearly convinced that her "arrangements" appeared to be working out nicely.

Now though, with Tess off to bed, Kit was suddenly nervous. Without the older woman as a buffer, would the fragile peace between Kit and Alex shatter?

Carefully she marked her place in the book she'd been pretending to read and stood up. The cozily decorated sitting room suddenly seemed cavernous—the distance she would have to cross to reach him, miles. Slowly Kit began to walk toward him and each step she took sounded out as a warning in her brain.

Alex rose as she approached and she felt the strength of his gaze on her. An almost mesmerizing glint shone in his eyes and she couldn't have looked away if it meant her life. When she reached the small rosewood table, Kit took the chair opposite Alex.

"If you don't want to . . ." he said as he dropped into his own chair.

"I'd enjoy playing, Alex," she said and only hoped that she'd be able to concentrate on the chessboard.

A long moment passed. The air between them seemed to crackle with the heat of a freshly laid fire.

Her breathing ragged, she jumped slightly when Alex finally splintered the silence.

"As you can see," he said in a voice rough with need, "Mother's left you in quite a quandary."

It was a full minute before Kit realized that he was referring to the chess game. Dutifully she stared down at the intricately carved, hand-painted set of chessmen. She swallowed heavily, touched one piece with her fingertip, and said, "Yes. She has. I'm about to lose my king, aren't I?"

"Possibly," he conceded, "though in chess, anything can happen."

As in life, she told herself and arbitrarily moved one of her rooks.

"A bold, yet chancy move," Alex whispered and leaned one elbow on the table. "Are you one for taking risks then, Kit?"

"If the need arises," she answered quietly and kept her gaze locked on the play board.

Alex's long fingers curled around one of his black knights. He moved it to a new square and captured the rook she'd only just placed there. "A risk is not always worth taking."

"Sometimes," Kit whispered, "it's better to follow your instincts than to question yourself too carefully." She reached out and slid her queen halfway across the board.

"A dangerous practice," Alex countered, "instinctive responses can be . . . *inaccurate*." He reached for his bishop and began to move on her queen.

"And yet"—Kit's voice lowered even further—"instinct—what we feel—is all we truly have that is uniquely our own." Slowly she lifted her queen and moved it diagonally five spaces. When she released the piece, Kit looked up into Alex's eyes and said quietly, "Your queen is in danger."

Frowning, he stared down at the board. After a long, silent pause Alex looked back up and met Kit's gaze. "Any move to save my queen would put my king into jeopardy. Yet without her, the game is almost lost anyway."

"Yes," she said and knew they were talking about more than the chessboard.

"How do I save my queen without sacrificing the king?"

"Perhaps you can't."

"And if I choose *not* to make that sacrifice?"

"The game is over."

"And my queen?" Alex asked.

"You must decide your queen's destiny, Alex."

Kit pushed herself to her feet and kept her eyes on him as he too rose. She'd suddenly had enough of talking in circles. "Good night, Alex."

He looked as though he might argue with her leaving, but then apparently changed his mind. "Good night, Kit."

Leaving the sitting room as quickly as possible, she hurried across the darkened, more dimly lit hall and fairly raced up the stairs.

He was coming. She was sure of it.

Kit tugged at the silk ribbons tied beneath the bosom of her deep lavender silk dressing gown. The flimsy garment covered a nightdress so scandalous Kit blushed when she wore it. But wear it she had. Each night since her marriage.

When she'd first discovered it among the items of clothing ordered from Mrs. Talbot's shop, Kit had known immediately that Alex himself had picked it out. It was not a gown most husbands would choose for their wives—but then, at the time, he'd wanted her for his mistress.

Kit moved to the doors leading to her private balcony and swung them wide. She stepped out onto the cold stone floor and the soles of her bare feet scraped against the rock. The ocean breeze caressed her and the cold, damp air lifted her hair and swirled it around her like a cloud. Gooseflesh crawled up the length of her arms and skittered down her spine. Reluctantly she turned her back on the night and returned to her room. As she closed the balcony doors once more, a gentle knock sounded.

"Come in," she said, her voice as hesitant as that knock.

The forest-green door opened and Alex stood in the shadowed doorway. His features tight, he stared at her with a raw hunger that shook her soul.

He stepped over the threshold and closed her door firmly. With his back pressed to the oak panel, he turned the key and Kit inhaled sharply as the lock shot home.

"Kit . . ."

There were so many things to be said. So many things she wanted to understand. And so many more she wanted to say to him. But for the moment, all she needed was to feel his arms around her again.

Slowly, deliberately, she pulled the ribbon tie free and let her decorative robe slide from her arms. Kit carefully stepped free of the silken puddle and watched Alex's eyes devour her.

His heart had stopped. He wasn't breathing. But Alex knew he wasn't dead because his body was on fire.

The lavender gown. How often he'd wondered if she'd worn it. And what it looked like on her. But the reality was even more beautiful than the image his mind had created.

Sheer, fragile silk clung to her every curve. The bodice of the gown reached high enough to barely cover her rigid nipples and between her breasts the fabric plunged nearly to her abdomen. Stretched across the creamy texture of her flesh was a spiderweb of violet lace.

And though he couldn't see it, he knew very well that the sides of the gown were open, held together only by wisps of ribbon.

Alex's palms itched to touch her and still he hesitated. The moment he'd walked in the door and seen her wearing that gown, he'd been sure that he hadn't misunderstood their odd conversation downstairs. And yet . . . there was still so much unsettled between them. Was he wrong about her? Did he dare do as she'd challenged and trust his instincts? Was he ready to risk losing the game?

As his brain struggled for answers that wouldn't come, Kit began to walk toward him. Her slow movements created ripples in the silk that gave her every motion a liquid look. Caught by her beauty and his body's response to her, Alex was rooted to the spot.

Until she touched him. She laid her palms flat on his chest and Alex's heart began to beat again. Thudding against his ribs, the frantic pounding of his heart echoed the throbbing in his groin. His arms closed around her slim body and pulled her tightly to him. Running his hands over the smooth, flesh-warmed fabric of her gown, Alex inhaled her scent as if it were the breath of life.

Hungrily he dipped his head and claimed her mouth in a frenzy of need. She answered his passion with abandon and in seconds he'd released the ribbon ties of her gown and bared her body to his eager touch.

There wasn't time for niceties. He didn't have the fortitude to go slowly, carefully. Alex was in the grips of a desire that demanded satisfaction. He buried his mouth in the curve of her neck and gloried in the feel of her fingers winding through his hair. She pressed herself into him, and when her warm breath and then her tongue touched his throat, Alex groaned and let the fire consume him.

Sweeping her up into his arms, he took three long strides to her bed and stretched her out on the down mattress. She seemed to sink into the softness and his only thought was to join her before she could escape him.

He tore his clothes off and lay down atop her. Every inch of her body touched his. Flesh on flesh, he moved and she shifted with him, rubbing their bodies against each other until neither of them could wait another moment.

Kit spread her thighs wide and drew her knees up on either side of him. Her palms moved over his back as if memorizing the feel of him. Alex slid himself down her body until he was able to draw one of her nipples into his mouth. It leapt into rigidity with the first touch of his tongue, and when he began to suckle at her, her hands cupped the back of his head and held him in place.

He was burning. And every time he touched her, the flames grew hotter until he was sure he could feel the heat licking at the edges of the bed. Reluctantly he pulled away from her breast and rose up to his knees.

She lifted her legs and wrapped them around the small of his back, arching her hips as she did so. Through passion-glazed eyes, Alex looked down at her as his fingers moved to caress the dampened flesh between her thighs.

Kit's body jerked and she tilted her head back into the pillow. Her hips rocked against his hand and Alex answered her silent demand. While he slipped his fingers inside her, his thumb moved over the now hardened nub of flesh. As she writhed in time with his caresses, Alex let the wonder of it fill him.

He watched her features as she strained for completion and he knew that he would never be able to touch her enough. If they were together for a hundred years, it still wouldn't be long enough for him to have had from her all that he needed.

Need. The single word flashed through his mind and in an instant he recognized it for the truth. He needed Kit Simmons MacGregor. As he needed air and water . . . he needed *her*. Without her, there was nothing.

He moaned at the mere idea of a life without her. Quickly then he pulled his hand from her, lifted her buttocks slightly, and pushed himself inside her body.

Kit gasped and arched her back. Her legs tightened around his middle and her fingers clutched at his shoulders.

As if he could prevent her ever leaving him by becoming a part of her, Alex thrust deeply into her. So deeply finally that he was sure he had touched her soul.

When her body trembled and his name left her lips, Alex gave in to the incredible release he'd been holding in check. Driving into her one last time, he poured himself into Kit and prayed that she *did* love him.

Fifteen minutes later, still locked together, Alex rolled over onto his back. His hands moved down her spine lazily and it was a few more moments before Kit lifted her head and smiled down at him.

He opened one eye and looked at her uneasily. "Did I hurt you?"

She dragged her fingertips down the length of his throat before saying softly, "Did you hear me cry out?"

Now the other eye opened as well. "As a matter of fact, yes."

Kit gave him a crooked smile. "But not in pain." It was more wonderful than she cared to admit, having him back in her bed. Now, she was grateful to Tess for having handed over the chess game. She smiled to herself, remembering the veiled conversation she'd had with Alex only a short while ago. Perhaps, she thought, he was ready to move on beyond the ugly things they'd said to each other so many days ago. "I see," she said softly, running her fingers through the patch of black curls on his chest, "you decided to follow your instincts after all."

There was no answering smile from him. Only his hushed voice admitting, *"This* time."

A bubble of regret formed around her heart. So. Nothing had changed after all. He'd come to her solely for his physical needs. Why couldn't he let go of the past?

Was he going to punish her forever for the lie she'd had to tell? Was he *never* going to forget? A small slice of anger began to thread its way through the sorrow rising up in her. Why couldn't he understand? Why couldn't he see that she'd only done what she'd had to do?

Suddenly determined to reach him, Kit told herself that she would keep him there . . . in her bed . . . until she discovered the *real* reason behind his stubbornness. She simply couldn't believe that he would throw away their chance at happiness because she'd lied to him in order to survive. "Alex," she said, her palms on his cheeks, forcing him to look at her, "can't you see that I did what I believed I had to do?"

A shutter of blue ice dropped over his eyes, but even in the cold, Kit imagined she could see a spark of hope. It was as if he *wanted* to believe her, but something was preventing him.

Her body stretched out atop his, she felt his warmth and knew that was all she'd ever have of him if she couldn't make him talk to her. She plunged ahead. "After I'd come to know all of you, I realized that you wouldn't put me out in the street—or take Rose from me." Speaking faster, more desperately, she added, "But by then, I didn't know how to confess the truth without branding myself as a liar."

His hands stopped their idle movements on her flesh and Kit felt immediately chilled. The hope burgeoning in her breast began to wither, but she wouldn't let it die without saying the *one* thing she wanted him to believe more than any other.

"I *do* love you, Alex." She laid her fingertips across his mouth. "And I think you love me."

Alex's hand curled around hers and pulled it from his lips. "Please don't."

"But why? Why won't you believe me?"

"I believed someone else once. Long ago." His eyebrows lifted and a mockery of a smile curved his lips. "I may not learn my lessons quickly, Kit. But I *do* learn them."

"Who was she?" Finally, she told herself. Finally they were getting to the heart of his distrust. She only hoped she was strong enough to see the revelations to their conclusion.

"Who doesn't matter. It was *what* she was that taught me about 'love.' "

"Tell me," Kit demanded. Though the last thing she wanted to hear, while her body still hummed from his touch, was a story about a lost love . . . it had to be said.

Alex rolled to one side, successfully breaking their intimate bond. Moving to the edge of the mattress, he swung his long legs off the bed and braced his elbows on his thighs.

Kit felt his absence down to her soul. Staring at his bent head, she tried to brace herself for what was coming.

In a cold, flat tone, Alex told her about Althea. Instinctively Kit reached for him. Her fingertips stroked the small of his back and she flinched when he shifted away from her.

His voice went on and with each word he spoke, she was aware of a new distance forming between them. She felt his humiliation. She heard the pain of the old wound as he opened it. And Kit sensed that though he was still within arm's reach, he was farther from her than he'd ever been.

She saw it all so clearly as he described it. In her mind's eye, she saw a youthful Alex, listening to the woman he loved insult him to her friends. She watched him as he discovered that his money was all that mattered. She felt his pain and in that moment Kit would have given everything in the world for five minutes alone with the vicious woman.

What damage had been done by a stupid, selfish female!

As he finished his story, Alex pushed himself to his feet slowly, tiredly. Kit watched him as he snatched up his clothes and silently got dressed. The spell was broken. Their time together ended.

And this time Kit was fairly certain that it would never be different. He would never be sure that she loved him for himself alone. He would never completely believe in her. Trust her.

For the rest of her life, she would be battling his memories of one spiteful woman.

Alex walked to the door and quietly unlocked it. His hand gripped the gleaming brass knob, but before he turned it he glanced back at her. Even from across the room, Kit saw the sadness in his eyes.

Through a mist of sorrow, she heard him say softly, "Good night, Kit. I'll see you at breakfast."

Then he opened the door, stepped through it, and was gone.

Too restless to return to his room, Alex went down the main stairs, across the hall, and outside. He walked at a furious, punishing pace and didn't even realize where he was headed until he'd reached the cove.

Under a clear, cold sky, Alex sat on the rocks and watched the rising tide. He knew the cove as well as he knew his own house. And the knowledge told him that soon he would be cut off. Trapped in the crescent-shaped cove until sunrise when the tide would subside enough to allow him passage. It was what he wanted—needed. Solitude. The time to think. To examine the mess he'd made of his and Kit's life.

His mind raced with memories. Of Althea. Of Kit.

The roar of the sea faded into insignificance as his mind began to churn.

It was as if talking about Althea out loud had forced him to really *look* at his past clearly. Objectively. Oh, the pain and humiliation were still there, but now Alex realized that the "love" he'd felt for that vapid young woman was nothing compared to the feelings Kit inspired in him. Over the years, he'd concentrated so on the wound, he hadn't looked at the cause. Althea. How long had he held the image of that woman in his mind, painting every other female in his life with her brush?

And what had he really known, at the tender age of twenty, about *love*? As he recalled it now, he acknowledged that his feelings for Althea had been based on her beauty and the raging lust he felt to possess her. Was that love?

No.

Alex snorted a regretful laugh. He had allowed a boy's humiliation to color his entire life.

And what he'd done to Kit in the name of his own pain shamed him. Even knowing she was a virgin, he'd gone to her bed, used her, then threw her offer of love aside like so much garbage.

How could he have been so stupid?

She'd never been interested in his money. Only in security for the child she considered her own. Yet every time she tried to explain that to him, he shut her out. Not once had she asked him for money. Why, Alex had friends whose wives had practically bankrupted them within a week of the wedding! Hell, Kit hadn't even wanted the damned clothes he'd ordered for her!

The froth of an incoming wave slapped against his boots and he drew his legs up, clear of the water. He wasn't worried. He knew from his boyhood that the rock he'd climbed would keep him above the swirling water. Staring down into the black sea, Alex heard Kit's voice clearly in his brain. She'd said that one had to trust one's instincts.

Take the risk.

He smiled slowly, the grin easing up his features like a long-forgotten friend. She was right. He had to trust her. She was his chance at the kind of life he'd dreamed of. *If* she would forgive him for his stupidity.

And after the way he'd treated her, Alex knew that was a big *if*.

Harsh, driving wind pushed at him, pressing him into

the rocks. Icy damp covered him and sea spray shot up and settled over him. Alex welcomed it all. He felt . . . *alive* again.

He spread his arms wide and laughed aloud, the sound booming out to join the crash of the waves against the rocks.

Cold gripped her.

Deep, bone-chilling cold.

There was nothing left.

Kit drew in a shuddering breath and scooted off the bed. Despite her hopes, she knew now that nothing would change. His mind was made up concerning her. He'd decided that Kit was no better than the other woman who'd betrayed him.

The only difference lay in the fact that this time he'd married the betrayer. A bitter smile crossed her face as she realized that he no doubt considered it making the best of a bad situation.

But Kit wasn't ready to spend the rest of her life atoning for another woman's sins. She wouldn't lie with him, bear his children, and still be made to suffer distrustful glances.

Wrapping her arms about herself, Kit stalked quickly across the room to her wardrobe. Yanking open the double doors, she rooted around in the darkness until her fingers closed over the handles of her old carpetbag.

It was the only thing left to do.

19

At sunrise, Alex stretched his aching muscles, tilted his head back, and watched the dawn, smiling. When each soft, muted hue had swelled into brilliance, he jumped from his perch in the rocks into the frigid, knee-high surf.

Determined, hopeful, Alex slogged through the tide-water to shore. He had to see Kit.

At the house, he slipped inside quietly. It was far too early for anyone to be up and about. Alex shivered and briefly considered going to his own room first to get out of his soaking wet clothes.

With his next breath, he dismissed the notion. He wanted to see Kit. Needed to see her. There would be time enough later for other, less important matters.

The top stair creaked when he stepped on it and Alex winced. Moving stealthily, he went along the hall, heed-less of the water marks his boots left on the sky-blue carpet.

At Kit's door, he paused, thought for a moment, then knocked quietly.

No answer.

He frowned slightly and knocked again. He'd had no idea she was such a sound sleeper.

Still no answer.

Was she ignoring him? Well, his brain countered, if she was, he could hardly blame her.

Still, he thought, she'd been patient with him *this* long. Surely she could do it for another few minutes. "Kit?" he called in a hushed voice. "Kit, it's Alex. I'd like to talk to you."

Nothing.

Well, really! How on earth was a man supposed to apologize for being an ass if the woman won't open the door?

He gripped the knob tightly. She'd probably locked it. And if he was a gentleman, he wouldn't try to enter uninvited anyway. But then, that voice in the back of his mind spoke up again, asking, "Who ever accused you of being a gentleman?"

True, Alex admitted and turned the knob. He smiled to himself. Unlocked. Maybe she'd been waiting for him to come back!

As soon as he'd opened the door, he knew that wasn't the case.

Her wardrobe doors hung open, the lavender gown still lay on the floor, and her bed was empty. Dread began to worm its way through Alex as he crossed the room to the wardrobe. Quickly he pushed aside gown after gown and even in his haste, his brain noted that the only clothes missing were the ones she'd brought with her to his house.

All of the elegant, fashionable clothing she'd never wanted hung in front of him, a silent reaffirmation of how little she'd been interested in what his money could buy. Even as he acknowledged the truth deep in his soul, his brain refused to believe it. His mind continued to insist that she was there. Somewhere. Frantically he went about the room, searching for something, anything that might prove his suspicion wrong.

But finally, Alex was left with no choice but to admit the undeniable fact.

Kit was gone.

He was too late.

Dropping to the mattress, he stared at the puddle of purple silk on the floor. He had no one to blame but himself for any of this. She'd been far more patient than he deserved.

His right hand curled into a fist and he slowly began to pound on his own thigh in a steady, rhythmic beat.

Why now? he asked himself. Why did she have to leave now? The absurdity of it all struck him and a strangled laugh choked from his throat. At the same time he'd been in the cove, realizing that he wanted her more than life—*she'd* been here . . . *packing*.

Ridiculous! his mind insisted. Why, if this had been written in a book, he would have laughed at the very notion of such an unlikely coincidence!

But, he reminded himself, this wasn't a book. This was his life. And by God, he wouldn't let it end like this! He and Kit and Rose were going to be a family if he had to drag the woman . . .

Rose!

Alex jumped off the bed and raced out of the room. Heedless of the noise he was making, he ran down the length of the hall to the little girl's room. Had Kit taken the child with her?

He burst through the door, startling the nursery maid out of a dead sleep. While the young girl blinked and gaped at him as though he were mad, Alex hurried to Rose's bedside. A heap of blankets lay in the middle of the mattress. Alex's heartbeat staggered, caught, then began again more steadily as the toddler peeked out from under the mountain of coverings.

"Papa!" the little girl crowed and pulled herself upright.

Alex lifted the child and held her close. The soft, sweet baby scent of her surrounded him and he was immediately humbled. He should have known. Kit had put Rose first since the moment he'd met her. Of course, she wouldn't take the child away from a safe home.

God, he groaned silently. She'd left him her child. She trusted him to take care of Rose. Even as badly as he'd treated her, Kit still trusted him. Hopefully—she still *loved* him as well.

"Mama go 'way," Rose said suddenly, her eyes filling with tears.

"Alex?"

He turned to see his mother, still tying the belt of her robe, standing in the open doorway.

"Alex? What is it? What's happening?" Her gray-streaked hair lay in a neat braid across her shoulder, but her features were a mask of worry. "Is Rose all right?" she said and stepped into the room. "Alex! You're soaked through!"

"Yes, I know." He turned back to the girl in his arms.

"What is happening here? I demand to know!" Tess came closer but he didn't look at her again. "Put that child down, Alex. You're getting her wet and she'll catch her death!"

He hadn't thought of that. Carefully he set Rose back on her bed. How did Rose know that Kit was gone? Had she come to see the child before leaving? "Did you see Mama go?" Alex tried to keep his voice calm, quiet.

"Uh-huh." She nodded, sniffed, then gave him a bright smile. "She come back now?"

"No, Rosie. Not yet."

"Kit's gone?" Tess cried and stepped up beside her son. "Where? And why?"

He ignored her.

"Why she not come back?" Rose asked.

"Because she's not ready."

"Why?"

"Because she needs to have a little trip."

"Why?"

Good Lord. He could hardly tell the child that Mama had left because Papa was an idiot! Besides, he didn't have the time for this. He needed answers. He needed to know where to start looking for Kit. There was no telling how much time had passed already since she'd left the house.

Dammit! Why wasn't Kit here when he needed her?

"Did Mama tell you where she was going?" he asked, hoping to get Rose away from asking why.

"Uh-huh!" She yanked at his shirtfront and lifted her right leg in a useless attempt to climb up his chest.

"Where?"

"Onna train . . ." Rose shook the handful of wet shirt she held. "Rose go too?"

"Not this time, sweetheart."

"The train?" Tess echoed. "Why on earth would she

take the train?" Pushing at her son, the older woman demanded, "What have you done to her?"

"Nothing that can't be fixed . . . I hope," he said and bent down to place a kiss on the top of Rose's head.

Alex ran out of the room, headed for the main staircase. There was no time to lose. She had to have taken the early morning milk train, which meant she already had more than an hour's start on him. Of course, the milk train made dozens of stops between here and London, he reminded himself, to pick up the day's supply of milk from local farmers.

He smiled to himself. He could find her. He *would* find her.

"Alex! You wait one minute!" his mother shouted and he heard her running right behind him on the stairs. He simply didn't have the time to talk to her.

"I'll tell you all about it later, Mother!" he called back and threw open the front door. Leaping over the steps, he sprinted toward the stables.

Tess reached the empty doorway out of breath and furious. How dare he not tell her what was happening in her own house! And how dare he mistreat Kit to the point where she was forced to leave in the dark of night!

She sniffed audibly, tightened the belt of her robe, and took a single step to follow her son. A hand on her arm halted her. Glancing over her shoulder, Tess looked up into Michael Harris's sleepy eyes.

"Don't," he said firmly.

"But, Michael," she argued, "I have to tell him what he needs to do . . ."

"No," her butler said and drew her back into the warmth of the house. He closed the front door and smiled down at her. "Your heart's in the right place, Tess. But this is something they have to solve alone. The two of them."

"But, Michael . . ."

"Tess . . ."

"I *still* think the only way things will be straightened out is if I—" He cut her off in the most surprising manner.

He kissed her.

Pleasure snaked through her limbs and Tess felt like a young girl again. When the brief caress was ended, he pulled back, clearly horrified at what he'd done.

"Michael!" Tess stared up at the man she'd known so long and so well. In the last year or so, she'd found herself more and more drawn to the dignified man who stood before her now with sleep-ruffled gray hair. It didn't matter one whit to Tess that the man she cared for was her butler. But she'd never thought he would work up the courage to cross the servant-mistress barrier between them. Now, as she watched him, a slow wellspring of delight spouted inside her.

"Madam," he said, his voice hollow, "I *beg* your pardon. Naturally, I will tender my resignation at once. Please forgive my—"

This time, Tess pulled his head down to hers. And when the long, tender kiss had ended on a sigh, Tess laid her head on her butler's robe-covered chest.

"Oh, Michael," she whispered happily, "you certainly took your time about this!"

Stunned into speechlessness, Harris wrapped his arms around the woman he loved. Resting his chin on top of her head, he smiled.

*   *   *

Kit sat perched precariously on a small stool in the corner of the train car. Hardly a comfortable way to travel to London, she thought. But it was the fastest way she knew to leave Alex behind her.

Tears welled up in her eyes as she realized that he wouldn't even know she was gone for another hour or more. And when he did know, she asked herself, what then? Would he care? Or would he be grateful that she'd removed herself and solved his problem for him?

And Rose. How it hurt to leave the little girl. She could still see the toddler's wide green eyes staring at her. She heard the child's whimpering cry as she'd left the room. Kit knew that for the rest of her life, she would be seeing that tiny, tear-streaked face in her dreams.

Her breath caught and Kit buried her face in her hands. She had to stop torturing herself. She'd done the only thing she could do. As much as she loved Alex, she wouldn't spend the rest of her life miserable just to prove it.

But what if you're with child? her brain taunted suddenly. Kit sat up and let her hands fall to her lap. A baby. Alex's baby. A brief flash of hope leapt up in her breast before she squashed it deliberately. As much as she would have loved Alex's child—she would say prayers nightly that she wasn't pregnant. Lord knew, it would be hard enough for her to make her own way. She could never support a child on her own.

Heavens, if Kit *was* pregnant, no one would hire her. She would eventually be forced to return to the Mac-Gregors for help . . . and even the *thought* of that was too much to bear. No, she told herself and lifted her chin defiantly, God wouldn't let her be pregnant now. He just wouldn't.

"You all right, miss?"

Kit jumped and looked up at the open cargo door as a man clambered down the outside ladder and swung himself into the car.

"Yes"—she nodded, forcing a brave smile—"I'm fine. Thank you."

"Shun't be too much longer now, miss." He bobbed his head and his black hair fell across his eyes. "On'y a couple more stops to go now!"

"Thank you."

"Oh, ta." He grinned at her and lowered his tall, rail-thin body onto the floor near her. "Ain't often I gets comp'ny on this trip. Most times, I just talks to meself."

Kit nodded and as the man went on talking, his voice faded away. She stared out at the passing countryside and heard the iron wheels clacking on the tracks. They seemed to be saying, "Go back, go back, go back."

20

The train shuddered to a halt and Kit looked out at the tired faces of the local farmers. Each of them stood beside a cart and horse. And on the carts were huge metal containers filled with milk.

As the trainman and the farmers went about the now familiar ritual, Kit stared off into the distance. Morning light filled the countryside, laying down a pattern of shadows beneath the hedgerows. A sea breeze swept across the open compartment, teased at Kit through her threadbare shawl, and disappeared.

She tilted her head back to look at the sky and noticed the position of the sun. It was higher now and she told herself that the MacGregor household would be awake. Rose would be in her room with the nursery maid, having her bowl of porridge while her uncle and grandmother would meet in the dining room.

They would help themselves to the covered dishes on the sideboard and once seated, Alex and Tess would notice that Kit was late. Alex would wonder if she was avoiding him and Tess would worry. Probably Polly would be sent upstairs to fetch her and only then would they discover her missing.

She inhaled sharply and let the mental image dissolve. That life was behind her now. It would be best if she left it there.

Only minutes later the trainman grabbed hold of the ladder, leaned out, and faced the engine. He waved one arm wildly in a signal that he'd finished his business and Kit braced herself for the train's lurch of motion.

Chugging and wheezing, the old engine puffed its tired breath into the morning air and groaned as it began to move again. She'd been on the train over two hours and she would have been willing to wager that they hadn't traveled more than ten miles from Cliffton. At this rate, she told herself, she might have been better off walking.

From a distance, Kit heard someone shouting. Had the trainman forgotten one of the farmers? She bit back a sigh. Undoubtedly, they would have to go back.

"What's that bloody"—the trainman glanced at her sheepishly—" 'scuse me, miss. What's that fool doin' then?"

"Hmmm?" She wasn't really interested, but she felt she owed him courtesy, at least.

His fingers curled in a death grip around the ladder's rungs; the man leaned out into the wind to get a better look at the tracks behind them.

"There's some id'jut gallopin' after us on the biggest, blackest 'orse I ever seen!"

An idiot? On a horse?

No, Kit thought. Impossible.

She heard the shouting again and this time it was closer. More familiar.

"He wants us to stop!" The trainman snorted. "Id'jut.

The milk train stops for milk. Not for every Tom, Dick, and 'arry what's got a 'orse."

The idiot wants the train to stop?

Something incredibly like hope flared up inside her and Kit systematically beat it back down. If it *was* Alex on that horse—if he *did* want them to stop—it was for reasons of his own and nothing to do with her.

She chewed at her bottom lip nervously and waited for the trainman's next report.

"The damn, 'scuse me, *darn* fool's gonna kill that 'orse of 'is, ridin' 'im like that! Why 'e's all a lather!"

"Damn you!" the angry voice shouted. "I know you see me! Stop that train at once!"

Alex?

"Would ya listen to that, then? 'Oo's 'e think 'e is? The bloody, 'scuse me, blessed king?"

As a matter of fact, Kit thought . . . Yes, he does.

She stood up and braced her legs wide apart in an effort to keep her balance on the rocking train. Laying her palm on the rough wood planks of the car, she stared at the opening, waiting.

"Look out, miss!" the trainman called, backing away. " 'E's comin' up!"

As she watched, she saw the head and neck of a beautiful black horse appear alongside the train. Riding that animal, bent low over the horse's neck . . . was Alex. But this was an Alex she'd never seen before.

As his horse strained to keep up, Alex grabbed hold of the train ladder, kicked free of the stirrups, and swung himself onto the train.

The huge animal, free of the man guiding it, turned away from the train and was quickly lost to sight.

Kit stared at Alex in stunned silence. His hair stood out about his head, his clothes were filthy, and he looked as though he hadn't slept. He also looked furious.

"Good God, man!" he bellowed at the much skinnier fellow. "Why didn't you stop the damned train?"

"Milk train stops for milk. And only milk."

"Oh, for the love of . . ." Alex pushed his hands through his hair and turned to face Kit. "You left me!"

"Yes."

"Why?" He shook his head quickly. "Never mind. I *know* why. But why now? Why not last week? Or *next* week?"

Kit glanced at the fascinated man beside her husband, then looked away again. "What difference does it make?"

"You'd be surprised!"

"What do you want, Alex?" she asked, suddenly weary of defending herself to this man. "I haven't taken anything that belongs to you. Of course," she added quietly, "you're welcome to examine my bag."

His features tightened and a curious shade of red crept up his neck. Whether it was shame or rage though, she wasn't sure.

"That's not why I came," he said.

"Then why?"

Alex opened his mouth to speak, snapped it shut again, and glared at the stranger in the car. "Would you mind terribly leaving us alone for a moment?"

"Oh! Uh . . . I don't know . . ."

Kit spoke up quickly. "There's no need for that."

Whatever he had to say, he could say it in front of a witness.

Alex scowled, then shrugged. "You're right. It doesn't matter. Stay."

The other man crossed his arms over his narrow chest and slowly slipped to the floor. Bracing his back against the wooden wall, he watched the couple in front of him with avid interest.

Alex took a half step, swayed as the train took a bend in the tracks, and stopped.

"Kit, I want to say something . . ."

No more, her mind cried. Hadn't too much been said already? Aloud, she told him, "We've said enough, Alex. Both of us."

"No. You don't understand."

"What is it? You want me to come back to the house? Pretend that we're a family? Pretend that half a marriage is enough for me?" Kit shook her head and blinked at the threatening tears filling her eyes. "No. It's *not* enough and I'm tired of pretending."

"That's not what I mean, dammit!"

"Don't shout at me."

"Sorry." He pulled in a deep breath and said quickly, "I love you, Kit."

She hadn't expected that. And to her surprise, it wasn't enough. Easy to say, the phrase only had meaning if the person uttering it believed the words.

Hope fought with pain in her heart and the pain won. What was it, she thought, that he'd said to her? Oh, yes. Quietly she gave his words back to him. "Undying oaths are quite tiresome, Alex."

He blanched, crossed the few feet of space separating

them, and grabbed her upper arms. "Don't, Kit. Don't repeat the words of a fool," he muttered thickly.

"Alex," she started and shook her head.

"Kit, don't leave me." His hands cupped her face and his gaze moved over her like a dying man looking for heaven. "Dear God, don't leave me."

She reached up and held on to his wrists. Through her fingertips, Kit felt his racing pulse. His eyes were haunted, wild.

"I was in the cove all night," he rushed on, his thumbs tracing patterns over her cheekbones, "calling myself all kinds of a fool. Over and over, I relived everything I've said and done to you. And if I could change it, I would."

Her lips trembled and Kit resisted the urge to wrap her arms around him. He'd fought this thing between them. Now it was up to him to make it right again.

"When the tide finally receded, I ran to the house but you were gone." His head dropped back on his neck for a moment and then he raised it again to look deeply into her eyes. "I died, Kit. I know I did, because I felt my heart stop. Your room, the house . . . dammit, the whole *world* felt empty with you gone."

"How did you know where to find me?"

"Rose."

"Is she all right?"

"Fine. She misses you."

Kit nodded and tried desperately to swallow past the knot in her throat.

"Come back with me, Kit. Be my wife. Be Rose's mother." Alex leaned close to her and kissed her eyelids, the bridge of her nose, her cheeks. "Help me to give her brothers and sisters." His mouth touched hers briefly. "Love me, Kit, and let me love you."

"Alex." Kit gazed up into his eyes and saw everything she'd always hoped to see. He'd come after her. He'd swallowed that pride of his in one gulp.

He loved her.

"Say yes, Kit." Alex dipped his head and kissed her long and thoroughly. When he pulled back, his breathing was ragged. "Dear God, I love you. Have for the longest time. Hell, I even sent John away because he was paying you too much attention!"

Another surprise.

"He probably won't be speaking to me by the time he returns," Alex conceded. "But I don't care about anything else but you. Please say yes, Kit. Please don't leave me alone."

She lifted her hand and touched his cheek. His eyes closed and she felt him tremble. When his deep blue gaze was fixed on her again, Kit slowly nodded. "I'll come back. I love you, Alex. I always have."

Pent-up air rushed from his lungs and he sagged into her embrace. His arms tightened around her until she couldn't breathe and only then did he loosen the pressure just a bit. "I love you, Kit Simmons MacGregor."

He kissed her and Kit felt the difference in his caress. This time, he was holding nothing back from her. He was offering her all that he was and all that he hoped to be.

" 'At's luvly, just luvly," a voice cracking with emotion spoke up from the corner.

They broke apart and turned as one to face the trainman. Tears rolled down the man's face and he wiped his nose with the back of his hand. " 'At was luvly indeed, sir."

"Thank you." Alex's lips twitched at the compliment.

"Miss," the weeping man said, "you're doin' the right thing, you are."

"I know." Kit grinned at him.

"Why," the man went on, "when I tell my missus what I seen in 'ere today, she'll be that 'appy. Likes to 'ear nice stories, she does."

Kit laid her head on Alex's chest and listened to his heartbeat beneath her ear. And as he held her, she finally noticed that his clothes were clammy and freezing.

"Alex?" She leaned back and looked up at him. "How did you get so wet?"

"It's a long story, love." He pulled her close again. "I'll tell you when we get back home. All right?"

She nodded and snuggled in close. The word "home" had never sounded so good before.

"We need a celebration or somethin'," the trainman announced. " 'Ow about a cuppa milk? Free of charge, o' course?"

FREE
Romance
(a $4.50 value)

Send in the Coupon Below

To get your FREE historical romance and start saving, fill out the coupon below and mail it today. As soon as we receive it we'll send you your FREE Book along with your first month's selections.

Mail To: **True Value Home Subscription Services, Inc. P.O. Box 5235**
120 Brighton Road, Clifton, New Jersey 07015-5235

YES! I want to start previewing the very best historical romances being published today. Send me my FREE book along with the first month's selections. I understand that I may look them over FREE for 10 days. If I'm not absolutely delighted I may return them and owe nothing. Otherwise I will pay the low price of just $4.00 each: a total $16.00 (at *least* an $18.00 value) and save at least $2.00. Then each month I will receive four brand new novels to preview as soon as they are published for the same low price. I can always return a shipment and I may cancel this subscription at any time with no obligation to buy even a single book. In any event the FREE book is mine to keep regardless.

Name _____

Street Address _____ Apt. No. _____

City _____ State _____ Zip Code _____

Telephone _____

Signature _____
(if under 18 parent or guardian must sign)   **11705-6**

Terms and prices subject to change. Orders subject
to acceptance by True Value Home Subscription
Services, Inc.

Recipes from the heartland of America

THE HOMESPUN
❧ COOKBOOK ❧

Tamara Dubin Brown

**Arranged by courses, this collection of
wholesome family recipes includes tasty
appetizers, sauces, and relishes, hearty main
courses, and scrumptious desserts—all created
from the popular *Homespun* series.**

Features delicious easy-to-prepare dishes, such as:

Curried Crab and Shrimp en Casserole

1 large can crabmeat	1 pint milk
1 can shrimp	2 tablespoons butter
2 tablespoons flour	1 teaspoon curry powder
½ teaspoon salt	1 tablespoon chopped onion
1 tablespoon chopped green pepper	

Cream the butter and flour. Add milk. Cook over slow fire,
stirring constantly until slightly thickened. Add salt and curry
powder. Stir until smooth and remove from fire. Put onion and
pepper into cream sauce and mix well. Shred crabmeat and clean
the shrimp. Spread a layer of crabmeat in casserole and cover
with a layer of cream sauce. Repeat with shrimp and cream sauce.
Repeat this until all is in the casserole. Bake at 300 degrees for
30 minutes before serving.

A Berkley paperback coming February 1996